He Wore His Shooting Mittens with a Slash in the Right Hand for the Trigger Finger . . .

There was no snow yet, and a stiff wind had put texture into the surface of the water as it froze. Gun moved to the southeast, staying just off shore, keeping his eyes on the place where the scrubby growth ended at the rocky waterline, his right index finger on the trigger guard of his 870, his thumb on the safety. You had to be fast in this game. Not as fast as you had to be against a Nolan Ryan, maybe, but still mighty quick. The hares liked to hide low in willow clutches or the shadows of fallen hackberries at the edge of the ice. They'd crouch there, invisible, and when your boots got close enough or loud enough and they couldn't stand the suspense any longer, they'd bolt.

In this case the rabbit waited too long—until Gun was just yards away—then shot out from the clawlike roots of a dead elm. The hare ran twenty yards to the right on ice and cut left toward shore as Gun panned with it. It leaped and landed off kilter on a patch of smooth glass.

Squeeze, pump, there, and the rabbit exploded into a roll it wasn't meant to come out of.

"My Lord," Gun said. He was not looking at the dead hare. He was looking ten yards behind it, at a man's head frozen in the ice. . . .

Books by L. L. Enger

Comeback
Swing
Strike

Published by POCKET BOOKS

A GUN PEDERSEN MYSTERY

STRIKE

L.L. ENGER

POCKET BOOKS

New York   London   Toronto   Sydney   Tokyo   Singapore

An *Original* Publication of POCKET BOOKS

POCKET BOOKS, a division of Simon & Schuster Inc.
1230 Avenue of the Americas, New York, NY 10020

ISBN: 0-671-74481-X

First Pocket Books printing July 1992

10 9 8 7 6 5 4 3 2 1

POCKET and colophon are registered trademarks of
Simon & Schuster Inc.

Cover art by Stephen Peringer

Printed in the U.S.A.

For Nick and John

Thanks to Bill Brice,
who read these pages
with an eye to the Northern ground.

STRIKE

First thing every morning, last thing each night, down on the cold oak floor, fists on bare wood, back straight as a Louisville Slugger—in this manner, twice a day, Gun Pedersen did a pair of push-ups for each and every year of his life. He'd been at it since the morning of his tenth birthday, thanks to his dad, who'd been doing the same thing since *he* was a kid.

I got a present for ya, boy, that'll hold you for the rest of your life, if you've got what it takes.

That was thirty-eight years ago now, exactly. Which meant this morning he had to do two more push-ups than he'd been doing every morning for the past year. And it still mattered to Gun whether or not he had what it took.

They weren't easy this morning, not by any means, and he had to bribe himself through the last ones with a perfectly imagined taste of morning coffee, dark and uncomplicated. Then he got up and put on his first layer of winter shooting clothes: gray wool undershirt and long johns coarse enough to make you remember you had them on, every move you made, and silk socks to keep your feet slippery and blister-free inside leather boots.

1

Gun's muscles ached pleasurably at the back of his upper arms and deep in his chest where they attached to the ribs. Funny how just two more could make a difference when you were doing so many already, but they did, every birthday the same, the pair of new ones doing to your arms and chest what a fastball with poison did to your eyes in spring training—tricked them, leaving them surprised and bent on revenge. Tonight they would come even harder, the push-ups; he knew this from experience. Then tomorrow he'd start to make up ground. Two or three more days and the ache and stiffness would be gone for another year.

Standing at the kitchen counter in his underwear, Gun ground coffee beans, then filled the metal pot with water cold from the tap and lit the gas flame on the right rear burner. He sat down at the kitchen table and let his fingers roll a Prince Albert. The sun was not close to rising, but after a cigarette, coffee, and a bowl of Wheaties, there'd be enough light seeping in through the pines to see and kill a couple of furry stew hares.

It was a decade, more now, since Gun Pedersen had left his Tigers and baseball. For most of those years the quiet and the clean water and air had done their job, leaving him alone with himself and face to face with the man he'd become during seventeen seasons of applause, leaving him no recourse but to stare that man down until he could once more live with him in peace. It hadn't been easy. Ten years it took to forgive himself for what his wife could have pardoned, if she hadn't died. And then, just when he'd finally let himself think of starting over with somebody else— somebody he didn't deserve and knew it—he'd gone and complicated things.

He ground out the pinched stub of his cigarette into the clear glass Hamm's Beer ashtray, then stood up and went to the stove to pour out his second pleasure of the morning. The thermometer outside the window read minus nineteen, mighty cold for mid-November.

The telephone rang.

It was an old-fashioned black desk-top model and he picked it up and set it on the pine table in front of his chair, sat down, and took an appreciative sip of coffee before lifting the receiver on the fourth ring.

He said, "It's early," knowing who it was, and glad she'd called in spite of himself.

"Happy birthday," said Carol Long. "You might have told me."

"How'd you find out? No, don't say it—you've been talking to Mazy." Mazy was Gun's grown daughter, a journalist living in Minneapolis who figured her dad must be crazy for not making things right with Carol months ago.

"Baseball card. Nineteen seventy-nine, no, eighty."

"The last year I played."

"Not a happy picture, either. The way your cap's pulled down, and your eyes, God, like, 'Stay away from me with that camera.'"

"I'd say you've got it right, Carol."

She was quiet, and Gun let the silence stand. He knew he should help her—he wanted to, wished that he could—but something wouldn't let him.

"So how does it feel?" she asked. "Being a year older." Her voice trying to sound cheerful, valiantly trying.

"Ohhh, I don't know. Like something's happening I don't approve of but can't put a stop to. They always feel like that for me. Every year I tell myself it's all perfectly normal, happens to everybody, these birthdays. Doesn't help, though. When it comes right down to it—and I mean this—I don't think we were meant to get old."

"Old? Try middle-aged."

"Whatever you want to call it. It's wrong somehow. At least for me. I wasn't meant for it." Gun heard but only partially regretted the irritation in his voice.

Carol said, "I didn't call to argue about getting old."

3

"I know. You called to see if we're on for tonight."

"Well, yes. But when we talked, I didn't know it was your birthday. I mean, don't feel obligated. You've probably got other plans."

"Nothing much," Gun said, "but yes, I do." When Carol had called offering to cook for the evening, he'd said sure, forgetting what day it was. Being with Carol on his birthday, though, would somehow feel too cozy right now. Give her the wrong ideas. Or if they were the right ideas, the timing was wrong. "Can I take a rain check?" he asked.

Carol's quick laugh didn't hold any humor; all the well-intentioned cheer was gone out of her voice. "A what? Gun, you should hear the way that sounds. A rain check. Sure, I suppose I could give you a rain check, but you know what? I won't. I'm not giving you any such thing. No. The offer's good for tonight only, and then it's *void*. All right?" Her words sounded as flat as struck lead.

He had seen Carol angry and knew how she looked about now. Her eyes like a pair of green headlights—large, bright, and unblinking—her jawline as cold and sharp as fractured ice. He made a lousy effort to redeem the situation. "Look, Carol, you're taking this wrong. We'll just have to try for another night, that's all."

"Have a beautiful birthday," she said crisply, and hung up.

Gun put the receiver down carefully, checking his impulse to slam it home. He forced himself to finish his coffee slowly, then got up and took his Model 870 Remington from the gun case in the knotty-pine living room. He rubbed down the blued barrel and shank with an oiled rag and lay the shotgun and a handful of number six shells on the kitchen table. In his bedroom he put on green wool trousers, a flannel shirt, and a pair of leather boots with heavy pile linings.

From the closet next to the front door he took his goose-down parka and the waterproof shooting mittens with a slash in the inner part of the right hand for the trigger finger. He'd gotten the mittens a year ago after going for geese in Manitoba and finding himself in a surprise blizzard one morning, sitting in a cattail blind next to an ice-fringed lake, thousands of Canadian geese and tons of wet snow tumbling in all together. He'd taken his limit easily, and also frozen most of his fingers walking the two miles back to his pickup, his leather gloves soaked through and useless.

Gun stepped outside. The sun was rising out of morning color into a hard, white winter shine. He walked alongside his log house, past the pile of chopped and split oak, and down to the lake, which had frozen up rock solid last night, at least around the edges. A few more days of this kind of cold would have people dragging their fish houses onto the bars and reefs where the angling was best, and by mid-December there would be whole little shanty towns of fishing shacks.

The walking couldn't be better. No snow yet, and a stiff wind had put texture into the surface of the water as it froze. Gun moved to the southeast, staying just off shore, keeping his eyes on the place where the scrubby growth ended at the rocky waterline, his right index finger on the trigger guard of the 870, his thumb on the safety. You had to be fast in this game. Not as fast as you had to be against a Nolan Ryan, maybe, but still mighty quick. The hares liked to hide low in willow clutches or the shadows of fallen hackberries at the edge of the ice. They'd crouch there, invisible, their little noses jumping, and when your boots got close enough or loud enough and they couldn't stand the suspense any longer, they'd bolt. Zig-zag away on the ice, right, left, right and gone, up into the scrub again.

They were tougher to land than pheasants or overhead geese, and of course not nearly as nice on the palate. But when it came to stew, Gun held a hearty fondness for the hare. A morning simmering away in

5

the pot with plenty of vegetables and some red wine, and you had yourself a meal.

In this case the rabbit waited too long—until Gun was just yards away—then shot out from the clawlike roots of a dead elm. Immediately Gun had the round steel bead just ahead of the white flash. The hare ran twenty yards to the right on ice and cut left toward shore as Gun panned with it. It leaped a dark bump on the lake's surface and landed off kilter on a patch of smooth glass, its rear legs splaying out then pedaling for traction.

Squeeze, pump, there, and the rabbit exploded into a roll it wasn't meant to come out of.

"My Lord," Gun said. He was not looking at the dead hare. He was looking ten yards behind it, at a man's head frozen in the ice.

2

The eyes, thank God, were closed, which made it easier for Gun to move in for a better look. He knelt down several feet away. The head stuck up from the ice like a trophy kill on polished oak. The lips were slightly parted—about to speak, it seemed—and the color of holiday beets: ripe, purplish red. The teeth inside looked nice and straight and well brushed. The cheekbones, chin, and jawline were sharply defined, masculine. The hair was long and black and fanned out all around behind the head, some of it locked in ice. The man was Indian, Ojibwa. Young. Gun had never seen a body frozen, and the skin, which looked more like molded plastic than something organic, gave the face an ethereal, ageless quality.

For the smallest instant, a hopeful voice in Gun's brain told him this was a prank, a fabricated head planted here to put the fear of God in the unlucky finder. Then a large raven flapped down and landed just yards away, cocked his head and clicked his beak, greedy. Gun waved his arms and said, "Shhh, get outa here," and the raven pulled back into the air and settled next to another on a branch of the dead elm tree on shore.

7

Gun looked back down and saw a wound on the dead man's right temple and a line of blood that led to a frozen pool inside the right ear. He felt a sudden helplessness press against his lungs. He took off his mittens, reached out and touched the man's forehead. Then his hair. He couldn't remember touching anything as cold. He stood up and saw dimly through the ice that the man was sitting on the floor of the lake, his arms wrapped around himself, his back supported by a large rock that came just short of the lake's surface. He looked like a boy comforting himself after a hard scolding.

Gun took off his red parka and carefully covered the body. From the branches of the elm tree the pair of ravens scolded him. *Leave, leave, leave now,* they said. Gun lifted his Remington, clicked off the safety, and leveled the steel bead just over the top of the bird on the right. He squeezed the trigger. The barrel jumped and the raven tumbled. Gun pumped and chambered another shell. His shooting eye found the second bird already lifting away, and he pulled the trigger. This bird dropped too and landed ten feet from the first one, its legs paddling the air with such fury and anguish Gun almost felt a little better.

Without a parka he could feel the cold moving fast through his flannel shirt and wool underwear. An involuntary shudder went through his body. He picked up his spent shells for reloading and the dead rabbit too—no reason to leave it for the next pair of ravens—and set off on the ice, continuing in the same direction, southeast. Already he was nearly a mile from home, and Dick Chandler's place was half that distance away.

As the cold tightened its hold on him, his walk became a slow jog and then an all-out run. In his mind the image of the frozen head was replaced by that of the barrel stove in Dick's kitchen, ripples of heat coming off it. Then he was at the edge of Dick's yard and his sled dogs—smoke-colored huskies, a few big malamutes, a single blazing-white Samoyed—were staked out on the bare dirt, yapping away at him, begging for breakfast.

They both looked surprised—Dick and his boy, Babe—when Gun came gasping into their kitchen without so much as a tap on the door. They were sitting at the cedar table eating a breakfast of French toast and Babe's famous venison sausage, and Dick looked up, his tongue going after a golden stripe of syrup caught in his mustache.

"Hungry?" Dick said. Then, "Criminy, man, where's your coat?"

Gun crossed to the corner where the stove was and stood as close to it as he dared. It was going strong, thumping away, giving off waves of brutal heat, the draft wide open. When he'd stopped shaking enough to speak in a steady voice, he said, "That sausage—I could smell it all the way out on the ice. What do you put in there, anyway, Babe?"

As usual, Dick spoke for his son, who merely looked at Gun out of his round face. Dick said, "Secret formula. Babe's mother, she made him promise never to tell." Dick always called his former wife "Babe's mother," or had ever since she'd up and gone back to the reservation years ago.

"Smells something like, um, cinnamon," Gun said, thinking, *It's no hurry, he's dead and he's going to stay that way,* wanting to put this off for another minute, until the cold was farther behind him.

"Not even close, Gun, not close." Dick reached into his mouth with the hook which served as his right hand and extricated something, a piece of gristle or bone. "Babe," he said, "take that rabbit there and clean it up for Gun." With his left arm, which also ended in a steel hook, Dick pointed at the dead hare Gun had dropped on the stack of split wood next to the stove.

"No, that's all right," Gun said, but Babe was on his

feet already, his fingers freeing the knife from the sheath he wore on his belt. The boy picked up the rabbit and took it to the kitchen sink, where he performed the quickest evisceration Gun had ever seen. A precision cut and a snap of wrist hollowed the animal. Another couple of minutes and the skin was separated from the red-muscled carcass.

"You needing the fur?" Babe muttered. His wide mouth and cheeks were smiling, but his eyes didn't rise higher than Gun's chest. They were brown eyes, dark brown, liquid and dangerously somber. He was more his mother than his dad, people said.

"You keep it, Babe."

The boy dropped the carcass into an empty bread bag and laid it back on the pile of wood.

"Good soup it'll be, too," Dick said. He went to the stove and poured coffee into a large mug shaped like a pear. "So, here you are without your coat on," he said, handing the coffee to Gun, who was still at the stove. Dick sat back down and sliced a fat chunk of sausage from the helping on his plate. The knife and fork were like natural extensions of his metal hands.

"There is a dead man in the ice," Gun said. "Right out there." He nodded out the window toward the lake, which was barely visible through a stand of white pine. "Just found him."

"Holy Mary and all her children," said Dick Chandler. "Dead, you say? Or hurt bad?"

"I'm standing here getting warm, Dick. What do you think?"

"Dead as dirt."

"He's in the lake. Rock solid."

Dick lowered his fork, a wedge of sausage still on it. With one steel hand he wiped his mouth politely, using a cloth napkin. "Fisherman, you figure? Bet my ass, one of those guys up from the Cities, all the right gear and doesn't know lake ice from a picture window."

"He wasn't fishing," Gun said. "Doubt if he was up

10

from the Cities, either. And my guess, he didn't drown."

"What, you know the guy?"

"Nope," Gun said, "but *you* might—or maybe you, Babe." Gun looked over at the boy, who was at the sink, rinsing his knife under a stream of water. His dark eyes were holding to Gun's now. "Ojibwa," said Gun. "And pretty young. Looks to me like somebody hit him real hard."

Dick got up and took a green wool coat down from a peg on the wall next to the door. He put on a pair of rabbit mittens and pulled a dirty Twins cap down low on his head. Gun had never seen the man wear anything on his head but a baseball cap, even in weather like this; his ears must be immune to cold. "Get on your coat," Dick said to his son.

"We better call the sheriff before we go down there," said Gun.

"Lotta good that'll do."

Gun walked over to the black rotary phone on the wall. "Want me to call?"

"I'll do it." Dick made a sound in his throat like a weasel in a trap—a scratchy low growl with an edge of whine to it. "Get the poor bastard out of bed, pull him out of his bad dreams." As he dialed the number, he said to Gun, "Help yourself to a coat there, if you can find one big enough. The beaver, maybe."

Gun was able to stretch the long-cut fur coat across his shoulders and still get it buttoned, but the arms petered out well above the wrists.

"Come on, come on," Dick said into the phone.

Babe didn't wait for his dad and Gun, but opened the door and slipped out by himself. Gun went after him.

"Babe?" he said.

The boy kept walking, heading down toward the frozen lake.

"Let's all go down together," Gun said. He caught up to the boy and put a hand on his shoulder. "Let's wait for your dad." The sun was free and clear, though not much good for heat anymore. Babe looked past Gun straight into it. His face had strong bones but still held the roundness of boyhood, and Gun saw a soft mustache trying to darken his upper lip. He wasn't the kind of kid you could hope to protect from life, but Gun thought, *Please don't let it be somebody he knows,* even though chances were better than even that it would be. Babe Chandler spent a good part of each year with his mother up on the reservation—a community small enough that if you weren't related to someone by blood, you were likely related by marriage or trouble—or both.

Babe looked from the sky to the lake, his eyes tightening. Gun turned and saw, through a space in the pines, the red spot on the ice where the body was covered by the parka. Then Dick banged out of the house, shaking his head and scratching his stubbly chin with one hook.

"Coming right out, the good sheriff says. We'll see." Dick made the trapped weasel sound again. "I told him where to find us. And I told him to leave the bottle behind." He spit into the snow.

"You're hard on him, Dick."

"Somebody's gotta be. The man won't pull him*self* together."

Babe started down the slope toward the lake, hands in the pockets of his camouflage parka. Dick and Gun moved quickly to draw even with him, and the three walked silently through the line of white pines, then down through the scrubby growth on the shoreline. Gun saw half a dozen large ravens resting patiently on the bare limbs of the dead elm. Five yards from the red parka, Gun lifted a hand. Dick and Babe stopped. Gun walked forward and raised his red parka away from the head.

Dick took off his dirty Twins cap and said, "Oh, Julius."

Babe clamped his bottom lip in his teeth. His eyes

looked busy and full for a moment, then he smiled. "It doesn't look all that bad," he said, and took the parka from Gun to cover up the head again.

There wasn't much to do but go back to the house and drink coffee until Sheriff Durkins showed up. Babe wouldn't talk. He sat quietly with the men for a few minutes, then got up and disappeared out the back door.

"He'll be in his little cabin back there for a while," Dick said. "That's okay. That's Babe." He took a long deep breath and rubbed his eyes with his steel hands. "Ah, shit. It had to be Julius."

Julius, Gun learned from Dick, was Julius Marks, Babe's older friend and idol. Like Babe, he was half-Ojibwa, half-white, and moved in and out of both worlds.

"How come I never saw him around?" Gun asked.

Dick leaned forward in the kitchen chair and fiddled with his Twins cap. "Where the two of them spent most of their time together was up on the Rez. Fishing, shining deer, spearing in the spring melt, God knows what all. And it's only been a touch this fall that Julius started spending any time with us down here. Not a bad boy, neither. Not bad at all, Gun." Dick exhaled, long and miserably. Out the back window of the kitchen, just visible through a winter-thin hedge of untrimmed caraganna bushes, stood the one-room cabin Babe had built with no help from anybody two years ago at age fourteen. He'd used eight-inch balsam and notched them together neat as Lincoln Logs. Scrap plywood from a local sawmill for a patchwork floor and roof. Shingle odds and ends from the Stony lumberyard. Cost him nothing but the few dollars he spent on windows, irregulars Dick found for him up at Marvin in Warroad. With a good oak fire, the little cabin held its own against the coldest nights; Gun knew this because on a couple of occasions he'd seen smoke and stopped in to check on the boy. Not that another man's son was any of Gun's business, but there were times you couldn't help but think Dick cut Babe too much slack.

"I can't say I'm surprised, though, Gun," Dick continued. "Julius knew how to make trouble. Though I don't think he ever meant anything by it. I remember one time, oh man, he was maybe eleven, twelve years old, and I took him and Babe fishing. This was up on the reservation, just before Margaret left. Babe would've been about seven. We're out on the ice, nothing to block the wind, and the crappies fussy as hell, nothing good enough for 'em. The boys started getting antsy and cold and I said, 'Go run up some heat for yourselves, stamp around a little.' So they took off. And I plain forgot about 'em. Took my limit of crappies, finally, then I started looking around for the boys, and where do you think they were?"

Dick laughed and pushed his cap back onto his graying head. "Huh? I'll tell you where they were. Hooting their butts off in Frankie Little Mink's fish house. Putting that Irish retriever of his through the coldest workout of its life. See, Frankie'd left them in charge there and gone off looking for the hot spot, and the boys had that poor dog diving into the spearing hole after sucker minnows. I walk in there and the animal's shaking like hell, and so are the boys, they think it's so great. And Julius yells at me, 'Watch this, Dick,' before I can get a word in, and he throws a handful of suckers into that hole, live ones, and the dog goes right in, head first like a kid off the high board. Just disappears. Gone.

"Now think of it, Gun. I'm going, 'Holy balls, the dog's not comin' back and guess who's gonna end up paying for him?' I mean, the animal's worth a few hundred clams, right? And the boys—or Julius, anyway—he's bent over the hole clapping his hands and yelling, 'Here boy, here boy,' and smiling the whole time, plugged into a live socket. Babe's standing above him, his eyes going back and forth between the

14

hole and me. And me, I'm about ready to grab the both of them and drop *them* down the damn hole, when I see this red flash and the setter bursts up through the hole in the ice and scrambles up onto the floor. Shakes himself all around and starts in whining at the bucket of suckers for more. That's when Frankie Little Mink comes in and asks what in frozen tarnation is going on."

Outside, a car door slammed. Gun stood up from the table and went to the door. Through the window he saw Sheriff Durkins walking slowly up to the house, his eyes on the ground in front of his feet.

One of Dick's steel hands lifted in the air and came down hard on the homemade cedar table. "And that was Julius," he said.

3

Jason Durkins had been county sheriff for just a year, which was long enough to live through a full four seasons of political weather. In a matter of months his popularity had gone from stratospheric to below sea level and out of sight, and the way things looked now, out of sight was where it was going to stay.

He'd taken over last spring when Sheriff Bakke—well liked, grandfatherly, hopelessly inept—slipped off at the urging of the county board into early retirement. Right away Durkins made his mark. He busted a long-standing boat-heist operation, then put a stop to the keggers in Stony State Park. Most everyone, Gun included, thought Durkins was just what the county needed. Hard working, tough as they come, not afraid to make enemies.

People loved to talk about the young man's background: growing up street smart in Chicago, going to cop school right after high-school graduation and getting a job in Minneapolis, the youngest guy on the force, taking a slug one night in a north-side drug raid. Durkins wasn't averse to showing off the scar he had above his right nipple, either. Gun himself had seen it twice in Smitty's Barber Shop—a red welt the size of a fifty-cent piece, and above it, Durkins's hands lifting his T-shirt, his grinning face staring into the long mirror behind Smitty's single chair. But he was a young man, and Gun forgave him.

After all, he had his priorities straight. He'd left the city for his bride, who had two kids from a previous marriage; he wanted a quiet, safe place to raise a family. Moved north for the deputy job under Bakke, and then when the old man quit, took the special election running away.

Everything looked fine, too, until his wife left to join her ex in Seattle. Left the kids as well. And when she didn't come back, the story went, Durkins threw up his hands and gave in to the bottle, each morning pissing away his courage after last night's drunk. People counted him out. Gun wasn't so sure.

Yeah, he might drink too much sometimes. But whenever *Gun* had seen him he'd been sober. And you had to give the guy credit for doing a decent job with the two kids he'd been left with. A small town could be tough on a person who life's been tough on, is how Gun figured, and if it was true that Durkins had had a few before his kid's open house at school and threatened to put a teacher's head through a window for calling him on it, that was too bad. Maybe the teacher had it coming. To Gun's way of thinking, it was too early for all the talk of throwing Durkins out. The man needed time to find his balance. He needed people to leave him the hell alone for a while.

Of course Dick didn't see it that way. Dick hadn't tried drowning himself when *his* wife had taken a hike, years ago. Dick had just gone on making his pots and jars and plates and bowls, turning them at the wheel with his two bare feet, firing them hard in his backyard kiln and selling to the summer people and the retailers up from the Cities. Dick didn't brood or screw up, and he sure didn't whine. Which up in this part of the world meant a lot. Dick *handled* things, and figured other folks better do the same.

Gun pushed open the door and told the sheriff to come in. Durkins looked bad. His blond stubble was a few days old and his eyes were puffy, like miniature bagels with too much leaven and only slits for holes. His tan trousers had yellow egg stains and one of his boots was partly unlaced. As he moved past Gun into the kitchen he pushed his metal-rimmed glasses higher on his nose with a trembling finger. Dick, still at the table, shoved a chair out carelessly for the man to sit on. Durkins eased himself down like somebody looking to save strength.

"You made it," said Dick. "Good of you."

Durkins ignored Chandler's tone. "I drove down on the access and had a look. You know who it is?"

"Julius Marks. A friend of Babe's from up on the Rez."

Durkins's bagel-eyes widened, and for a moment Gun could actually see what color they were. Dark blue. "I'm sorry," Durkins said. He glanced over at Gun, then back at Dick. "Was Julius here last night?"

"Nope. Haven't seen him in a couple weeks. Last I heard, he was doing some logging for a brother out there on the Emerald Tract. Working hard, too."

"Well, he took one hell of a blow last night, I can tell you that," Durkins said. "The young man didn't freeze to death. God, I'm sorry."

"I know you're sorry, sheriff. You said that. Now what other questions've you got for me? Or Babe, you'll want to talk to him."

"No," said Durkins, getting to his feet. "Fact is, I better be on my way."

"You what?" Dick asked.

"Go into town, write this up, and call the BCA, get them out here." He zipped up his green parka.

"What, you come out here and ask me two questions, and Julius out there in the ice like a frozen carp. What the hell kind of a cop are you? What do you mean, 'Call the BCA'?" Dick was on his feet now, moving to block the door.

"Bureau of Criminal Apprehension," said Gun, standing. "The state fellows. Take it easy, Dick."

"Take it easy? Don't tell me 'Take it easy.' This guy here's supposed to be the sheriff and he comes out here all smooth and calm, like somebody just stole the bubble-gum machine out of the bowling alley. Take it easy, yeah. That's Babe's friend Julius out there in the goddamn lake with a dent in his head and this sorry-ass soak tells me 'Let's call the BCA.' He wants to go home and drink to his wife, is what he wants. Doesn't want to bother himself. Get somebody else to do the work."

Durkins tried to flank Dick and reach the door, but Dick stiff-armed the taller man. Durkins held his ground. His eyes came open wide again and sparkled, angry.

Dick said, "Yeah, sure, hit me now, yellow son-of-a-bitch. Just because I'm telling you the facts. No wonder your old lady split. Couldn't put up with your pouting."

Gun tried to get between them but couldn't move fast enough. The sheriff threw a straight right hand at Dick Chandler's belly but Dick swept it away with his left forearm and brought the other flat against the side of Durkins's head, dropping the man to his knees. Dick hit the sheriff once more, left elbow on right ear, and Durkins fell hard to the kitchen floor. Gun stood back. Dick hadn't allowed his steel hands to so much as touch the other man.

"Now get the hell away from my house and on home where you belong," Dick said. "I don't even want to hear about you again."

Gun helped the sheriff off the floor and outside. Durkins leaned heavily against him on the walk out to his vehicle. "I wish I wouldn't have done that," he said to Gun.

"You're both alive. Shake it off."

"I'd be mad too, if he'd been a friend of mine," said Durkins. "Can't blame him."

Gun opened the door of the Blazer. Durkins sat and looked up at him through his bagel slits. "If I just wasn't so damned worn out, Gun. I'm sorry, but I'm shot."

Gun said, "Doesn't matter how bad you feel, you've got a job to do."

"I know."

"I take it you'll call the family, then. Tell them about their boy."

"First thing, don't worry." Durkins pulled the door closed and started the engine. He rolled down the window. "Can you do me a favor?"

"I might."

"Talk to Babe. The way his dad thinks of me, there's no point in me trying to get anything out of him. I'm thinking of all the stuff going on up on the Rez. Gold-strike rumors and the mining boys. Warrior Pim, that mess. And maybe this Julius kid fits in somehow. See what Babe knows. Or at least try."

"I'll talk to him," Gun said. He had been going to anyway, but was reassured to know the sheriff had at least thought of it. "And I'll tell you what I learn."

Durkins threw the truck in gear. "Gun? Thanks."

Gun walked around the end of Dick's large clap-board house and back to Babe's cabin. A thin stream of woodsmoke rose from the metal chimney. Gun knocked at the narrow door Babe had made from wainscoting left over from Dick's kitchen remodeling project. The door had been cut perfectly and no light came through around the edges. The wainscoting was white pine and varnished with a clear gloss. The single step up to the door was a blackened railroad tie into which had been carved the profile of a bear up on its hind legs.

Babe unlatched the door and drew it partway open. He didn't seem anxious to have Gun inside, but Gun stepped past him into the tiny cabin and helped himself to one of the two old metal-tube kitchen

chairs. The inside of the building was no larger than
Gun's own kitchen, maybe twelve by twelve. A barrel
stove hummed away in a corner, a kitchen table stood
square in the center of the floor, and an army cot
made up tightly with a Hudson Bay blanket was
pushed up against one wall. Above the table a Coleman lantern hung from a log runner. All around the
room on the uppermost row of logs was a border of
carved birds, painted black. The birds were in flight,
and Gun's eyes wanted to follow them in their coun-
terclockwise progress around the room.

"Can we talk?" Gun asked. Babe hadn't moved
from the door. He had his hands stuffed into the
pockets of his blue jeans. His eyes, fixed on one of the
flying birds, were as shiny as black river stones.

"I guess," Babe said quietly.

"How about sitting down, then? I'd be more comfortable. You might, too."

Babe took his hands out of his pockets and walked
over to the table, moving smoothly, like an old
machine with newly greased bearings. He sat down.
He wore a flannel shirt that fit him well and showed
off the adult strength of his body. He may have gotten
his mother's face, but he was built like his dad.

Gun tried to think of what you said to a sixteen-
year-old kid whose friend has just turned up dead, but
nothing sounded even close to right, so he settled for
nothing. Waited for Babe to talk. It took about five
minutes. Then the boy's eyes dropped down from the
dark birds and crashed into Gun's.

"Couple days ago," he said. "Last time I saw him."
He spoke carefully, honoring each word.

"You didn't see Julius last night?"

"No."

Gun could feel the boy's eyes trying to pull away.
"Folks are gonna ask a lot of questions."

"Okay."

"Like who had it in for Julius? And they're gonna
figure you're the one that might have an idea."

21

Babe shrugged, but his eyes didn't look away. He seemed to be gaining confidence.

"You were as close to him as anyone, weren't you, Babe?"

"I guess."

Gun leaned back in his chair and ran his fingers through his short white-gray hair. *Come on, Babe.* "Julius have anything to do with Warrior Pim and his group?" Gun asked. "They're getting a lot of people riled."

Babe laughed and his eyes finally broke free. He shook his head, seemed to relax. "Pim wants the pure-of-heart. Full-blooded minds, you know? Anybody found any gold up there and Julius'd probably be the first one to go after it. He doesn't believe in Pim's dreams. Indian when he wants to be, that's Julius. He doesn't take sides."

"Tell me about the last time you saw him."

Babe got up and tossed two chunks of wood into the barrel stove. He had to put on a pair of leather gloves in order to open the hot cast-iron door. Around the outside of the stove, heat lines threw everything out of focus. "A couple days ago. We did some work together." Babe took an apple from a windowsill and the knife from its sheath. He came back to the table and began to skin the fruit. "Want some?"

Gun nodded. Babe drew the blade through the center of the apple, halving it, and pushed it across the table. He looked up at his flock of crows, followed them around the room with his eyes. "We had a job," he said, chewing. "We did some work for that geology guy that works for DDH. You know, he's got that weird house up by Union Lake?"

"Schell," Gun said.

Babe nodded. Crosley Schell was smack in the center of the fight between the reservation Ojibwa and DDH—Diamond, Day, and Hammond, Inc.—the mining company that for the last year had been test-drilling on land shouldering the Rez. Some were saying Schell had found traces of gold in the old cores that had been taken out of the land years before. Then last month Warrior Pim had started telling his dreams of apocalypse—the earth, attacked by men on steel animals, opening its wide mouth and swallowing up every living thing. There were plenty of Indians who listened and believed: enough people to create a political force. They called themselves Spirit Waters. Pim had put up a buffalo-hide tepee in the middle of the only road leading to the drilling sites, felled a few trees to form a blockade, and invited others to join him. They did. A couple hundred or so.

Gun hadn't been up there himself, but he'd talked to his daughter Mazy, who'd done a story for the Minneapolis paper, and to Carol Long, who edited the local *Stony Journal.* Within days, whole families had followed Pim, and Spirit Waters succeeded in shutting down DDH's test-drilling. According to most accounts, the standoff with DDH had brought revival to the reservation, a new interest in the traditional ways: drums and chanting, sacred visions, shaking tents.

"What kind of work did you do for Schell?" Gun asked.

Babe shrugged. "Painting, stuff like that."

"You painted his house, you and Julius?"

"Storage shed, barn, whatever you call it. Where he keeps all those old core samples somebody took out of the ground way back. He's been going through them for DDH. You know."

"Did Julius's people know he worked for Schell?"

Babe shook his head. "We didn't *work* for Schell. We painted his damn barn. We laid some sod. That's all."

"His family didn't know, then."

"Maybe, maybe not. Julius doesn't care what people think. He does what he has to do to get by."

Gun leaned forward and caught Babe's eyes. "Babe, listen to me. Julius is dead. He's not coming back. You hear me? Somebody probably killed him. And I'm

23

asking you now—why would somebody want to do that? Think about it. All right?"

Babe blinked, then shut his eyes. He took a deep breath and lifted both hands to his face, then rubbed his eyes with his fingertips.

"You think about it," Gun said. "When something comes to you, we'll talk. Babe, all right?" He reached across the table and put a hand on the boy's shoulder. Babe lowered his head and turned away, but he let Gun's hand stay where it was.

4

Gun took his rabbit home and threw it in an iron skillet, whole, with butter and onions and garlic. While the rabbit browned and the kitchen warmed with the smell of it, Gun cut up potatoes in two-inch squares, sliced a pair of tomatoes, half a dozen carrots, and part of a cabbage. He added water to the skillet, a healthy squirt of red cooking wine, then the heap from his cutting board, swiping it into the pan with the cleaver. He put the skillet back on the stove, salted and peppered the right amount from habit, covered the pan, and turned the burner to simmer.

At the kitchen table he rolled a Prince Albert, consciously attending to the process this time because it felt good—the crisp paper at his fingertips and the grainy line of tobacco, roll, lick, twist it tight, admiring his work and holding it close for a sniff, then putting it to his lips and lighting up. There were times you had to slow down and pay attention to the familiar, let your mind empty itself of the big grand stuff. Let it rest and wait, taking in light from the south windows and the sound and smell of slowly boiling stew, the taste of tobacco on your tongue. Then, when your mind was good and ready, it would start to fill up again with the important things: the people you knew, and your obligations to them. And when that happened, and you were thoroughly back in the world, a feeling would come to you—after leaving for just that little snap of time—that life was about to become very fast and complex.

Gun got up and brought the telephone back to the table. Carol Long answered on the second ring. She sounded pleased. Vindicated? Couldn't he leave her alone? "It's not about tonight I called," Gun said.

"Oh."

"Somebody died last night in the lake, right out here. I found him an hour and a half ago. I think he was murdered. You'll be wanting the story."

"Do you know who it is?" Her pitch dropped about an octave, as it always did when the subject got around to business.

"A young man from the reservation. Ojibwa. He's a friend of Babe Chandler's. Julius Marks."

"I'll be right out. Who's there now?"

"Dick. Durkins came and left already. He's bringing in the BCA, and you can bet they won't be another hour or so."

"Will you be home?" Carol asked.

"No, actually. I've got errands in town." Gun was going to say good-bye, but for some reason he got a picture in his mind: the two of them, he and Carol, sitting in his dark kitchen, purple moonlight entering through the window and throwing her shadow against the pine wall. He said, "Carol, I want you to come over tonight."

"Change of plans?" she asked lightly.

"Yes." Or a change of heart.

"Me, too. I mean, I changed *my* plans after we talked. I've got somebody else coming over . . ." She waited a long beat before adding, "for an interview."

"Who?"

"Crosley Schell. Know him?"

"I'd like to. What time is he coming?"

"Nosy, aren't we?"

"Darn right. Do you wish I weren't?"

Carol coughed. "Early evening," she said. "Why don't you come, too? Not for the interview, but later on, say nine o'clock. We'll be wrapping up by then, and I can introduce you. When he leaves, well, we can stare at the fire for a while. Maybe even talk. Who knows?"

Gun was back from town by noon and ate two bowls of stew, wishing he'd left out the third clove of garlic. At one o'clock he lay down for a short nap and woke up at four, the low afternoon sun glaring at him through a west window. He got up and phoned Sheriff Durkins, who answered after too many rings to count.

"I talked to the boy," Gun said.

Durkins made sloppy noises in his throat.

"He didn't say much, but I think he might come around. Said he didn't see Julius last night. One interesting thing, though. He and Julius've been doing some odd jobs for Crosley Schell."

Another throat clearing and the sheriff had his voice. "Ah, that *is* something to look into."

"Did the BCA come out?" Gun asked.

"Yeah. They were quick, too, getting here and leaving. Didn't find much. Pair of prima donnas, thought they were God's gift to . . . something or other." The sheriff coughed again, a deep blast that sounded like a soul ripping loose. "They chipped him right outa there and now I guess they're poking away at him down in Bjorstrum's basement." Bjorstrum was Stony's undertaker.

"They seem to think Julius got himself bludgeoned to death," Durkins went on. "Imagine that. Big discovery on their part. Took about three hundred and twenty-nine pictures of the poor bastard. Had this German shepherd drug hound sniffing around."

"How come you're not down there with them?" Gun asked.

Durkins was quiet for a moment. "Oh, I figured they were up to it. And they don't make for good company."

"Suggestion," Gun said. "You might want to have a talk with Crosley Schell. Babe and Julius did some work for him, Babe told me. Schell could know something helpful."

Durkins sighed. "Thanks, Gun, I'll do that. I'll get him tomorrow."

"How about the kid's family?" Gun said.

"Got hold of his parents right off. Or his dad, at least. The man took it bad too. Came right down to Bjorstrum's and had a look to make sure we had it right. He took a swing at one of those BCA guys, who started asking the poor man questions. I mean right there with the body shivering on the table, still frozen and sitting up, you know? Like, 'Did your kid have a drug problem?' Shit like that. And the old man gave him a good one in the kidney before I could hustle him off. I took him down to Jack Be Nimble's and put enough beer in him to settle him down, then enough coffee so he could drive away. Helluva nice day, is all I can say. And now I gotta be home because Mrs. Solum's at a shower this afternoon and I'm cooking for the kids. Hamburger and macaroni hot dish. Bet you're jealous, Gun."

"You could tell."

"And tonight when Mrs. Solum gets back and the kids are asleep, I'm gonna go out and get so drunk I'll sleep all the way through the hangover."

"Good luck."

"A guy's got to get away from it once every little bit, any way he can."

"So when are you going up to the reservation, start looking into this?"

"Hey, don't worry. Monday I'll be at it. Of course, the BCA's on it too."

"Let me know what you learn."

"I'll do that," said Durkins. "Geez, I wish people

around here would give me a break. Quit crossing the law, at least for a week or two. What I'd like to know is, why'd I ever leave the city?"

Gun set down the receiver, thinking, *Well, character is a hard thing to read.*

Carol Long had recently bought a roomy bungalow of brick and lakestone on Stony's Lake Street, and Gun pulled to a stop in front of it at ten after nine, according to his pocket watch. The engine of his old Ford truck dieseled a half-dozen times before giving up. Carol's Mazda two-seater sat outside her garage on the short driveway. A Renault that Gun had never seen in Stony was parked across the street beneath a streetlight. The living-room end of Carol's house was lit up and Gun walked to the door and knocked.

She opened it right away. She looked good, better than Gun wanted her to look, considering she hadn't been alone tonight: high color in her skin, lipstick running to the orange side of red, which made her straight-cut shoulder-length hair especially dark and full. The few wandering strands of silver in her bangs seemed to radiate light.

"You look nice," Gun said.

Carol took his arm and brought him in. Her fingers pressed hard before letting go. He glanced to the right, saw the fireplace cold, then ahead to the dining room where a man of moderate height and slim build was rising from his chair at the end of Carol's maple table.

"Hard to believe you two haven't met," Carol said, taking Gun's parka. "This is Crosley Schell. Crosley, meet Gun Pedersen."

Gun shook the man's hand. Schell's smile seemed automatic and very used, the lines on either side of his mouth jumping right into place. His light blue eyes were heavy lidded, content, almost sleepy. "I've always, always admired you, Mr. Pedersen. A real pleasure, believe me."

"I've wanted to meet you, too."

"Let's sit down," Carol said.

"I really can't stay more than a few minutes longer," said Schell. "Not that I wouldn't like to," he added, looking at Carol. "But as I said, I've got to get back to Crystal. My Siamese. I'm afraid she's allergic to the new herbs I'm trying to grow. They're imported from the rain forest. Anyway, it's eyedrops every two hours for the poor girl, and I've already been gone for three. She'll be livid."

"What are the herbs for?" Carol asked.

"Oh, you'll laugh at me."

"No, no. Will we, Gun?"

Gun just smiled. *Not out loud, Carol.*

"Okay," said Schell, seeming pleased at her interest. His sleepy eyes got sleepier for an instant, then he yawned, blinked, and shook himself. "They're not hallucinogens, first of all. Fact, you really don't feel a thing except for this heat that sort of stays with you afterwards." His eyes woke for an instant, showing some humor. Not too much. "It's supposed to put you in touch with yourself. Phone call to the soul."

"Does it work?" Carol asked. What a reporter.

Schell laughed. "Work? I expect it does. Mr. Pedersen, you look skeptical." Schell's brow wrinkled up and his mouth made a series of quick puckering motions.

"Not so much that as I am disinterested. Don't let it bother you."

Schell stood up. "Of course, most people are more comfortable leaving these things alone. And you can imagine how that limits their access to the universal mind."

"It's troublesome," Gun said.

Carol stood up, too. She tapped the table with her fingers. "Gun"—she was serious—"coffee?"

"Thanks," Gun said. He looked at Schell. "You heard about the Marks kid?"

The man closed his eyes and raised one hand. "God, yes. Hasn't everybody by now?"

"You know him?"

"I knew him a little. He and the Chandler boy . . . well, you'd know about that if you've talked to Dick. The fact that they did some work for me. You're his neighbor, right?"

"What'd you think of him? Julius, I mean."

"Other than the fact that he was a thief, I thought he was a fine young man. I don't suppose Babe told you that part."

Gun shook his head. "Why don't you?"

Schell eased himself back into the chair. "I haven't talked to anybody about it yet. Maybe if Durkins were in better shape I would have given him a call. As it is, I was planning to talk to the boys myself. I say boys, but my guess is, Julius was the one. Babe might have known, might not've."

"What do you think they took?"

"I don't think. I know. Couldn't have been anybody else. I have this little collection of guns, nothing especially valuable, but a few decent pieces. One day I went into town—Julius and Babe were painting the barn. When I got back that night I noticed the gun missing. A Colt Python revolver. Three-fifty-seven Magnum. Eight-inch barrel with a vent rib. Stainless steel. A pretty thing."

"And you're sure no one else took it?"

"I saw it that morning when I dusted. That evening it was gone."

"You should have at least called Dick," Gun said.

"I should have called somebody, yes. But I didn't. And now it doesn't seem very important, does it?" Schell stood up again. "Carol, it's been lovely," he said. "You ask beautiful questions, and don't forget the standing offer. It'd be a thrill to show you around my house. I think you and Crystal would hit it off."

Carol smiled. "You give a good interview," she said.

"Hey, I'm just glad you're doing it. If people know enough, they'll understand I'm not in this for the money. I want to be sure all sides are treated fairly,

Pim's group included. No one needs to be taken advantage of here." Schell followed Carol to the door and put on his coat, which she had retrieved from the closet. Gun stayed at the table.

"I want you to know, Carol, DDH is grateful and so am I."

"You shouldn't be." Carol's face tightened, and fight came into her emerald-green eyes. "I'm doing a story, not a press release. *I* don't even know how the piece is going to turn out. It could be you won't like it."

Schell laughed sleepily and opened the door. "It'll turn out fine. The facts will speak for themselves." He turned back into the room and waved at Gun. "Good night, Mr. Pedersen."

Gun lifted four fingers from the table.

5

Carol shut the door and leaned back against it. She bent her knees and allowed herself to slide down the door until she was sitting on the Oriental welcome rug. Her mouth was lax, her head slumped forward, but her eyes were stand-up, shoulders-back, chest-out sharp.

"Long day?" Gun asked.

Carol gave him a wide parody of a smile. "You know how to make things real comfortable," she said.

"Thanks." He smiled back.

"Baseball charm school?"

"No. Years of my own company."

Carol propped her chin in her palms, fingers covering her cheeks. She ran her hands through her black hair. "You might have been a little polite. For my sake. This is my house, after all. He was my guest. As you are."

"I'm sorry," Gun said.

"Sure."

"I am—for your sake. I didn't mean to make you uncomfortable."

"That helps a lot."

33

"I didn't like him," Gun said.

Carol shrugged, tilting her head to one side. "He's a very smart man who's walking a very tight rope. Give him some credit. Most people working for a company like that are going to alienate every Indian on the reservation in a month. He's been around for almost two years now, testing those old cores."

"And he's only got half the reservation mad at him."

"Some of the Ojibwa claim he's their friend," Carol said.

"Because he drinks tea from the rain forest?"

"No." Carol's voice was sharp. "Because he tries to understand what they believe, how they think. Which I think is admirable."

"Maybe."

"What do you mean, maybe?"

"You think the guy's for real?"

"Who's to say he's not?"

"Just asking," Gun said.

"Sounds to me like you've made up your mind."

"All right, all right." Gun felt like the night was about ten words from getting away. He held up his hands, palms out. "I'll take your word for it. The man is for real. And I'll grant him his smarts. Everything I hear, it's been God's own job doing that testing for DDH without getting killed. He's gotta be doing something right. But tell me . . ." Gun was following Carol into the living room now, accepting her motioned offer to sit down on the pillow-backed couch. "A gun collection? The guy drinks herbal tea. He's got a cat named Crystal. He talks about the universal mind."

"So, he's complicated." She sat down next to him and moved in close. He could smell her; she was the South Pacific tonight, a little salt but mostly the soft hint of flowers. "I know somebody else who's complicated," she said, smiling. "It's not that unusual. Now, do you want to talk about Crosley Schell or do you

34

want me to go after the dessert I put in the freezer this afternoon? Don't forget, it's your birthday."

As she stood up and left the room, Gun noticed the lilt was back in her stride, the one he'd seen when he first met her. The one that told him she was pleased with herself and didn't care if people noticed or if they didn't. Gun, for his part, always had, even if his attention of late had been divided.

The problem was, if you weren't ever-diligent, if you dropped your guard at the wrong instant, you could take one square on the heart and go to your knees, blinking and trying not to love it too much. If you got your wits about you fast enough, you could get up and get away before she put you all the way down. Move too slowly and well, that was it. Gun knew from experience. A decade ago he'd moved too slowly and lost his wife. This time he'd gotten up after that first blow and kept moving—his will, if not his whole mind, fixed on Carol.

From the kitchen came the sound of the coffee grinder, then faucet water going into the glass coffee-pot. Carol sung a Garth Brooks tune, her voice low and roadhouse convincing. Gun leaned back into the sofa's soft pillows. He whistled to match Carol's pitch and fell in with the melody. In his mind he went down to the water and peopled an old wooden boat with Crosley Schell, frozen Julius, Dick and Babe Chandler, and Jason Durkins. Still whistling, he took the oars from the oarlocks and threw them on shore. He gave the boat a mighty shove into open water and set a stiff breeze blowing out. Then he sat down on a rock and watched the little boat and those crowded into it getting smaller and smaller until they were almost nothing—somebody else's neighbors, somebody else's friends, somebody else's concerns.

When Carol floated into the room and used her lips to silence Gun's whistling, the boat disappeared into a sweet-smelling bank of fog.

* * *

Ten minutes later, reluctantly, Gun agreed to let Carol go after coffee and dessert.

"I'm not hungry, though," he said, holding on to one of her fingers. She was standing above him, trying—though not too hard—to pull away.

"Yes you are." She leaned down and stared into him. "It's right there, right in there. I can see it." Her smile fled, then, and her eyes entered his with such force it almost hurt. He let go of her finger. "Be right back," she said.

And she was, with a tray of steaming china cups and china dessert plates heavy with thick black wedges of something that belonged behind glass in a restaurant whose name was unpronounceable.

"Take it away, can't afford it," Gun said.

"Guess the flavor." Carol meant the coffee. It was a game they had, and one Gun could rarely win. In fact he always lost. His eyes, even after ten years away from baseball, were fast and true, but his nose had never excelled at anything. He leaned down into the steam rising from the cup she'd placed in his hand. He waggled his nose in it. He pretended to concentrate, crunching the muscles in his forehead. He hummed. He cocked his head. He had no idea what the flavor was. Coffee was coffee.

"It's a combination this time," said Carol, waiting.

"Clue?"

"Let's see." She sipped from her cup and thought for a moment. "It'll go well with dessert, but it won't be redundant."

"And what's for dessert?"

"Coffee ice-cream pie with fudge frosting. Real fudge."

Gun groaned his pleasure. "Not redundant?" he said.

"Well, the coffee part is, of course. But other than that."

"Wow, great clue."

"Hurry up, guess."

He picked two flavors out of the blue. "Irish cream and French vanilla," he said.

Carol blinked and her lips came open. She scowled. "You went back there and read the labels. When did you do that? You sneak."

"Admit it, my nose is superior."

"Your luck, maybe."

"That, too." He tasted his coffee without taking his eyes from Carol's. He said, "I was almost jealous when I got here tonight, seeing how good you looked."

"Almost?"

"Okay, jealous."

They drank their coffee and ate their coffee ice-cream pie. The fudge frosting was black and rich and as chewy as caramel. Gun wanted to speak but feared being more—or less—than honest. Carol Long was not the kind of woman you could soothe for the sake of the moment. He shook his head over his plate, which was still heavy, and pointed the fork toward his mouth. "This is . . . I don't know. Any of the words I could find would insult your powers. Mmmmm, I like it."

"Gun—are you really back?" Carol asked.

He looked down into his cup but felt her eyes on him. "I'm here," he said. "Not there."

"For how long?"

Turning to the large picture window that faced the street, he saw snow falling outside. The flakes were visible only in the cone of light that descended from the streetlamp and had turned the windshield of his old truck white, covering up its pattern of cracks. Gun thought of the hole in the ice where Julius Marks had spent last night. His last night. It would have frozen over again by now, and by morning the new snow would leave the place unremarkable. He thought of Babe Chandler lying on the narrow cot in his cabin surrounded by wooden blackbirds, and his father Dick fifty yards away, alone in the house. He brought his eyes to bear on Carol's face: her good chin and perfect lips, the bottom one full, the top curved and delicate. Her deep, lovely green eyes.

He said, "I wasn't ever gone, Carol. Not really."

"It sure felt like it to me."

Gun shook his head. In the tone of her voice and the look in her eye she made it seem as if he'd committed the worst sort of betrayal. It hadn't come to that; he hadn't allowed it to. He'd been careful as a priest, or nearly. He set his coffee cup and his plate of dessert on the low table in front of the couch, took Carol's dessert, too, and set it down. "You haven't kissed the birthday boy," he said. "One for every year, that's the rule."

"Our desserts," said Carol. "We can't let them melt."

"It'll be a shame, won't it?"

The letter's timing was sweet-edged spooky. It was all by itself in Gun's rural delivery when he finally got home. Two in the morning, new snow putting a pretty bookend on the evening with Carol and he pulled the old Ford up next to the box, and opened it. The envelope had an eastern postmark. He thought: *Someday, somewhere, something ought to be simple.*

The letter had no salutation, just started straight off at the top of the page and nailed him. Black ink on white paper in a clear, female hand.

The night we sat out on the deck of Billy's boat, I asked you if there was someone up north who was important to you and all I got was silence. A big impressive silence, too, and it ought to have said as well as words what the situation was, only it didn't. Maybe I was too grieved over Billy to understand the obvious. Maybe the grief and that Florida humidity was messing with my standards of decency and I thought I could take you for a while—you know?—and the hell with your commitments. Listen. If you had only stayed then, Gun, just stayed a little while, I would have let you go. Do you see? Bereaved and desperate, that was me. I'm a scriptwriter, don't think I don't understand my own actions, but understanding only takes a person so far. You were a good thing, and I knew it. I would've settled for temporary.

But the pages keep turning, don't they, and I seem to be getting through the tough midsection of the storyline. I'm all through expecting it to be Billy every time the phone rings, I can play a hand of poker on the set these days without crying when I draw the queen of diamonds. It still jolts me some when I wake up suddenly in the night, hearing the house creak like when Billy used to let himself in on one of his surprise visits. But I'm healing.

And there's work. "Movie of the Week" last week was a script of mine—don't worry, I know you won't have seen it—and at last I'm getting a shot at cinema. Tri-Star, big budget, filming next spring in Toronto. Story involves a ballplayer. Wait and see.

Or don't wait. You don't have to. I'm saying this again as if we were still sitting there at midnight on the deck, as if I'm still interested and wondering. Are you alone now? Do you want to be?

Another big impressive silence, and I'll know for sure. But if you come looking, show up here or on location, then be warned that I'm over Billy now and healthy. Come near me again, Gun Pedersen, and I won't settle for temporary. I promise you.

Diamond

He read it through once. Slowly. More than that and he'd be up for hours, he knew it, sitting at the kitchen table while the sun worked its way round to this side of the planet. Sitting there thinking about ways to go wrong, and how easy it would be, and how a man might enjoy it until his next planeload of truth and good hopes fell down from the sky in flames.

6

The phone call came early.

Gun was buried in the deepest kind of sleep, and partly because of that, partly because he'd recently switched bedrooms on account of a well-placed leak in the roof, he had to ask himself a hard question: *Which side of the bed do I get out on?* He chose the left and swung himself hard into the log wall. His kneecap howled. He rolled to his right and hit the floor running, smashed his little toe on the doorjamb.

No moon or stars tonight, so no light coming in through the windows. No light to see by. Limping and hurting, Gun reached the phone in the kitchen by feel. "Yeah," he said into it.

"Babe's gone." It was Dick, and he sounded grim. The lighted clock above the refrigerator said four thirty.

"What do you mean, gone, Dick?" Gun knew the boy was used to coming and going according to his whims.

"I mean gone, as in, he snuck off like a criminal. Can you come over? Now?"

"Fifteen minutes," said Gun.

"Dress warm. She's way down out there and not coming up any time soon, I hear."

In spite of the temperature, the Ford started on the first crank and Gun drove the near-mile to Dick's place through the silver glitter his headlights made of the light snow falling. There were a couple of inches of new stuff on the ground.

Dick's face was centered in the lit-up window of his front door, and his eyes stared out from deep inside his head. "I got up at four to use the can, couldn't sleep," he said, letting Gun into the kitchen. "I looked out the window back there, like I do. Make sure Babe's got a proper fire, especially on a night like this, but I didn't see any smoke. Looked like a cold chimney, so I thought I better take a walk and check on him." Dick was bent at the wood stove, shoving two-foot chunks of oak through its open door. He looked up at Gun. "I found his cupboard cleaned out, his little closet too. Took damn near everything he owns. Plus *my* little cash fund, what I keep in a little pot underneath my bed. My bed, damn it."

Gun nodded toward Babe's cabin. "Mind if I have a look?"

"Not necessary," Dick said. "He's headed for one of two places, which is why I called you. I can't follow both trails with just two legs." Dick stood up and took his parka from the back of a kitchen chair, shrugged himself into it, and moved toward the front door. Gun stayed put next to the wood stove. Dick looked back at him. "Okay, go ahead. Ask your question," he said.

"I thought Babe did this kind of thing a lot. You're always saying how he likes to roam, stick his nose into the woods and follow it around for a few days, is how you tell it."

"This time's different, Gun, besides the money he took. He normally's got a way of telling me when he's gonna leave. He'll get ahead on chores, for one thing, split up enough wood to last me a while. Another thing, he always leaves his cabin neat as a widow's parlor, cleaned up and sparkling. He's a fussy kid that way. But not this time. He's never gone and left his place such a mess. Come on, if it's gonna make you feel better we'll have a look." Dick pushed out the door and Gun followed, thinking of Crosley Schell's missing revolver and hoping Babe wasn't into something a whole lot bigger than petty theft.

The tiny cabin was chilly. The stove held a few still-glowing coals but mostly white ash. The place wasn't as bad as Dick had suggested but it hadn't been straightened much, either. Outdoor magazines lay scattered beside the cot, which was tossed over with a heap of blankets. Dick opened the door of the small cupboard to display its empty shelves, then pointed to a pair of nails on the wall above the stove.

"See there? That's where he hangs his frying pan and cook pot."

"And you know where he went," Gun said.

Dick nodded. "One of two places. Depending on . . ." He scratched at his head with one steel hand and looked up at the crows on the wall, then shut his eyes. "Shit," he said. "What do you think he's messed up in, my kid?"

"What do *you* think?"

Dick seesawed his neck. His eyes were still closed. "I'm telling myself it's got nothing to do with Julius. Or if it does, it's just a matter of Babe getting upset, scared. Needing to get away. He's like that, you know. Like his mother. She'd leave, too. Just take off whenever the mood hit her. She left us a couple dozen times before that last time when she didn't come back. She'd go up to the Rez and stay with her family for a few days, sometimes a week, then show up back here, no warning, waltz back into her kitchen and make supper. Chicken, that was her comeback food. Usually had one with her, butchered from her family's yard."

"You think Babe's up there?" Gun asked. "Or going that way?"

"He might be, yeah. Fact, I'm sure he is—if he's clean. Julius, see, he might've had a few differences with his people, but that Marks family—everybody up there on the Rez—they know how to close ranks. Babe wouldn't go near the reservation if he thinks they're even gonna imagine they smell blood on him."

"And what if he thinks they will?"

Dick raised one steel hand and pointed it at Gun. He shook it like somebody with a real hand shakes a finger. "If I'm wrong—and I don't think I am—but if I'm wrong, and my kid has something to do with this shit, then the only place he'd go is up to Shorty Heller's. You know Shorty?"

"I know who he is," Gun said. Shorty Heller had a lodge up on the North Shore. People called it the Babe Ruth lodge, because during the thirties Ruth had made a habit of going up there once a year for the fall fishing.

"Well, Shorty and I go back the distance. Forty years now. He was good to me when I was an ornery kid that didn't deserve it. Hired me on out of reform school after he saw me play second base. That was the summer I was thirteen. I had hands, then." Dick grinned. "But he made a hell of a difference to me, Gun. I spent five summers with him. Dock boy and such. And my kid and I've been up to see him every year for the last sixteen—well, since Babe was born. Shorty's got a way with the young ones, see, and he reached in and grabbed onto my boy's tough little heart same as he did mine. I'm telling you, Gun, if Babe's in real trouble, he'd trust Shorty before he'd trust me. I'm ashamed to say it."

"What's Shorty going to do if Babe shows up?"

"Tell him the right and wrong of things. Then let him decide for his own self what to do. Shorty's not gonna put the dogs on him. If Babe wants to run, Shorty'll say, 'Okay then, run.'"

"How does he get there, Dick? It's a good, what, hundred and fifty miles down the road?"

"Hitch. He's done it before. Highway 30's a straight shot over."

"He could be there already," Gun said, but Dick was shaking his head. "You called Shorty?"

"Yup," said Dick, "but, shit, I'm not sure if Shorty's coming clean with me over the wires. I'd have to see the old devil's face."

"Let's say Babe's headed for the reservation. Is he going by thumb?"

"I highly doubt it. That stretch of road between here and there's got more state troopers and local cops than my woodpile's got rats in the summertime. Babe'd be thinking 'Stay clear of Highway 7.' Nope. If he's going that way tonight, then Babe's a runner, wearin' out his boots. And the weather what it is, the cold and new snow and all, he's not gonna make it up there by morning, not by a long shot." Grinning, Dick clicked his steel hands together in front of his chest. "And I can tell you where he'd lay up at first light."

"You better, if that's where you're sending me."

"Here's the thing. If he's in real trouble, then *I* want to be there. If he's not, well . . . then he's not. Which means I'll head for Shorty's."

"And I go where?"

"Nowhere—" said Dick. "Unless you promise me something. That you won't call Durkins in. I want *him* out of it till this is all over."

Gun shook his head and checked his pocket watch. Five-fifteen. "Sorry, Dick. If you don't want my help, I'll go home. I can't make that promise."

"The man's no good to anybody. You should be able to see that, Gun."

Gun leaned back to stretch out some of the sleep stiffness still left in his shoulders and back. "And we're no good to anybody as long as we're standing around here. Probably won't need Durkins anyway."

Dick sucked air and blew it out his nose, a disgusted bull. "Okay," he said. He opened a small drawer in Babe's kitchen table. He removed a pencil and a tablet of lined paper. "I'll draw you a map."

Gun knew the spot, more or less. He'd been there years ago in the fall, tracking a gut-shot deer. It was ten miles northeast of Stony Lake: a forest of old bur oaks about a mile square that gave way on the north to a tamarack bog, the whole tract of three or four hundred acres belonging to a doctor from Minneapolis who'd once taken cartilage from Gun's left knee. The deer population had always been healthy—the oaks providing forage, the tamaracks protection—and Gun didn't feel badly for taking advantage of his acquaintance with the doctor. Acorn-fed venison was the best cold-winter food he'd ever come across.

A rail line cut through the property north to south and served, Dick said, as the trail Babe and Julius had often used to come and go, shining deer. The land was about halfway between Dick's place and the reservation, a good resting place if you were going to the Rez by foot. No one lived on it, the doctor never even came around, and though deer shining was illegal outside the Rez, nobody bothered the boys. They put up a little shack half a mile south of the northernmost property line and stayed there overnight sometimes, dressing their harvest.

All of this background—the poaching, the trespassing—Dick had explained without apparent remorse, and Gun, who was driving north with the sky just beginning to lighten on his right, understood that the natives of the region didn't see game laws as applying to themselves so much as to outsiders who might not have proper respect for the land's goodwill.

Gun knew when to leave the highway when he saw the rusting carcass of an early sixties Cadillac with two big fins in back, one of them tipped sideways. The dead car flashed at the edge of Gun's vision and he braked to a stop. He threw the Ford into reverse, backed up, and eased into the ditch. He crept past the Cadillac and gunned the truck up a slight incline between a useless telephone pole and a crooked bur oak, then into the woods. He drove blind for twenty or thirty yards before he could make out old tire tracks beneath the new covering of snow.

He drove slowly and carefully. Several times his tires lost traction on hillsides where snow greased the smooth dead grass. Once he had to back up fifty yards to gather speed for an uphill run, hoping as he climbed that when he reached the top there'd be no surprises. No fallen trees, no sudden drops or turns.

At the dry slough marking the line between the bur oaks and the tamaracks, Gun stopped the truck and got out. He knew Babe's shack was close by. He walked to the railroad grade, scrambled to the top, paused for a moment between the tracks to consult his inner compass, and started off on a straight line toward a particularly tall tree that said to his mind "East."

The clearing was less than a hundred yards away. And sitting right beneath his guiding tree was a small dark shack shaped like a lean-to, with a roof that started high on one side and slanted nearly to the ground at the other. A heavy gray line of smoke rose from the tin-can chimney, the kind of smoke you get from damp wood burning slow.

Gun made a wide circle around the shack, taking his time. There were no windows. No back door. The shack was nothing but a sleep shelter made of scrap boards gone dark from the weather. Gun stood at the door for a minute, wishing Dick had been the one to come here. He wasn't at all sure what to say to the boy.

He hadn't decided on an opening line when he heard Babe start humming inside. The melody was simple, repetitive, and familiar, calling Gun back twenty years to his daughter's childhood, and as the words entered his mind—*this old man, he plays one, he plays knick-knack on my thumb*—Gun's concerns about what to say disappeared. He smiled and began to hum along. He knocked.

Inside, Babe stopped humming. The door creaked open. Just a crack at first, then it swung in. Babe stood like somebody about to get hit, his arms in front of himself, protective. He wore a heavy wool shirt, no shoes. His dark eyes were fierce in concentration.

"It's only me," Gun said. "What's wrong, Babe?"

The boy took two slow steps backward, making no sound. Gun crossed the rough-sawn threshold and entered the shack, which was dark and clogged with the heavy smell of the damp fire. The low ceiling forced him to hang his head. Babe slid to Gun's right, his eyes moving to the doorway, greedy to leave.

"Stick around," Gun told him, "we've got to talk."

"I don't think so," Babe said. He dropped his head, feinted left, spun, and ricocheted toward the door. Gun's hand reacted on its own, catching the seat of Babe's trousers. Gun lifted him kicking into the air and swung him into the room, dropped him on his butt. Babe swore and bounced back up. Gun reached behind himself to push the door closed, couldn't find it, turned. The instant he looked away he felt a burning thump on the right thigh and went to one knee. Then Babe was out the door and gone, running in bare feet across the snowy clearing and disappearing into the trees. Gun pushed himself up and went after him.

There were tracks to follow, of course, bare footprints spaced widely at a gallop, slowing and closing some as Gun reached the trees. The boy's feet would freeze in minutes. At the clearing's edge something bright in the snow brought Gun to his knees. It was mostly hidden in the snow—a stainless-steel revolver with a long, long barrel. Gun stood up and put it inside the zipper pocket of his parka.

"Babe!" he shouted, entering the woods. "Come on." He followed the footprints into and out of a shallow ravine with jagged rocks then over a small hill covered with tight red willow growth. He was calling out and moving as quickly as he dared on the uneven ground.

He lost Babe's trail briefly as the tracks disappeared into a dense stand of young straight aspens. The trees were about five inches in diameter, not large enough yet to have thinned each other out, and growing among them were bushes with hardware-store nails for thorns. Gun had to crouch low in order to find Babe's footprints, took a thorn in the cheek, and thought, *Why in God's great earth is he leading me in here?*

He got his answer right away. A whipping sigh sounded just to his rear. He started to turn, felt something snap tight around his ankle, and then his body flipped clean over like an egg timer. The trees around him hung upside down, bouncing and bobbing, then came to rest, still upside down. He felt blood charging into his brain and the flesh of his face pulling oddly toward the top of his head. His parka slid up around his armpits, the big revolver working like an anchor in his pocket.

He was hanging by one ankle from a rope tied to the supple trunk of an arching aspen. He'd seen the trick a dozen times in Western movies growing up—the old

Indian snare—but somehow he'd never imagined himself in the white man's role.

Slowly he reached into his trouser pocket for his jackknife, careful as he put it in his hand not to let the knife slip past and fall to the snow. He opened the knife and tested the blade against his thumb. Adequate. He squeezed his abdominals and folded his body upward toward his roped ankle. He moved slowly, half-expecting something in his gut to give way. Everything held.

Just as he caught hold of the rope with his free hand, he moved his forehead into a thorn. He dropped back down, the whole length of him whipping out straight. *Ouch, damn!* and he lost the knife to the snow.

He arched his neck backward to catch sight of the knife, saw it right away, blade up in the snow. He tried to stretch for it. The very tip of his finger felt the tip of the knife. He reached again, making himself as long as he could. Still, just the fingertip.

"I can't believe this," Gun said out loud. He let his body rest for a minute, all except for the joint of his knee, which didn't appreciate the stress of Gun's two hundred and forty pounds pulling it apart. He was thankful it was the right knee. The left one might have given way. By now, of course, Babe would be back in the shack, getting his shoes on, putting his things together for flight. The boy would get a good head start and there'd be no way for Gun to catch him before he made it to the reservation, or wherever he was bound for.

Gun shook himself loose, trying to summon another half-inch or so of stretch. Once more he reached for the knife, reached with every fiber of himself. It wasn't possible. The knife stayed where it was, useless in the snow. Gun's trapped foot began to tingle and go numb. He couldn't feel his toes. He could see that the rope on his ankle was tied in a slip knot; it would only get tighter the longer he was hanging. A charley horse started up in his right hamstring, which was tired now from keeping a check on his knee joint.

"Don't come down on that blade a'yours." The voice came from Gun's left. A low soft voice, flat, like the kind owned by someone not used to talking. Gun twisted to see who it might be and saw no one. Not at first. Then a dark shape behind a bush of thorns moved and rose.

The man wasn't especially tall, but big nonetheless, broad in the shoulders, long from neck to waist. His head was large and square, but his features were small and set very close together in the center of a huge face. He wore a fur hat and a denim jacket with a filthy sheepskin collar. On his feet were hide mukluks.

"Go ahead and use it," Gun said, pointing to his knife in the snow.

But the man pulled out a knife of his own, a skinner with a leather handle and a blade in the shape of a crescent moon. He moved close, grabbed hold of Gun's knee, and pulled down against the springy tree trunk to bring the rope to within reach. He severed the rope with a quick swipe of the blade, making no effort to ease Gun's fall to earth—just slashed, then glided away into the heavy thorns and new aspens.

"Thanks," said Gun, but the man was gone already, even the sound of him.

Gun reached for his numb right foot and began to rub it back to life, glad for angels.

8

Gun's rule was never to talk to friends about their kids. He figured you could talk what you knew, and for him that didn't include the subtleties of child raising so much as the look of a hanging curve ball. Or an empty house. Come to think of it, he didn't talk about those much either. Still, kids were another universe, especially a kid that could matter-of-fact mess you up the way Babe Chandler could, dangle you neat as a dressed buck and slip off that way. It was embarrassing.

He pulled into Chandler's under a cold mushy sky and found Dick in the cluttered dark of his garage, a pair of empty five-gallon buckets swinging from one of his hooks. He raised the other hook hello.

"Dogs get an extra meal tonight," he said. "I'll be gone tomorrow."

"Headed for the reservation?" *Delay, delay.*

"Kid is strong, Gun. Too damn strong. You know his mom's up there. Her family."

"Mmm." Gun pulled the white paper sack from his pocket.

"And Julius, too, his people are there." Dick huffed,

lifted the lid of an old chest freezer, reached in with his free hook.

"There's this you should know about Julius, Gun. I liked the kid, liked him a lot, but God cradle his soul, he was a problem." Rising up, Dick showed Gun three gray fish the length of his forearm, carp from the big gray scales of them and the surprised round mouths. Nicely hooked at the gills until Dick dumped them in the buckets, tails up. He saw Gun watching and said, "Look, no gloves."

Gun took the big revolver out of the sack while Dick went fishing again. When he surfaced with three more carp, Gun said, "This look familiar?"

Dick squinted. "Well, it has a barrel and trigger. I'd say what you got there is a pistol. Mighty big one too."

"I took it away from your boy. He was at the hunting shack."

There was a push lawn mower behind Dick and he sat down on it without looking, right on the Briggs & Stratton. Gun felt like a rookie again, the look he was getting.

"I take it you didn't bring him along back with you," Dick said.

"My own fault. Did you teach him that snare business?"

Dick smiled. "Get swept up, did you?"

"Like Fess Parker among the Comanches. It was blasted uncomfortable."

"He can be," Dick said, standing now, getting back in the freezer, "an eerie child."

"What about the pistol?"

Dick didn't hesitate long. "Well, he stole it, I expect."

The dogs were tethered in front of their stubby shelters, a crescent of them strung out on the lake-shore fifty yards from the house. Hearing Dick on the path and anticipating carp, they set up an enormous howl, eleven dogs with names like Lion and Kudu and

Vulture. "The hell of it is, I've never been to Africa," Dick said. "Guess the reservation'll have to do."

Gun followed Dick on the sloppy path from dog to dog. They were pullers all right, bred in the Northwest Territories and built low for their weight. Two had wolf in them, Dick said, look at the silvertip hairs on their backs. He'd bought them for lead dogs but they didn't have the calm for it though they had the strength and stamina. To each dog he gave a frozen carp and a loving curse and a few strokes with the steel-smooth curve of his right hook. The howls subsided to high-breaking whines and Dick shook out the empty buckets.

"Old Julius," he said. "You can pick your own friends, you know, but not your boy's. 'Course you can maybe *in*fluence your boy, pass along a bite of good judgment or two, not that I ever had a surplus of it myself." He talked without bitterness or apparent anxiety, as though his son were out camping in June instead of running alone through the woods in early winter. "When Margaret left, went back to her family on the Rez, I took him up there all the time. Summers, holidays. He always felt more Indian than white, hell, I feel that way myself, so I encouraged it. He made friends."

"What was Julius, five years older?"

"Something like that. Babe was probably six, seven, and he comes home talking about this big kid he was palling around with. I figured, what's to worry about? Heroes never last, they get bored with it and tell the little squirts to go find someone their own age."

"My guess is Babe kept up pretty well."

"His trouble is he's always kept up well. Something about Babe, he was a baby for maybe his first three years, and then he was a little boy for about a week and a half, and then he turned serious. Got to be the little man."

That, Gun guessed, would've been about when Margaret left home.

Dick said, "That was about the only argument I never used on her, 'You leave, you'll wreck the boy.' He and I were such buddies I figured he could take it." Dick tossed Gun one of the empty buckets. "Here, pull your weight."

Gun waited a little and said, "You have any ideas about Julius? Was he into something that's got Babe scared?"

"Julius had enough larceny in him so it might've been plenty of things. He burgled somebody or pulled some little swindle, maybe Babe was along." He stopped, regarded Gun with a patient eye. "And I'll say this, I don't pretend my kid is an innocent. He's smart for his age and strong, and for the sake of one's purity that's not always the right combination. The reservation's an easy place to get away with things."

"He's just sixteen," Gun said.

"Tell me about sixteen, Fess Parker."

They slogged back up the path under the early-closing November sky, a single overlaying cloud making everything gray as carp scales, a damp wind at their throats. They broke from the main path and went up through a thin stand of aspens and came out at Dick's little round-roofed barn. "Put your hand on the door there," Dick said. "A little higher up, there. Warm, is it?"

"Comes through the gloves." Looking down Gun saw the snow had shrunk back away from the metal shed, leaving a shallow wet strip like a moat.

"Go on in. Light's on the right."

There was one jungle-breath gust of heat when Gun opened the door and then it was bearable. The pair of hanging light bulbs showed plain unfired bowls and redstone bisques lining racks of metal shelves, tall blue-brown glazed canisters with lids leaning at their sides, some of them with lettering: MINNESOTA WILD RICE. "Damn tourists," Dick said, "you got to tell them what goes inside, or they won't buy it." At the far end of the room crouched the monster, Dick's wide brick kiln. It sat in the shadows with its square steel door cracked open. The room got warmer as they approached it.

"I shut her down this morning," Dick said. "Twenty-six hundred Fahrenheit, though, she's like an angry wife, the way the heat resides." He stretched forth to hook the door's steel handle, set his feet wide and pulled slow. It came creaking, the door rolling on casters set into tracks on the floor. Dick was muttering "Easy, easy," and Gun saw that attached to the inside of the door were the guts of the kiln itself, its firebrick shelves. They slid out cooling into the room, shelves of glazed plates that ticked like a griddle taken off the heat. Dick smiled, showing gold.

"Not at all bad," he said. He reached for a plate and levered it up gently in his hooks. It was white, edged with a thin powder-blue rim.

"Nice," Gun said.

"It was Babe who took that government truck a couple years ago. Remember that?" Dick was talking now while he looked at the white plate. Gun could see heat coming off it in the yellow light.

"Guess I missed it."

"So did the government. You recall that reservation textile shop, got the grant to make canvas tents for the army? It was gonna bring prosperity to that little Rez town, Four Corners. Well named, incidentally."

"Factory closed, as I remember."

"It did. They made ten, twelve shipments maybe, got good and far behind on their contract, which is what comes of trying to make a million tents with a few Indians huddled around an attic full of old Singers. The army figured, shoot, it was a good try and not bad PR for a week or two, and they pulled out." Dick put the white plate down and hooked up another, holding it up against the weak light. "Second or third shipment, though, the feds sent the big truck to get the tents, and the driver's an Ojibwa from Leech

Lake. More PR, some smart front-office guy thinking if he sends an Indian to the Rez on a job, maybe he'll run into a friend or two, talk 'em into joining up. And sure enough, the driver runs into a buddy of his, only it's Julius, see; and Julius pounds him on the back, snagging his keys because he's good at that, passes them off to Babe, and then Julius hauls his old pal twenty miles to the nearest beer. While they're gone Babe gets in the old government truck and drives away into the woods."

Dick was grinning. "Told you I hadn't much judgment. I still think it's funny."

"Must have a happy ending."

"Missing truck actually got written up in the Minneapolis paper, with a few factual mistakes. Paper linked it to this Spirit Waters outfit that's up there now, keeping the mining people out. Painted it heroic, you know; the idealistic Ojibwa people, making a statement against the military."

Wrapping up now Dick got busy with the plates, handling the still-hot glazeware with surprising speed, laying each piece out on the shelves to his right. "Best part was, the Spirit Waters people never denied it. They were looking for ink at the time, I guess. The feds found the truck a couple days later, no harm done. 'Course by then every Indian boy who wanted one had got himself a nice new tent. You ever see one of those? Army issue?"

Gun said, "Spirit Waters is getting the ink *these* days, hey? Warrior Pim and his visionaries."

It took the smile from Dick and he slowed momentarily in his work. "I don't like it much, Gun. Nothing's happened yet but you name me a place where Indians have tried to stand off whites and won." He looked up. "I'm going there in the morning, up to the camp."

"To see Babe."

Dick huffed a sigh. "I didn't tell you this—but

Warrior Pim? He's Babe's cousin. Margaret's brother's boy." Dick finished clearing out the kiln then almost recklessly tore down the firebrick shelves, sweeping them steel forearmed into a box.

"Do you know," he told Gun, "I was a lot slower at this when I had hands."

9

Dick Chandler drove a tiny burgundy Subaru with tall, narrow bucket seats and doors that Gun thought he might be able to put his thumb through if he tried. "It's called a Justy," Dick said, fighting the steering, "because it's Justy nuff, and nothin' more."

They'd left before sunup, moving away from Stony Lake on Highway 7 to the north. "You notice how there's no direct route to the Rez? Like nobody lives up there." Dick saw a pothole in the headlights, swerved and hit another—bigger—one that darted into the beam. "Damn near true, too."

Gun said, "You don't think he had any trouble."

"Nope." Dick heard what Gun wasn't saying and added, "I'm not being coarse about it, I just know Babe. The boy *lives* in the woods, Gun, and he left well stocked. If he knows where he wants to go, he just shuts his eyes and he's there. Where I *think* he is, I think he's at May Marks's place. Julius's cousin, the three of them were always together."

"You don't think he's with Pim? At the blockade?"

"We'll stop there first; it's closer. May's place is a little more north." Dick glanced at Gun. "You ever met Warrior Pim?"

"Nope."

"My guess is he's not what you'll expect." Dick let that float in the quiet between them as the sun came awake at last, sending its stretchers up over a rim of black pines. The rays reached up deep bright and slow, the color of sunflowers seen through a glassful of honey. It was, Gun thought, a sunrise made to be watched with a woman. They drove northeast as the morning got bigger around them and Dick said, "Hand me some of that coffee."

The blockade had none of the imposing look Gun felt should accompany the word. It showed up suddenly in front of the Subaru when they were still a mile from the reservation, visible at first only as a few fallen trees and parked cars, like a storm had come through in the night and clogged the road. They slowed, drove in close. Three sagging Chevrolets were parked in the ditch, rigored over with hard frost, as was an orange Opel from 1974, headlights intact and round with shock over having survived into the '90s. Straight ahead stood the blockade itself: a handful of jack pines, not big ones, cut and dragged across the county blacktop. Through gaps in the mangy barrier, a couple of trailer houses showed, the universal pale green of their vintage, and some angular white shapes Gun knew from the storybooks of boyhood. Tepees.

Dick pulled the Subaru over and shut it off. No one was visible. Gun rolled his window down and smelled cold woods, wet campfires.

"What do we do, you suppose?" Dick said. "Knock?"

"Stretch first." Gun wrung the door open and felt himself creak going upright. The cold helped; overnight the clouds had blown off and the sun was ten minutes up, blazing and worthless. He straightened his arms, waved them, did a deep knee bend. He was reaching back through the window for the thermos when a quiet tan shape loped around the near end of the blockade.

"The Devil in church clothes," Dick said. It was a dog, tall as a young deer even with its head held warily low. Short tan hair and a nose unnaturally shiny and a large head rounded on top like a man's. The dog drifted toward them with its hind legs sliding out to one side.

"Booger!" screamed a child's voice. The dog stopped and raised its head. There was motion in the green scrag of the barrier and a girl's face pushed through. "Boo*ger!*" she said, drawing the word into a threat. Seven, eight years old, Gun thought. The dog blinked and growled at Gun. He said, "Go on, pooch," and dog and child retreated.

"Well," Dick said, "we won't have to knock."

Though as it turned out they almost did. Following Booger's path around the blockade they saw the whole encampment of a couple of dozen or so tepees, smoke coming up from the tops, and a mess of trailer houses, one wearing a TV antenna strapped on with what looked like leather belts. Still there was no one; even the girl had disappeared. Dick led with a measure of comfort, as though he knew the way, and Gun realized that though Margaret had left years ago, some of these were her people, and that gave Dick an undeniable claim upon them. If Babe were here, great, he'd have his chance to explain why he ran. If Babe hadn't come, they'd check with May Marks. If he wasn't there, it'd be time to worry.

"Morning, you sonsabitches."

On the other hand, maybe it was time already.

"Ease up. Not pointing at you. Go on up to the trailer." The speaker was a tall Ojibwa in a brown canvas hunting coat who had stepped out suddenly from a hidden place in the barrier. He would have been handsome if not for a wide, red mouth distorted, it seemed, by anger or bitterness. And if not for the 30-30 he was carrying; that had an unhappy effect.

"We're looking for Babe Chandler," Dick said. He raised a hook and the flash of it caught the Indian's attention. "He's my boy, decided all of a sudden to take a vacation. I thought he might be here."

The man scowled further. "Dick Chandler," he said. His mouth worked quietly, lips moving subtly here and there as if poking around for the language. Finding it took a while. At last he said, "May Marks. Her you should talk to."

Dick glanced at Gun. "The boy's not here, then? Did he come here at all?"

But the Indian said nothing more. He seemed to be performing a retreat inside, a sudden catatonia, his eyes going inward and his attention to a place of rest and dark and no words, though his lips kept moving. Gun saw this and said to Dick, softly, "He mentioned the trailer," nodding to the nearest one, that with the TV antenna.

The man seemed not to notice as they walked past him. Still Gun couldn't help but see how the 30-30 rode in the Ojibwa's wide hand, palm covering most of the rifle's bolt action, trigger finger extended along the stock underneath. Even with the mind engaged elsewhere, hand and rifle stayed relaxed and balanced. As if, Gun thought, they'd been together a long while.

The pale green trailer had no steps beneath the doorway and they stood on the frozen muck looking up. The door had a tiny square window up high, showing them a brown-stained ceiling and a round white-glass light fixture, broken. Dick reached up, rapped a metallic beat on the door.

Deep in the trailer a dog exploded. A big dog, a lot of bass in its bark.

"Booger," Gun said. The noise shut off abrupt as a slap and they waited in silence. Chickadees darted in the dead branches of the barricade, singing their winter song—a high note bending mournfully, followed by a straight.

The door opened soundlessly and the girl looked down at them. More like twelve years old, Gun thought, and with no small measure of adolescent haughtiness. She had black hair yanked back in a ponytail, narrow, almost Asian eyes, a lofty mouth that would have the boys hating themselves in another year or two. Saying nothing she reached to her left and produced a short ladder of nailed-up two-by-fours. She lowered it for them and disappeared.

They climbed up into a clean kitchen bare of both food and people. The slim cheap cupboards had no doors; there was no stove except a new green Coleman on the Formica table, its lid closed. A trailer-house hallway, dark as a tunnel, led away from the kitchen and from it came dog noises and the rhythm of untroubled conversation.

Dick said, "Hello?"

A door opened, letting out the girl's laughter, and a man Gun judged to be thirty-five strolled into the kitchen. Not more than five-ten, slender and smiling. Big round wire rims over eyes slanting in, like the girl's.

"Dick," he said, the smile going a little stiff. He nodded at Gun. "Who's this?"

"Gun Pedersen, meet Alfred Pim." Dick's voice had slivers. "I agree, Alfred, *Warrior* sounds better."

But Pim was beaming, ignoring the sarcasm. "Gun Pedersen. I *heard* you were out here someplace—didn't you screw up that megamall, little time back?"

"Loon Country Attractions."

"Chamber of Commerce forgiven you yet?" Behind the glasses Pim's eyes sparked with genuine glee.

"Dick," Gun said, not liking the digression, "is looking for his boy."

The nailed-up ladder bumped against the trailer and the tall Ojibwa entered, looking back in the world, still with the 30-30. Pim turned to Dick, his voice gentle.

"I want you to go with Sparrow now."

"What? The hell I will!"

Sparrow was at Dick's side suddenly and gripping Dick's upper arm.

"It is necessary," Pim said. He pointed at Gun. "Pedersen will stay a little."

Sparrow was very alert now and Gun saw Dick knew when not to resist. Before going though he put his face close to Pim's. "Listen to me, *Warrior.* I'm not here for fun, I'm here because Babe's great pal Julius Marks froze in the ice and then Babe took off. It scares me. Now if he's here, I want to talk to him, goddamnit, not play at deciphering the mysterious Indian. Do you get this?"

Pim considered Dick a moment, looked in his face, said quietly, "I have not seen the boy."

Then Sparrow was ushering Dick away, Dick not fighting but not going quietly either, saying: "I lost my wife to you people twelve years ago, Pim. Now maybe I'm losing my boy, too." He held back against Sparrow suddenly, stopping the bigger man, and looked back at Pim. "And you're as white as I am," he said.

The door closed and they were alone, Pim looking at the linoleum. He stayed that way a long time with the sun coming in hard now through the frost on the east window. When he looked up again his eyes held sorrow Gun could almost feel.

"Angel," Pim called. "Angel, come in. We'll need some coffee."

The girl came from the dark hallway and seeing them in the same room it was plain she was his daughter. She had a red bag of Eight O'Clock Bean

Coffee in one hand. Not looking at Gun or her father, she set about the Coleman stove.

"I don't need anything," Gun said.

"You do," Pim told him. "You need to sit and listen now, because in this business of Babe Chandler I have very unhappy news."

10

"Maybe," Gun said, watching Angel spoon grounds into a black tin percolator, "you ought to have given your bad news to Dick, instead of sending him off with the sleepwalker. It's Dick's son, Dick's news." Though he realized somehow it was what he'd expected, once Dick had gone. The protocol of trouble: don't tell it to the man, tell it to his friend.

Pim sat and looked at his daughter while she set the flame high under the pot. She worked with a narrow efficiency and force of motion Gun found familiar. Pim said, "I mean Dick Chandler no disrespect," and added, quietly, "You shouldn't speak of Sparrow so. You don't know him."

This was true but beside the point. Still standing Gun said, "If you're going to tell me about Babe, then do it."

"Two nights ago," Pim said, "we had that light snow, an inch or so. It had to be after midnight; Angel was in bed, and the dog went spooky outside. Groaning, kind of, like somebody was coming that he knew. Not barking. First I thought it was Sparrow maybe because we had him guarding that night, but Booger never makes noise around Sparrow, they're too close.

And I thought, *What is this, some boys from town?*
They don't like us, these guys. Want nothing more
from this ground than for gold to show up and ten
million tons of equipment to come in and eat up the
earth like a shovel eats shit, and we're sitting here in
everybody's way. So I went out the back door without
a light and there was Booger groaning away happy and
somebody scratching at his belly."

"Babe Chandler."

Pim looked up, surprised. "No, it was May . . .
Marks. I told you, I haven't seen the boy."

For some reason Gun found himself embarrassed at
having assumed Pim was lying. Angel poured coffee
into a white cafe mug and he sat across from Pim and
reached for it.

"I hadn't seen May in, man, five years," Pim said,
more reminiscence in the remark than he'd probably
intended to put there. "I brought her in here. She was
freezing, no coat, hands all stiff. Couldn't talk hardly
and that"—he smiled—"ain't May."

"The night Julius died."

Pim picked up his coffee, sipped it like a scholar.
"Angel, it's wonderful. Thank you very much. If you
could attend to Booger, now—" From down the hall
the dog barked as if hearing its name, and Angel went.

"She'd just seen him die," Pim went on. "Saw him
fall through the ice after Babe Chandler hit him." He
was quiet, his eyes ashamed. "I didn't want to say it.
Dick has enough against us already."

"Sixteen years old," Gun said.

"This is what I think. Babe probably didn't mean to
kill Julius, just make him hurt some."

"She's sure it was Babe?"

"Babe was staying with Julius. The three of them
were on their way to Chandler's to drop Babe off. Big
argument on the way, she didn't understand it. They
wouldn't tell her what it was about. Babe made them
stop the car before they got to his house, they were
going to settle it."

"How'd they get out on the lake?"

Pim patted his pocket and extracted a Camel and scratched up a light. He sucked it slow and it straightened him, like strength. "Julius," he said, "didn't want to fight. May said he was laughing, 'Keep away from me, half-breed,' that stuff. She'd seen them fight before. Julius knew Babe's temper and liked to get him going. And when they stepped out of the car Babe took after him right off. Sure he's a kid, but big and tough."

"I know about Babe." Gun felt the snare again, saw the trees inverted.

"Julius kept backing off. Laughing yet. May said Babe was shoving, shoving. They got out on the ice and were slipping around, Babe hitting hard with his fists now, no gloves on. She said that's when she started getting really scared. Then Babe popped Julius in the face and he slipped down on his knees and Babe just kept hitting and Julius trying to get away. He went through finally. She said they'd been yelling at first but as it got more serious they stopped and when Julius went through she didn't hear a scream or anything at all. Nothing. She said she kept watching for a car to come by, someone. Nobody did. She said Babe backed off away from Julius in the ice, then she slid over to the driver's side and took off."

Pim told the story heavy voiced, a brown palm flat over his coffee cup keeping in the steam, his dark eyes calm. A warm square of sun had crept across the Formica tabletop and Gun, feeling it now on his hand, realized the silence. He said, "Dick tells me they were best friends."

"It looked like it." Pim carefully placed a new Camel, closed his eyes, lit it. "Babe is my cousin, as you know, but we're not close. The fault of all my years wandering through your universities." For the first time in his voice, there was bitterness.

"My universities?"

"No. I'm sorry. I grew up here, understand, on the

reservation. If you read, you know what that means. I went away gladly, thinking I could go to any good school and major in Anglo and it would change all the footnotes in my history."

Gun waited while Pim inhaled again. He wished for Prince Albert and papers.

Pim blew smoke and then spoke into it. "Sparrow came for me, finally." *You shouldn't speak of Sparrow so,* Gun remembered. He waited, and his waiting seemed to please Pim.

"He found me in L.A. in a houseful of stupid children who spoke nothing but sociology. You ought to have seen him, that straight black ponytail. He has this big Bowie knife he was actually wearing on his waist. What he was then was fearless."

"He still doesn't look scared."

Pim smiled patiently. "He is afraid now, always. But not then. I'd never met him before, but I'd read about him, how he started up this radical bunch"— Pim grinned—"that the papers called Indian eco-terrorists. I have to say that appealed to me. I'd been four years in graduate school."

Gun shook his head. "And you followed him home." There had to be more to it than disillusionment.

"It wasn't so simple. He came to me because he'd met my grandmother—"hesitating now and putting out the Camel—"she had dreams—no, visions, I should call them what they were. Things that concerned us. I won't tell you details. But Sparrow had met her, gone to visit her in the home, and she pointed him out to me."

Again, Gun waited.

"These things," Pim said, apologizing for it, Gun thought, "can be generational."

"Visions."

"Yes."

"Sparrow sought you out to be some sort of spiritual leader," Gun said. Trying to get used to this.

"Spirit Waters was his own vision. But he dreamed one night that his soul would be harmed in a battle for the land. The dream told him to find a successor." Pim stood. "I took it like you'd take a new job, like it was a career change. I was pretty close to white by then; I didn't understand."

"Now you do?"

Pim went to the door, opened it, lowered the ladder for Gun. His voice was quiet and held no anger but no humor either as it had before. "I had been back a month when the visions began to happen, the way they did with my grandmother. I would stop them now, if I could. Yes, I understand."

The mud was going soft with sun outside the trailer. Dick was nowhere, and so most likely was Sparrow. An old Indian in a yellowed union suit and a goose-down vest sat on a pine-log bench outside one of the tepees, eating a Twinkie. He smiled at Gun and said, *"Boujou."*

"Morning."

"Pedersen," Pim said. He was standing in the open door of the trailer. For the first time Gun noticed his socks, zippy green ones, eye snappers. He said, "I'm sorry for Dick, about Babe."

11

"Pim," Gun said, under power again in the Subaru, "thinks Babe killed Julius." It was a crummy thing to have to say and he burned a little toward Pim for not telling Dick himself. Dick was driving stiffly, hooks at ten and two o'clock on the wheel. He didn't answer.

"Claims May Marks saw it happen," Gun said. Watching Dick, he saw the line of his jaw slide forward, set itself. There was silence and Gun realized this was a possibility Dick had already thought of. What did a man imagine now, with his kid running scared and dangerous?

They drove northward into reservation territory, toward May's, watching the big straight pines deteriorate into tamarack and crippled willow scrub. The sun was racing up and actually working good now like God had reached over and switched it on. It warmed Dick into talk. "So what did you think of Mr. Sparrow?"

"Pim says he's faded some."

"First name is Jefferson," Dick said. "I remember when they broke his head, it was at that sad-ass demonstration in D.C. over the Alaska oil business.

71

Wrecking the wilderness. He got billy-clubbed, still's trying to wake up."

"Nasty."

"Version I got from Julius," Dick said. "You had maybe two hundred people walking around the Capitol holding up signs, I LOVE TUNDRA and such—like any of 'em ever saw it—and Sparrow thinks, *This is no good. People in Washington don't even* notice *marches.* So he starts going into the government buildings, he's gonna try to talk reason with someone. Except this was on a Saturday, there wasn't so much as a freshman Congressman on the whole lousy Hill."

"Maybe they saw the Bowie knife."

"So Sparrow trots around most of the day until he's tired and hungry and disgusted. I never been to Washington, but I get the mailings from the senator, and disgusting is real easy to believe. At last Sparrow's in some fine rotunda somewhere, he's lost for sure now, and it's been a long day. He finds a public bathroom; it's locked. The situation is severe. So he goes back to the rotunda and takes a dump on a floor mosaic of the American Eagle."

"That's disgusting."

"The security guard thought so as well. He was the fellow swung the club. Sparrow wasn't even zipped up."

They passed a small white sign on a leaning pole that declared, simply, 138. Dick said, "Living out here," shaking his head, and turned onto a soft sand track leading west.

Five minutes of boggy effort by the Subaru got them to a place where the sand hardened into road and swung wide around a patch of birch trees. Their leaves were gone but for a resolute few and the sun hit the bark white gold.

"One time," Dick smiled, shifting gears, "a Fuller Brush man came out here. This is in the seventies. Julius said his mom was so glad for the company she made him stay for supper. They had ham."

"For the Fuller Brush man?"

"It was an event. They didn't buy anything. Afterwards Julius got part of an old beaver skin out of his room, told the guy it was a scalp." Dick slowed and made a careful left onto a track so narrow, brush scrabbled at both doors. "Here we go."

They came out suddenly from the cover of brush and birch and low pine and entered a clearing that seemed only recently pioneered. There were no tepees this time, just trailer houses, set up level on blocks, the luckier ones with most of their windows still glass.

Dick pointed. "That one belonged to Julius. Don't know who'll be living in it now. It's a big family."

"They all live here? Aunts and uncles, old folks?"

"Say what you like about the Rez, some things they do right." Dick hesitated. "Gun, I want to talk to May myself first. Who knows, Babe might be there."

"You don't want him to think you brought the cavalry along."

"Thanks. Ten minutes."

Dick left the car running in case Gun needed heat. He didn't. He needed air. He let Dick turn the corner around the nearest trailer, a white one with rust running down the sides, then he shut off the car and stepped out. The air was sun dried, not cold. Cool. He could hear kids and dogs among the trailers. He saw a rooster atop a faded blue Buick, head bobbing. He decided to walk a little in this November-polished noontime while Dick reasoned with Babe, May, whomever.

Dick sure had calm in his genes, Gun would give him that. Gun's own daughter Mazy had been ungovernable too at sixteen, but that had been a whole different set of worries. Not the kind you got frantic about, because the fact was you had to be pragmatic with girls, take this punk boyfriend or that lousy attitude with a little flex in your step or you lost them forever. He'd lost Mazy that way once, more than once, but she was unusual, he got her back. Gun had never had boys. Until now he'd suspected they were simpler.

Dick didn't come back during Gun's first walk around the clearing. Gun had counted eight trailers and patted six happy hounds, nodded at a couple of kids. They didn't invite him in for ham. Dick didn't come back after Gun's second walk, which was more moseying than the first. He went to the Subaru where a quarter-size stick-on clock told him it had been more than an hour. He told himself reasoning was slow sometimes. From the northwest a breeze came abruptly and winter started showing through again, waiting. He noticed the dogs were quiet. It was bothersome somehow. He decided to go looking.

Nobody answered at the white trailer house. Between that and its closest neighbor, three kids—what, four years old—had surrounded a chicken and were making openhanded dashes at it. Gun asked them where May Marks lived and one straightened and pointed at the farthest trailer. The hen took a chance and darted past the boy, who dove after it too late. Gun said, "Sorry," and weathered the four year old's stare.

May's place still had glass windows. Gun stopped twenty feet from the trailer. The wind was coming heavier. A man opened the door and it was not Dick. Not Babe. Gun knew him though from his size, his square head and small features. From his confident efficiency of movement as he silently came down the steps. From the stubby half-moon skinning knife. What was different this time was the long slick of blood across the right cheek, and the smile that said it wasn't his.

12

The man made no attempt to hide the blood on his face. It was on the knife too, and he unself-consciously wiped it on his pants. Gun saw recognition start now and the man came for him, not stalling or talking, just stepping easily over the grass, no hurry. Behind him Gun saw a woman at the door of the trailer and her face was wet and quiet. Gun waited. The man came smoothly nearly to arm's reach, seemed to coil in midstride and struck. There was no seeing it. Gun stumbled back, grabbed his chest, found the second button on his coat sliced in half. Sweet God, what speed. And attitude. Look at the man stalking him now, no smile, just doing his work. The knife had switched hands somehow. *Watch the blade, watch it, see it,* and he saw it lacing up toward his chin and in dodging lost his balance. He went down with the half-moon rising above him and rolled to his gut, covered his neck with his wrists. He twisted, lunged at the feet, the legs, was astonished to be fast enough for once as the knife slipped past his spine. He got one of the man's knees in each hand and bent them outward. The man resisted, not understanding in the half-second it took Gun to push his limbs apart, but getting it the next moment when Gun smashed them together again. The knees colliding made a crunch like the end of someone's career, and the phrase "bone chips" jumped into Gun's brain. He stood and saw the man go down, big-eyed and breathless, hugging his knees. *Never miss 'em till they're gone.* Gun's lungs bucked in his chest. He left the man curled and went to the trailer. The woman who was there had to be May. She said, "In the tub," pointing down yet another trailer-house tunnel. He followed it and a rough sour smell, and arrived at a twenty-five-watt bathroom containing what was still in place and breathing of Dick Chandler.

The lone doctor at Indian Health Services in the town of Little Sun was a slight young man with an old man's cough who told Gun he might have driven too fast to save Dick.

"What?"

"You drive a little slower, don't rock him so much over these goddamn potholes, maybe the blood has a chance to clot," the doctor said. He had a mask on and tight rubber gloves, which he was trying to remove. They were slippery. "I stitched him up where I thought it would help." He coughed disease into the mask.

The waiting room was a long, narrow, converted coat closet with no windows. It was painted claustrophobic yellow. The Little Sun cafe was better. It was across the street and had four calendars on the wall. Gun remembered reading somewhere that the fare of America's back cafes could be estimated by how many calendars they displayed. One calendar, terrible food, two calendars, passable, and so on. Now here he was, four calendars right in front of him, and Dick across the narrow street waiting to wake up again, or not. Gun had a lot more time than appetite.

The pay phone up by the cash register had a Magic Marker sign on it, BAD PHONE, and he had to ask the waitress if he could use the one in the back office. She was black haired and timid about asking if it was a local call.

"Nope. Credit card."

She looked doubtful. She pinched up a lock of hair, squeezed it, stuck it in the corner of her mouth. He said, "Really," his exhaustion showing in the word, and she tilted her head, let the hair fall free of her lips and pointed at a door behind the counter.

Durkins was at home. He answered straight off. He was chewing something.

"Sheriff, it's Gun."

"Nuts. Can't a man finish his Cheetos in peace?"

"Dick Chandler's been sliced up. It's bad. We're up on the Rez, at the doctor's."

Gun heard the sheriff swallow and the far-off crinkle of a plastic bag and then Durkins said, "Tell it," and Gun did. Big man, fast, mukluks on his feet. Strange low voice, like the muscles that made it didn't get much practice. Squarish face. Gun stopped short of saying he'd seen the guy before, at Babe's deer shack in the woods.

"Aw, hell," Durkins said. "Dick's gonna come through it?"

"He's a strong one."

"And his kid's still missing. Poor bastard."

"He hears you say that, he'll come awake just to sit up and strangle you."

Durkins snuffed through his nose and told Gun thanks for the call.

Tabled again Gun watched through the window while a solitary mutt cruised up and down the main street of Little Sun. The Subaru was the only car in sight, parked over at the clinic. The mutt pissed on all four tires while Gun drank coffee that was two calendar at best, and at last the clinic door opened and the doctor emerged in a navy peacoat, heading for the cafe. Still with the mask on, considerate man.

"We're going to send him south," he told Gun. A

waitress appeared, faltered at seeing the mask, and failed to offer coffee.

"What? How?"

"Northwestern in the Cities will send the helicopter. He's stabilized, but we don't have facilities for this." The doctor coughed and the waitress, behind the counter, averted her face.

"Doc. He'll be back, normal again?"

"Take a while. He'll be sore. Don't make him laugh."

It struck Gun as the cafe door gusted shut that the doctor hadn't asked who did the damage, how it had happened. He hadn't even seemed surprised. Just stitched up the patient, waited for results, and informed the guy sitting across the street. He'd been dutiful and joyless and far too old. Like that cough was never going to go away.

13

By the time he got back to May's it was rubbing up against midnight and only two trailers in the little Marks settlement had lights burning. May's wasn't one of them. He tried there first anyway, overcoming the cold rock that formed in his bowels as he went up the steps. They were made of old wood held together with old nails and they squawked under his weight like an Indian rooster aiming to roust the whole reservation. They hadn't made a sound under the knife guy, not the way Gun remembered it.

When no one answered his second set of knocks he tried the door. Locked. He turned and wondered which of the two lit trailers he ought to try. As he watched, lights went way down on the one to the left, yellow to brown, then to black. Put a thing off long enough, your choice gets made for you.

It was her grandparents, in that last lonesome trailer, brewing a pot of green Lipton tea which the old man said would send them to sleep faster than living by a river.

"Come and sit," he told Gun. He was a wide, suspendered old man, his heavy hair just starting to silver. He didn't ask Gun's name.

The place was narrow enough but otherwise not like most trailer homes Gun had seen. Not cluttered. Just a few pieces of furniture. Plain oiled wood, solid.

"Have some tea," the old man said.

"No, thanks." But here came the grandmother with a ceramic pot, a handmade one of Dick Chandler's built up of slabs like a Frank Lloyd Wright. The woman was tiny and brown and careful. She had a lot of fine white hair, just brushed, which drifted over the shoulders of a deep blue cotton housedress like cumulus clouds over a bright lake in summer. She motioned the men to sit, poured tea for Gun, and watched him until he'd taken a sip.

"Look at her," the old man said, his voice going golden as he watched his wife.

Gun nodded.

"Yes. And deaf as this table," Grandpa said, knocking on pine. He shrugged. "I have to get my own beer now, when there's a ball game on. Get up and move around the house. You get used to it. What do you want from May?"

Gun took a slug of the tea. It wasn't awful. You couldn't look at it while you drank was all. "Did you know there was a man there earlier today? Two men. One of them cut the other, pretty bad."

Grandpa said, "I'm told the sheriff was here later, asking questions. The deaf one, of course, knew nothing about it." Under the flannel shirt his chest expanded slowly, big lungs in there. "And I saw the guy, too. Not the one who got cut, the other one. Sitting on the steps. He had some blood on his face. He was grabbing his knees."

"Do you know him?"

Grandpa ignored the question. Tilted up the tea, exhaled hard through his nostrils, narrowed his eyes. "I was trying to take a little nap. Couldn't sleep, see? Hadn't had any of this," he said, tapping the cup. "It seemed like there was some sort of thumping going on, kids playing with their little football or something.

So after a while I sat up and looked out and he was there, on the steps. He was white, white enough to make *you* look Chippewa. I think he was white because of some pretty hurt knees."

"But you didn't recognize him."

"Nah." Grandpa's upper lip moped downward over his teeth and he eyed Gun with horsey sadness. "Seen enough fellows over there. Quit paying much notice. White guys, most of the time." He turned to Grandma, whose back was turned. "Mama, sugar!" He shouted it out, but had no luck; she was over at the counter pouring milk into her own cup.

"You see," Grandpa sighed. He got up, took his tea to the counter and stood beside his wife, spooning in sugar.

Gun sat at the table, feeling himself settling. He'd had too much day, staying around to see Dick rolled into the helicopter and thinking then he'd go straight home; only turning and driving here instead, his hands on the wheel of the Subaru, just doing it automatically.

Grandpa had enough sugar in his Lipton now and was moving back to the table, his feet slow and regretful they had to carry him at all. He said, "We stay up too late. We're night people. Do you ever watch that Letterman?"

"Not when I can sleep."

The old man nodded. "You're still young. I am eighty-seven. Every time I lay down, my intestines tell me to get up again and make water." He shook his head, slugged tea.

"How long did he stay? The man with the knees?" It was good to know he'd hurt the guy. Bad to know he'd been able to walk away.

"What do I know? Did I know there was some poor bastard bleeding all over her bathtub? No, I laid back down and tried to rest. Got a little sleep. I had a good dream, too, that May was little again and I was younger. And don't you know, when I woke up, I was curious. Went over to her trailer. It was locked in the front and that's not usual. Around back the door was open but I saw footprints going away into the trees. I walked in a ways after them, but when the woods got thick the snow petered out. Could I track 'em? Listen: I say, shoot, go find yourself an Indian." He looked at Gun to see if he'd chuckle.

"Are you worried about her?"

"May?" A long, wheezy smile. "May'll be back. With May there're so many guys. What would they do without her?" The old man troubled himself to sit forward in the chair, losing the smile as he moved. "Anyhow, I followed them a ways in, and then I found some bear prints and followed them. It's getting late in the year for bears. When I got back the wife told me about the sheriff coming. I was glad to miss that."

Another gulp of tea took it down to where the bits of leaves swayed, down in the bilge, and Gun stood to go. Home was a good drive off and he still wasn't sure why he'd come; Durkins had already been and gone, and the sheriff probably had a name by now.

He went to the door and said, "Thanks for the tea." The old man ignored him but his wife, her back to him still, nodded once, firmly. You're welcome.

14

"Did Dick say anything about him? Does anyone even know his name?"

It was close to noon and Carol Long was on the phone, shaking him out from those warm flannel sheets just as he'd managed to sleep at last. She was using her I'm-on-deadline voice. Barely awake this way, it was almost more than he could forgive.

"Dick never saw him before," Gun said.

"He told you that?"

"Couldn't tell me. He shook his head. Slowly."

The line went still and he let her imagine it. Then she said, voice soft again, regular Carol, "Is he going to be all right?"

"It looks okay. There was internal bleeding but it's stopped. Face is sliced up good, tendons in his elbow severed, and he'll lose some mobility in his midsection. Take a long time to do any sit-ups."

"You're unconvinced."

Well, for certain. "He'd rather get Babe back safe than sit around healing up. Your kid takes off and something like this happens, it's going to work on you."

"What about May?"

"I couldn't find her when I went back. The knife guy either. She went with him, I guess. Or he took her."

"Babe?"

"No sign of him, there or at the blockade." He leaned down, rubbed his eyelids until the scratchiness faded. It'd been a short night, seeing Dick off in the helicopter, a swing back to the Marks settlement, the drive home. Lots of miles in which to think.

He said, "I think the knife guy is after Babe."

She was quiet. He could hear another phone ringing behind her, no one picking up. He said, "Do you have to answer that?"

"Go on."

"I saw him once before. I'd just caught up to Babe out in the woods." He related the scuffle, the snare, the unexpected rescue. "I didn't think of it then. Probably he was already chasing the kid."

"Why?"

"Right. Why?" He wanted to hang up and go back to bed. Nothing could exhaust you like *why*. He said good-bye and hung up.

Well, Dick was in the Cities, trussed all to heaven. May Marks was gone someplace, probably with the knife guy, whoever he was. Carol was on deadline. Probably, Gun conceded, he could do worse than going to see old Crosley Schell. Once in a while even beautiful human beings could tell you something of value.

Schell's place was a Renaissance man's for certain: the oddball octagonal house somehow seeming right at home there at the edge of forest, sided with clear, rough, vertical cedar, its roof black and round and pointed. It would look from a distance, Gun thought, like some Chinese laborer had cut down a perfect red tree and then covered the stump with his hat. Above it rose lacy tamaracks that looked wet and smelled of night coming soon. Schell's Renault was settled in the yard and next to it a square, blue, four-wheel-drive foreign make with a Hertz sticker on the back. A totem pole full of frog faces was planted at the entrance.

The front door was of some fine-grained wood so sturdy it might still be growing. It made you knock hard. Finally footsteps answered and Crosley Schell opened it, letting out music.

"Gun, again. Hello. Enter," said Schell, a little puzzlement in his features.

"Crosley." Gun ducked inside. No, not music. Just chords of some kind. Harp sounds.

"There's water on."

The inside of the octagon surprised Gun with its room and light. Cedar in here, too, and few interior walls; lots of windows. Good design, harps or not. Gun said, "Nice place," and became aware as he said it of the other man in the room. He was at the table, in a corner of the house that looked like the kitchen, quietly grasping a ceramic cup.

"Thank you." Crosley motioned. "Gun Pedersen, meet Izzy Rolph. We're old geology pals. Bedeviled the profs together."

Izzy nodded. He looked a little like Crosley at first but it was just the clothes, ankle boots over wool socks, the bright fleece zip-up letting you know how environmental he was. The fleece was the same blue as the four wheel drive.

Crosley poured and handed Gun his second unwanted mug of tea in twenty-four hours. This one had a loon on it. BOUNDARY WATERS. The steam smelled like flowers. Crosley said, "What brings you by?"

"Babe—"

"Still missing." Crosley shaking his head now, reaching down to scratch the cat that was twining around his ankles.

"—and this." Gun pulled the heavy Colt Python revolver from his coat pocket. "Thought you'd like it back."

Crosley put three fingers to his lips, a tentative Jack

Benny gesture. "Where'd you find it?" He took the piece gently and began turning it over.

"Babe had it. First thing after he ran off, I went out to a shack where he holes up sometimes. Dick told me where. Babe got away, but he left the gun."

"Well. Thank you." Crosley smiled and touched his lips again and set the Python down on the kitchen table. Izzy looked at it and then away. Crosley said, "Anything I can do for you?"

"The work he did for you. Him and Julius. What can you tell me about it?"

"They did a little painting, upkeep stuff. And Babe hauled some core samples for me. Look," said Schell, crossing the open room to a big desk with a long wooden box lying across it. "The cores," he said, lifting the lid from one and squinting at some letters inked on the cardboard. "These are from the old Vermilion Range. Drilled out in, let's see, 1928."

Gun hadn't seen drill cores before but they were as he'd pictured them: short, broken cylinders of gray rock, maybe an inch in diameter. They were laid out in rows across the bottom of the box.

"Unremarkable, aren't they?" Crosley said. Gun knew the tone of voice, tutorial, the knowing teacher about to tell the child what's really inside that ugly cocoon.

"I don't know," Gun said.

"That's the beauty. We don't know how remarkable they are, none of us does, and I'm the lucky guy who gets to figure it out. This piece, now"—Crosley selected a rod of stone—"came from forty feet underground near a little range town called Embarrass. And probably there's some good stuff in it. Nickel, copper, gold maybe. Only back then, mining was simpler. If the ore wasn't high grade and in big chunks, it wasn't worth going after. Now," Crosley said, "you find enough fancy specks in a rock, you can drop it in a hopper and get the stuff out. A whole *lot* of specks, it even pays."

"That's your job? Finding the specks?"

"So far I haven't found enough. Just hints."

"And DDH is test-drilling on the strength of those hints."

Crosley shrugged. "I guess so. It surprised me, I'll admit it. Frankly, I wish they'd waited. Saved themselves some working cash and me—saved me this discomfort with Spirit Waters."

Gun lifted one of the cores. It was cold, smooth, lead heavy. Not a glint on it. "How do you find the specks?"

"About the way you'd think. I have a hydraulic splitter to open the cores, then put the chips under a glass. The promising ones get sent out for analysis. Here, hoist the box once."

Gun did so. It was like lifting the old Ford.

Crosley said, "Strong kid, the way he horsed these things around. Come on, your tea'll freeze."

At the table, where Izzy still ignored the Python, Gun said, "Aside from Dick, nobody seems to know Babe well enough to guess where he's at. You have any ideas, I'd appreciate it."

"Gun, I don't know what you know about me." Crosley's eyes were as patient as harp music, clear as rose tea. "I get along with people. I communicate. Babe could've talked to me, only he didn't. Wish he had."

"Did he seem like he had trouble? Were there things he wasn't saying?"

Schell looked straight into Gun's face, giving him eyes the blue of early night. He had great sincerity and appeared to know it. "Babe is a peaceable boy. An Ojibwa."

Gun started to say that May Marks wouldn't agree, but Crosley interrupted. "It was Julius who had the temper," he said. "He actually started working here before Babe did. Liked to come over, hang around, pick up a little rock lore. Mostly he liked to smoke and tell lies. I cared for him."

Cared for him. The way this guy talked.

"They were pals."

"From what I saw, Babe wasn't much of a communicator."

Poor old Izzy gripped his tea without utterance. Gun wondered whether he was mute or just savoring the harp chords, which never seemed to get any louder or softer or, for that matter, to go away. A man couldn't think. It was like standing in a blizzard of dandelion fluff, trying to inhale.

He sat while his brain pried around for the next question. Oh yeah. "Crosley. Have you ever seen a big guy around here? Old ranch jacket, carries a skinning knife? Wears mukluks. Big square head."

"Big square head." Crosley chuckled. "No. Why?"

"Never mind." Gun stood to go. But Crosley seemed all at once to lose his good humor, and picking up the Colt Python said, "We got along. Why would he steal? From me?"

"Maybe it's how he communicates." Gun remembered his tea, took a quick taste and experienced regret. "Does it worry you, the stealing? He's a peaceable boy, right?"

But Crosley was hard to bug and quick to recover. He'd already gotten back all the blue in his eyes and was smiling softly. "You know, in all my years with the Indians, this is the first time one ever stole from me." Sounding like Jeremiah Johnson now. And looking a little like him too, Gun had to admit, that splayed-straw hair, the jaw, pulling it off. Izzy looked on, admiring. Crosley said, "When I live with whites, you know what? I have to put a lock on my zipper so no one'll take my pants."

And Izzy laughed. The sound of it was so unexpected from his solemn corner that Gun turned to look, which was why he was the first to see fire through the windows.

15

The fire was moving up the near wall of a long, wood-sided storage shed behind the house. It had a good jump and an audience of six or seven shapes that stood around with their hands up their jacket sleeves. A wet breeze blew but couldn't discourage the flames. The smoke was black and heavy. Crosley Schell shoved past Gun and into the red snapping light yelling, "Come on!" He had the Python in one fist and Gun thought, *Who's he gonna shoot first?* The shapes twisted a little, hearing him, seeing what he had in his hand. Indians from what Gun could see, a couple with black hair down their backs like in the old movies nobody believed anymore. Crosley stormed into them screaming, then tossed the revolver into the grass and rushed to the shed door and slapped at the padlock.

A long braided rug was airing on a clothesline and Gun grabbed it, heading for the heaviest flames. It was too late already and he knew it but there was Crosley kicking at the door with his foot (*What's in this thing, anyhow?*), Crosley like a little kid now, whining. Gun beat at flames above his head that only *whoofed* under the rug and then poured back at him between blows. Behind them the Indians watched, some of them taking seats now. Leaning against trees, elbows on knees, who's got the marshmallows. Turning, Gun saw Izzy's timid profile at one of Crosley's lighted windows. What a pal.

There were new sparks now as the fire grabbed hold of the roof above Gun and he backed away, the heat too much. Crosley had finally had enough too because he wearied all at once and made a dramatic, angry fall onto his butt. He turned and crawled an exhausted-hero crawl to where the heat wasn't and sat there, coatless, watching the shed go up. It was burning now as sturdily as backyard coals on the Fourth of July. The tamaracks were damp, good thing, the ground boggy. Crosley sat some more. Izzy stayed in the house. One of the Indians said, "Shit, man."

"Well, okay," Crosley said at last. He looked around, the firelight deepening the lines in his face. "I've seen some of you fellows before. Guess it's fair to say someone is unhappy with me. Who'd like to start?"

Listen to this, like it's a therapy group.

Under the fire the roof was swaying, showing bones.

"I've told you people what I know," said Crosley. "I've backed Spirit Waters. I've shared my information a hell of a lot more freely than my bosses back in the boardroom would like to know about. Now that you've screwed up two years' worth of sorting and paperwork"—Crosley waved at the shed—"I think somebody better tell me why."

"Did you find gold, Schell?" Now a voice Gun knew. Crosley knew it too.

"Sparrow. Where are you?" Crosley's voice skidded up a notch.

Jefferson Sparrow stepped from shadow into light. No rifle this time. He looked taller in the circumstances, Crosley on his butt, shadows stretching out all over.

"Did you find it?"

"No. Hell, no. What I told you guys, your Warrior

Pim, last time we met, was I'd tell you if I found it. What *is* this?"

Sparrow said, "I just wanted you to say it."

"No gold. No gold. There." Crosley got up finally. His pants were wet from the ground, sticking to his hind end, and he pulled them away. "You want to tell me why it was necessary to have this little cookout? What's going on?"

Sparrow rounded up what must have been all the articulation left to him and said, "We just wanted to get your attention."

Someone said, "And now that we have it, we're gonna go smoke. You too, man," he told Crosley.

The roof folded in at last, hissing and crackling. The walls were see-through, soon to follow.

"Schell's staying," Gun said. He felt their attention shift to him.

And then back as Crosley said, smiling, holding up his hand like Father Hennepin, "I'll go."

Schell was smiling gently as they came around him, a couple throwing arms roughly over his shoulders, and marched him to a blue, plateless Ford Econoline van parked behind the Renault. Several of the Indians were laughing. Not Sparrow. Just before stepping up into the van, Crosley faced Gun and said, "It isn't anything. I can deal with this." His face shone with sweat and self-esteem. "We shouldn't need the police," he said, and then he was inside with a bunch as jovial as ten jocks with a mathematician to slap around.

Gun watched the taillights shrink and fade; listened to the Econoline *chung chung* until it was gone and all that came back was the subdued crackle of the leveled shed. He thought about Crosley's confidence and about Sparrow's troubled eyes and the flattened way his voice sounded, then went inside and told Izzy to call the cops.

16

Sheriff Jason Durkins arrived after twenty-five minutes of Izzy walking through the house, kicking himself. "I had any balls, you know what I'da done?"

"Nope," Gun said. Izzy's head turned and Gun realized the man had been talking to himself.

"You know Crosley's a collector," Izzy said, waving at the locked case against one wall. "Revolvers, derringers, the whole shooting match. And every one of 'em works, he's real proud of that. What I'da done, I'da taken down one of those big Civil War issues, pistol with a barrel that long——" illustrating with his hands——"and gone down there. 'All right, you bastards, it's time to go.' You know?"

"Izzy Bronson," Gun said. *Death Wish.* " And that put the dimmer on Izzy's late-swelling courage. He looked at Gun, his eyes flaring anger for a moment, then his shoulders bunched and he fell into a kitchen chair.

"Any idea why they took him?" Gun asked.

Izzy shook his head.

"You know who those guys are, though, right? Spirit Waters?"

"He mentioned the group a few times. I never met

92

any of them." Izzy had enough fear and regret in his voice that Gun wondered just how involved the man was. When he looked up from the floor the anger was still there in his eyes, though it was quieter now and not aimed at Gun. "I can never understand exactly," said Izzy, "just how he does it. How he gets along with those people."

"What do you mean?"

"With the Indians. I mean, not to take anything away from him—I know what he's accomplished. But everybody paints him like some kind of anthropologist, like some kind of Margaret Mead. You know how every time she'd go off into the bush she'd come out again with some new lover? Crosley read *her* manual, all right." Izzy Rolph laughed through his nostrils, a snotty sound. "Man, I think this time he underestimated his Indian pals."

"Hold it. 'Read her manual'?"

Izzy got up and went to one of the dark windows, peering out sideways. "Well, if you're going to go native, go all the way, right? Like that totem pole. Like bringing home a squaw. Not that I wouldn't myself if a chance like that Marks girl came my way."

He spoke as if this was common knowledge, and Gun tried to keep things conversational. "Yup, May and Crosley. For how long now?"

Izzy shook his head. "Long enough so May's folks're starting to get over it, their girl shacking with a white guy. Shit, I don't know. . . ." He slumped in his chair and looked over at the dark reflection of himself in one of the large floor-to-ceiling windows. His face paled. He seemed to regret what he'd been saying about his friend.

"Those things, they can take a while sometimes," said Gun, standing. He looked away from the man to give him some room. Then he came in from another direction, saying, "What were you guys, schoolmates, was it?"

"Right." Izzy issued Gun a sharp glance that didn't

look right on him. "Geology majors, Rocky Mountain U. We've kept up, both being in the trade."

"And you work for who?" Gun said, going through Crosley's cupboards. Boxes of Celestial Seasonings, decaf Lipton Instant, chicken Soup Starter.

"I teach. Geology."

"Really." And cocoa, aha. "Enjoy it?"

"Yes. What's taking the sheriff so long?"

"County seat's a ways off." Gun found a saucepan, dropped in a teaspoon of sugar, a heaper of cocoa, and a squirt of hot tap water. "Hot chocolate?"

"Uh-uh." Izzy, irritable. "So how come you're so interested in all this? And in me?"

Gun stirred briskly. You had to get the mix just right, work the sugar and cocoa and water into a thick brown *roux* before adding the milk. He took the necessary time to do it properly. He found a mug that didn't say anything on it, poured, and tasted. It was rich and barely sweet at all, full of the right sort of bitterness. He turned and said, "It's just you, Izzy. You're such a fascinating guy."

Sheriff Durkins didn't want any cocoa either. He did want every detail Gun could offer him, two or three times over, and Gun fed them out patiently, watching Durkins do his job. He seemed good tonight, not smelling of anything stronger than the Swanson dinner Gun guessed he'd had for supper. He wanted names and Gun gave Jefferson Sparrow's; he didn't know any of the others. How many others? Gun had counted nine. Durkins asked for a description of the vehicle, got it.

"Plates?" the sheriff said, raising heavy eyebrows as if there was no way he could be so lucky.

"There weren't any."

Durkins shorthanded this down on his notepad and looked up at Izzy, who sat at the kitchen table looking cold and guilty. "Wait here," he said. "I'll want to ask you some questions." Then he nodded at the door and followed Gun out.

The freeze would come hard tonight. It had been overcast earlier but there was a big gap now and Orion was showing, as if the constellation had ripped a hole in the clouds and all the cold in the North was pouring through it.

"I'd sure like to know," Durkins said when they reached Gun's truck, "just what in foggy hell is going on here."

Gun found his key, got in, and started the engine. He rolled down the window and listened to it rattle inside the door. This cold, the old Ford kicked around a lot, gave you a body massage.

"You want to tell me about the guy who put Dick in Intensive?" Durkins said. "Not that it's my investigation, the feds pick up reservation accounts. Still, Dick Chandler, Babe Chandler, Julius Marks, and now his sister . . ." He looked at Gun, steady. "I'm in it, see. Up to the bags under my eyes."

Gun liked him for that. "Like I said, I don't know the guy. Big, fast, mukluks on his feet. I gave you this before. Dick'll probably be able to tell you more. In a few days."

"Yeah." Durkins tapped Gun's door with his knuckles and tried a smile. "So you didn't just ask this fellow his name."

"I was afraid he'd think I was making a pass at him."

Durkins grinned, then shook his head. "Now. Who's the guy inside? People I have to question, they always hate it when I know their names going in."

"I don't think he'll have much to tell you." Gun looked up at the house and there was Izzy's silhouette in the window.

"What's his name?"

"Izzy Bronson," Gun said.

Somewhere off the coast of daylight, Gun dreaming of a silent lifeboat full of pale-eyed boys sculling through fog and blue water, there was a small snap, as of a wet oar hitting flat on the surface in the distance, and Gun woke and knew the sound that woke him. Mice had come to his place at last this fall, after so many years without them, and he'd laid traps. Sunflower seeds brought them in all right, just like Jack had told him. Better than cheese, which worked in cartoons but not on these big-eyed field mice. Nope, they demanded something more agricultural, and they were getting it. "The mice start moving in, Gun, you been alone too long," Jack had said. "Pretty soon you don't mind 'em, and then in a little while you stop brushing your teeth, shaving. Cute little suckers, aren't they? And when it rains the water'll just run off your hair, won't even get it wet."

Jack could overstate matters; still, what Amanda would've done, hearing that scratching in the logs at night. Gun bought the traps.

He checked them after breakfast and found, sure enough, a squashed field mouse in the Victor between the refrigerator and trash can. He opened the door and pried the trap open, emptied the mouse onto grass which was so hard with frost it didn't even bend. Gun grabbed leather gloves, his black down vest, and watch cap. His axe stood just outside the door. He leaned back in on his way out to read the kitchen clock. Almost ten already. You could look for the lost boys all you wanted, but the woodbox still got low.

There was a weasel in Gun's woodpile that liked to crawl out from the middle of the hump and watch him split. Gun liked the work and he liked the audience, watched for it: the slender light-brown body moving like water in and out of the chunks, not a bone showing under that hide.

He picked five heavy rounds from the pile, pine logs more than a foot thick from a tree that had gone in a storm two years earlier and had enough age now to burn clean. He lined them up in a crescent before him, setting them solid so they didn't rock. He lifted the axe and stood with it at the hub of the half-circle of logs. He eyed the woodpile. No weasel. Felt the axe stiff and cumbersome under the leather gloves and took them off. Gripped the handle, good cold maple. Fingers loose, don't aim, watch the millimeter of center you want to hit and now up arc and down, through, part that block like the Red Sea. Hear that fine hollow *hock* as the slabs drop east and west. Look up.

The weasel was there. Sunnily perched on a chunk of birch, two-thirds up the pile and watching as if it were afraid of missing something. Gun gave the weasel a deliberate wink and saw the animal's raindrop-shaped head shift on its shoulders, away and back, its eyes on his.

The second log went easy, but the third had a sticky oval knot waiting for him down in the middle. He swung and it grabbed the axe and held on. He brought the whole log up on the backswing and slammed it hard on the ground. It held. He stepped on the log and rocked the axe handle until the blade squealed free and the cut snapped closed. He repositioned. Put his attention on the cut, knowing the knot would still be down there. He felt the chilly flex of the handle in his fingers. Made his mind a wedge in that cut, arced this time with speed that gave the blade a furry hum, and the log relented and lay back, cloven.

Gun looked up and the weasel was closer, halfway down the pile. Probably defensive about losing its home this way, a piece at a time, but somehow unable to resist the sound of the axe. It always came closer.

He finished up and stacked the pine wedges on the child's sled he used to haul them to the door. It was a Flexible Flyer, Mazy's old hot rod he'd paid twelve bucks for back in '73, trying to keep her from getting any older. She'd indulged him, used it for a winter when her friends weren't around. A good sled. A great wood horse.

At the door Gun smelled mouse, remembered, leaned down and picked up the flattened victim by the tail. The weasel was on the ground in front of the woodpile. Gun tossed it the mouse and picked up an armload of wood, feeling as he turned the weasel's eyes like two polished black bullets nestling up to the base of his brain.

He was meeting Carol at eleven, Jack Be Nimble's, where Jack had agreed to break protocol and make them breakfast, eggs, the whole show. You had to do that sometimes, Jack said; everything in life had its purpose, cholesterol included. "Makes you happy, makes you sleepy, encourages the occasional contemplation of your own mortality," Jack said. "A life unexamined, and so on." Gun didn't consider himself especially contemplative but had started to wonder if all these eggs had anything to do with his morning sit-ups. They seemed harder lately. He sat down on impulse just before leaving and did an extra set, seventy-five crunches. He swung on a jacket and went out to the Ford and drove off to see Carol, his gut muscles yelping behind the wheel.

They eased off though before he got to Jack's and pulling the pickup in through the thick birches he saw Carol had beaten him there by maybe thirty seconds. She'd parked her Miata, God love her, at the end of the building and was going up the boardwalk, away from him. Walking like that in a tailored black suit with a white shirt showing at the neck and a lot of blue scarf. Just enough white strays in all that black hair to let you know you'd better be serious. A superior sight, Carol striding; there were times Gun would rather watch her than talk to her.

Only here came Ted to screw things up.

Gun pulled in under a bare, leaning birch and saw he couldn't prevent a damn thing so just sat and watched.

Ted was a short-haired black mongrel as high as a hubcab whose thoughtless owner lived a quarter mile down the road from Jack Be Nimble's. He had a high voice, a narrow pinched yip you could hear with your windows rolled up and Garth Brooks yodeling in the cab. Gun had tried it. Ted had a passion for thin ankles and straps, and Jack had a pump-up BB pistol behind the bar for Ted.

But Carol today was having none of it. The dog was approaching from the rear, yipping, sneaking up on her and making sure she knew it, but she just kept going. Didn't turn around, go into a defensive crouch, didn't even speed up heading for the door. Her walk, if anything, got slower, more tempting, that compact behind ticking back and forth like a metronome winding down. The motion looked good enough to Gun but to Ted it was plain maddening, a pound of Purina after a hungry week, and the little mutt lost all caution and rushed at her, snapping his foolish teeth.

It was as if she were waiting for it. Gun had never quite known what to do with ankle biters like Ted;

maybe it was all his altitude, but Carol knew for sure and it came down to not being tricky. Hearing the rush, she spun, took a tiny efficient step for leverage and produced a Rockette kick that caught Ted between the front legs and an inch to the right of his breastbone. Carol's follow-through was so lithe and perfect—her knee not even bending as her leg continued up—that Gun almost didn't see the dog become a little black football, his white muzzle spinning into stripe, Ted rising and traveling outward until hitting the windshield of a tan International Scout parked near the entrance. It was Jack's Scout, didn't give an inch for such a lightweight missile and Ted lay on its hood with his legs splayed. Gun leaned back in his seat, watching as the dog blinked its eyes, separately, probably seeing two different worlds. Gun smiled. Sure, justice gets done from time to time, but not usually out there where you can see it. Not usually to Ted. He chuckled and looked for Carol, but she was already gone in with the door swinging closed behind her.

Jack Be Nimble's, LaSalle's place since before Gun built on Stony Lake the year JFK got shot, was of a vanishing type hereabouts. Little by little, Stony was attracting gentlefolk from the Twin Cities and beyond, persons who'd made their money cheap during the eighties and had decided to come north in the nineties to spend it. They came insidiously, welcomed by most locals who were still impressed by anyone who listened to classical music on their car CDs. The new people liked nonsmoking sections and nonalcoholic beer. They came to a place saying they needed a change, and then they changed the place to suit them. The bar-and-grill joints had been the first to go. If you didn't want ferns hanging from the ceilings and soft string music in the background, if you still ate meat and didn't mind that it wasn't 98-percent fat-free, you went to Jack Be Nimble's.

"Gun? Over here."

She was in a back booth, the knotty-pine glow making her tan even better than usual. All those years in Hawaii, it took more than a few Minnesota winters to make a paleface of her.

"Sharp," Gun said, nodding at her.

"Thanks."

He said, "What's that?" Carol had a notebook along but Gun didn't see a pen yet, that was promising.

"Don't worry. If we talk, something comes up I don't know yet, what am I supposed to do? Trust my memory?"

"Works for me."

They were the only ones there except for a slender kid of maybe nineteen who'd come in behind them and was already at the bar, eyeing the spigots. Miller Lite, Bud, Stroh's. A door squealed from the back of the place and Jack appeared. He headed for them white-aproned, rubbing his forearms as he came, like a doctor scrubbing up.

"With bacon, or ham?" he said.

"Ham," Gun said.

"With dry toast, wheat, margarine on the side," Carol said. "And poach the egg if you would, Jack."

Jack leaned into the booth and put his elbows on the table. He was short and solid as a side of pork and didn't have to lean far. He said to Gun, "This woman with you?"

"She is. It's a trial."

Carol said, "Do you want me sleek, or do you just want more of me?"

"Jack, poach the egg."

"It's poaching. Listen. I drove down yesterday and saw Dick. They're transferring him back to Stony in a day or two, but he's not gonna be home for a while. At least another week or two. You can imagine how happy he is. Anything turned up on Babe?"

Gun looked at Carol. "You're the reporter."

"Nobody's seen him. The police aren't saying so but

101

they like him better every day for Julius Marks. Apparently somebody up at the Spirit Waters blockade pointed the finger at Babe and said Julius's sister witnessed it. Now May's missing, too."

"Dick," Jack said, "is going to have trouble getting around for a while. It would be good if this were over by the time he gets healthy."

"What do you mean?" Carol said.

"Well, he still doesn't much feel like talking. But when he does, it's damning the law and damning the Indians, not to mention the guy who plowed up his insides. What he needs is Babe back again, and nobody around to blame for it all." Jack straightened, pushed a hand over his black crew cut. "There's the truth," he said, "from the mouth of a humble barkeep and egg poacher." He jogged his eyebrows and turned for the kitchen, his steps short and dignified, wiping the hairy backs of his hands on his apron.

Gun got up, went to the Bunn machine behind the bar and came back with a pot full of black coffee and two white cups. He set them down. He poured.

"Did you talk to Crosley yet? He get anything out of that little abduction?"

Carol looked at him flatly. She said, "It wasn't so little. He hasn't come back."

Gun fought the sense of surprise. Crosley'd gone off with the Spirit Waters group willingly, confidently. Probably'd made up, spent the night at the blockade, giving everybody hugs, improving race relations.

"The cops," she said in a careful voice, "went up to the blockade early this morning. Pim let on Crosley hadn't been there. They went in and searched the place, all those tepees, trailers. He wasn't there."

"Wait a minute. Was Sparrow?"

"Sparrow was there. So innocent he was rubbing his eyes. Saying, 'Crosley who?'"

"He was there last night. He took Crosley, or Crosley went with him—"

"I know, I read your statement."

Carol didn't miss much. It was scary sometimes.

She said, "Spirit Waters is playing some kind of game, but no one can prove it. You say it was Sparrow, Sparrow says it wasn't. Only other person who saw him, or the others, was Crosley. That friend of his, Izzy, says he didn't see enough to give a description."

"I guess he didn't." Izzy Rolph, pitching right in. Peek out the windows every few minutes, see how it's going. "So it's my account of things against Sparrow's."

"And Sparrow has a dozen friends pinpointing exactly where he wasn't."

"I would lie about this? Why?"

She gave him a smile and some of that sunlight her eyes could project when things under the surface got funny. "Maybe you're a bigot, Gun. A Nazi. Maybe you have assault rifles in your basement."

"Oof. That's me."

She sparked again like the sun on waves and he drowned there for an instant thinking, *What a talent, that with the eyes, if that could just hang on, if I could make it hang on,* but it faded then and she said, "Gun. Durkins is going to want to talk to you."

Oh well. He sipped coffee and Jack had made it right, a stand-up cup. "Again?"

"Well, you can see why. They didn't expect to get blanked up there this morning."

"Okay."

"So are the state cops. They say you haven't been answering your phone."

"I unplugged it."

"They still want to talk to you. Everybody wants to know who this guy is who cut up Dick."

"Me included. Durkins asked me about it. If I knew who he was, you think I'd be here?"

"No. But you think he's after Babe, and you think he might've taken May Marks away." Carol leaned toward him, saying it quietly though the place was nearly empty. "Gun, we need her back. Maybe what she has to say is something we don't want to hear, but we *need* to hear it. Even if it puts Babe Chandler in a tough spot." Saying this as Jack pulled up with two steaming plates, white enamel chipped gray here and there.

"Breakfast," Jack said. "A nonmenu item. Tip big." He thumped the fingers of his right hand, thumb and all three others, on the table. His index finger was gone at the socket.

After talking to Pim, Gun didn't know how badly he wanted to find May Marks. He didn't want to believe her story, didn't want it to cost him his sense of loyalty to Dick. Gun preferred simple goals: a friend's kid runs off, you go find him, everybody's all right again. He looked down at breakfast, yolks gold and gleaming but nothing tasting good in his mind now, all this muddy business. He said, "Carol? Tip big," and saw Jack smile, and that was good.

The kid at the bar had taken a key ring out of his pocket, a big one so people would be able to see it had MUSTANG on it and a picture of a rearing stallion giving hell to all who drove the lesser motorcars. He was tapping the key ring on Jack's mahogany bar. Snapping it triple time, one hard and two softs—*Bud*-weiser, *Bud*-weiser, *Bud*-weiser. Jack went over, plucked the key from the kid's hand, and handed it back to him, oh so gently, and drew him a beer.

Gun said, "Something else. Guess with whom Crosley shares his 'Music from the Hearts of Space.'"

"Who?"

"May Marks," he said.

18

"So it's Crosley and May," Carol said. She was at the wheel of her white Miata, looking like someone the people at Mazda probably paid just to drive around, while Gun hunched himself in with his knees face high. "It's interesting, but I don't know where it gets us."

They were back on Highway 7, reservation bound. Not because of who was there, but because of who *might* be: Babe Chandler, May, Crosley Schell. The guy with the half-moon knife.

"Maybe nowhere. Maybe the guy who cut Dick engineered the Schell abduction."

"He wasn't there, was he?" Carol glanced at him like maybe he'd withheld this part.

"No, but would he have to be?"

They drove a few miles, long enough for Gun to feel sore in the neck and regret going in the Miata instead of his Ford pickup. Not that two people could talk in the Ford anymore. Something in its digestion was going bad; it growled and horsed like a sick stomach.

"Maybe," Carol said, "it's significant that the two of them are missing together."

"Let's go to her place. After we try the blockade. Can't hurt."

She said, "Last time, it hurt."

Gun remembered as they approached the Spirit Waters encampment how the barrier of pines had appeared to him and Dick, previous visit. Like a sudden mirage: one minute they're driving sixty along the crummy blacktop and the next, a long, green wall shimmers up out of the road, and then you saw the old beaters parked in the ditch and knew where you were.

This was the same place, with an audience. They were still five miles from the blockade when an urgent whacking roar swelled up and swallowed the Miata's quiet engine, and a white-bellied helicopter overtook them from the rear. It swam straight over them and continued north, following the highway. Carol's nostrils widened slightly, the land-bound journalist being beaten to a story. She said, "Channel Eight."

Television people. Gun found himself looking stiffly at his car door. There had to be a handle somewhere.

"Are we even going to be able to get in?" she said.

Gun shrugged, an activity he had room for. "We got in before. Dick and me."

"That was before Crosley got himself snatched. Now our competition's the whole blessed Global Village." Carol tossed her head, hair bouncing so girlishly he wanted to reach over and play with it. Hmmm. Probably the wrong time, though.

The beaters were still there, had multiplied in fact and been joined by newer cars, a Lincoln, a BMW, a Honda. Most had reservation plates. Carol slowed, passing them, getting closer to the barricade. The air had a fuel taint. The white helicopter was parked off to the left behind a row of cars, its rotors bending toward cold ground, a woman standing next to it in makeup and a tan jacket talking with a guy wearing headphones. Another helicopter, green with EARTHNEWS 6 painted on the tail, sat with its crew farther from the barricade. What were they all waiting for? There was a TV truck painted with the CBS eye, a Dodge van with Minnesota Public Radio on the side, and a couple of sludgy-eyed fat men leaning against a brown station wagon with a steel thermos on top.

"No chance," Carol muttered. "It's a damned carnival." She found a narrow place between the station wagon and a GMC pickup hitched to a yellow horse trailer and wedged the Miata in.

There were horses in the trailer, a pair of them good and nervous, Arabians by their nostrils. The Mazda was so squeezed, Gun could only open the door a foot and had to lever himself out. He said, "If we have to leave quick, I'm going by pony."

One of the fat men set his coffee on the roof of the wagon and headed for them. He was pale as if just coming off a long winter, his cheeks like two over-turned soup bowls from the White China Diner. He wore a brown trencher the color of his car and looked unhappily familiar.

"Gun! Gun Pedersen! Bill Boise, *City Beat.*" His voice was seemingly the healthiest part of him and brought the other broad gentleman to attention. "You were out at Crosley Schell's last night? What happened?" A pen and steno had appeared in his hand from nowhere, *it's a miracle.* Those round cheeks lifted into ovals and pinked a little and he almost licked the tip of his Bic, Gun could tell.

"Bill, go away," Gun told him.

The other guy was jiggling toward them now, mouthing something like, Gun, clear this up for us, buddy. Carol pulled at his arm and he saw the tan-jacketed helicopter woman wending through cars toward him and her headphoned slave hoisting a camera. He hadn't thought of this, that he'd be a hot interview, part of the hot "Crosley's Gone" story, but it was damn plain to him now and it turned his mouth salty. He looked from Carol to the barrier of fallen pines, saw two Indian sentries sitting on the top pine wearing army fatigues and ponytails. Looking as if they wanted to be serious, but *boy* what fun getting to hold these rifles, and he took Carol's elbow and started for the blockade. Reporters flagged after him in the good name of journalism and he wondered if talking would be the right thing to do, and he smelled his own cowardice but stayed with it anyhow: *when the lepers get close, you go the other way.* They neared the blockade with media vectoring in on them like mosquitos to meat, and with a dozen yards between themselves and the sentries Gun heard the word "Go!" The dry pines rustled and a hound loped out at them, long teeth showing in its brown round head. The dog's chest reverberated in a growl like the Channel Eight whirly. Its nose glowed with moisture. Gun remembered to be polite.

"Hello, Booger," he said. The hound stopped, tilted its head. Behind him Gun sensed the freeze of reporters, Booger making them think here. You couldn't blame them, a beast this size. Keeping it quiet he said, "Carol, meet a friend of Pim's, and I think of mine." He went to one knee and the dog came up, sniffed, and remembered.

"Maybe he could go tell Pim to let us come in," Carol said. She was petting the dog now, Booger so tall she didn't even have to bend over.

"Better yet," Gun said. He stood quickly, snapped his fingers toward Bill Boise, *City Beat,* and said, "Go!" then watched Booger regain full froth and volume while chasing the man in the brown trenchcoat back to the safety of his station wagon. It set Carol of all things to giggling, and Carol was no giggler by nature. He'd have to ask her about it, but first they had to get inside the barrier, find out what the devil was going on here.

They headed for the east end of the blockade and were met by one of the sentries. He looked pretty serious now, as if he might know which end of that rifle to point after all. It wasn't pointing anywhere important yet, though, and Gun said: "We need to see Pim. Right now."

The smile came back and the guy said: "The hell? Pim sees nobody, not till the announcement's over."

Carol swallowed her last giggle. "What announcement?"

"That's what you got to wait to find out. Ain't you used to this by now, you reporters? Shit, man."

"This is about Crosley Schell?" Carol not giving up.

"Wait, like everybody else," said the sentry, pointing the rifle back past them now, showing them the way.

Okay, Gun thought, *we'll wait.* What announcement? And then heard Carol say, the lie coming from someplace in her he didn't know she had, "You tell Pim something. Tell him Gun Pedersen is here, and he brought another witness with him. I saw Sparrow take Crosley Schell."

The sentry frowned at that, said, "Shit, man," again and left them, jogging away toward Pim's trailer.

Carol looked triumphantly at Gun. The cold had added some red to her sunset tan and it fared nicely on her, gave the white smile some extra punch. He said, "What is this? And giggling, too."

19

The guy came running back in his army suit, badly
winded. Gun passed up the chance to say *'You look
fatigued'* and instead followed the path now being
pointed to by the rifle: toward one of the white tepees,
smoke chuffing from a brown-stained opening at the
top. The sentry stayed behind as they headed for it,
catching his breath, staving off further invasion. As
they neared the tepee, a canvas flap flipped open and
Warrior Pim stepped out. He was alone. He wore a red
hooded sweatshirt under a suit jacket of dark brown
wool. Blue peg-leg Levi's, deerskin moccasins that
looked brand-new. The jacket was buttoned at the
waist, some sweatshirt hood spilling out over the
lapels. He smiled and Gun found himself smiling
back.

"Gun, it's starting to feel like we're on opposite
sides. And it feels wrong."

"It is," Gun admitted, "and it does." A third
helicopter was arriving, blowing the world all to bits,
CHANNEL 10 painted on this one and WE CARE ABOUT
PEOPLE. They waited for it to settle down, out of sight
behind the barricade.

Pim said, "Carol Long? You are the witness?"

"Yes," Carol said, Gun wondering about the wisdom of this.

"Nobody saw you out at Schell's," Pim said, smiling some more.

Carol said, "Aha," and it made Pim smile even bigger. He said, "Warmer in the tepee," and ducked in ahead of them.

It seemed to be where Pim was living now. The fire sputtering softly in the center was built on a bed of gray ashes half a foot high. It didn't give much light but more came in through a top flap propped open by a straight birch pole. In the dark angled edges of the tepee, Gun noticed Pim's Coleman stove, a light-blue cooler with a white lid, and a box of Ritz crackers. An aluminum cot with a down bag spread over it was pulled up close to the fire and Pim waved for them to sit. The smell inside the place was clean wood smoke and some scalded odor Gun couldn't place.

"Milk?" Pim asked. That was it. The smell. "We're out of coffee. It's hard to get out to shop, nowadays." He was kneeling at the cooler, lifting up a yellow carton with a cow on the front, pouring some in a tin pan.

"No, thanks," Carol said.

"Gun?"

"Sure."

Pim used a stick to smooth some red coals at the fire's edge and laid the pan there to heat.

"Cups are under the cot."

Gun hooked up two mugs and handed them over. Pim pulled the cooler up to the fire and sat. He was quiet until the milk began to bubble and the smell of scald came up fresh. He took a handkerchief from the inside pocket of the suit jacket and used it to lift the pan from the fire. He poured slowly, saying quietly as he did it: "You were really there then, Carol? Watching the doings?"

It was an abrupt surprise for Carol and Gun watched her face while she decided whether to stay with the lie or go straight with Pim, who continued to pour. A splash of milk went down the side of a mug and dropped into the coals to rise again, a ghost of steam. Looking at Carol, Gun found he could not read her and this surprised him. Pleased him too.

"No. I wasn't," she said.

"I didn't think so," said Pim. He handed Gun a blue-steel mug, hot on the fingers, and faced Carol. "You are not the type to have stood back and watched. You'd have done something."

"I'm going to do something now," Carol said. She had her notebook suddenly, look-look-again, that same magic act as the fat man outside. "I'm going to write this down. I'm going to report that you've got Crosley after all. What you're doing is nuts, Pim."

Pim watched the notebook and her pen humming along, his eyes mild behind the glasses. He said quietly, "What do you think Crosley Schell could do that would hurt us? You're a reporter; find me a motive."

Carol was showing some exasperation, clutching the pen in stiff fingers. "Find gold, I suppose. Bring in the big shovels."

"Yes. And that's worse than it sounds."

Outside, a car horn honked and a few others joined in. It lasted a few seconds and died away to human voices, shouts. Gun said, "That you they're waiting for? What announcement is this?"

Pim leaned into a swallow of milk, closing his eyes in enjoyment, coming up with a foam mustache. "Let them wait," he said. "You white guys."

"They're expecting you to hand Crosley over," Carol said. "Nobody bought that denial of yours."

"So where is he?" Pim said. "Did anyone see him here?" He raised his eyebrows. "Tell me something. What do they think of Spirit Waters? The journalists, I mean."

Gun looked at Carol thinking, *Maybe it's time for another lie,* but her face said she was being played with and knew it, so screw the soft answer. "They think you're another in a long line of militant Indian groups trying to unscrew treaties that were broken years ago. That you're naive. Ill-equipped. That you speak vaguely about visions and saving the earth. That you're—" she painted her tone ironic—*"well meaning."*

Pim laughed lowly to himself, drained his hot milk and stood. "When my grandmother was in her twenties," he said, "she had her first vision. She spoke of it to my grandfather but he told her to quiet down. He was older, you see, he liked his wisdom from people with a lot of gray in their hair. But when I was small and visiting their house, she used to tell it to me. She told me that before I was old, the Ojibwa would again have to engage the whites in a battle for the land. She said a great needle would be brought to this ground" —Pim poked the earth with his toe—"and that whites would try to poke that needle through the skin of the world. Looking for gold."

"That was astute of your grandmother," Carol said, "but you know it wasn't an original idea. There'd already been a kind of gold rush nearby, over at Lake Vermilion. Eighteen-sixties. Only it didn't turn out. No gold in the ground."

"It isn't the ground that's important," Pim said. "It's the water, underneath. Straight down"—jabbing again with his toe—"straight down from where we are, maybe half a mile, there is an aquifer. A huge one, fed from a hundred million acres of wetlands in northern Minnesota and Ontario. An ocean's worth of water, and it's all pure. Never been touched. That aquifer feeds out in veins to the south, west, and east. Water starts here, it reaches both oceans. And the Gulf." Pim's face was glistening now though the tepee was cool. There was a taste of fire in his voice. "In the Cities, people are used to drinking water out of bottles. Go to the supermarket, pick up some water. Their kids think it's always been so. Do you know something? What we're standing on here, it's the biggest source of clean water in North America. It's the last clean well."

It was familiar Spirit Waters rhetoric. Gun had read it in Carol's paper, had seen it—edited into nonsense—on TV news out of Minneapolis.

Carol put her pen down. "They're not mining yet, Pim. They're exploring. They just want to look."

"That drill is the needle," Pim said. "The one my grandmother saw. If this goes on, they will poison the water. You know it could happen. Maybe not now, maybe not even soon, but it will happen. She saw it. 'The rivers in the earth will run with poison,' she said. And now I see it as well. I dream of it."

Gun said, "Poison?"

Pim sat down on the cooler looking suddenly worn, more like a man who'd just faced down a hostile press conference than one who still had to do it.

"Cyanide," Carol told Gun, "is part of the process used to extract gold—very fine gold, gold dust—from chunks of bedrock. The state people all say it's safe, it's been done in Canada with success. They haven't had very many leaks."

"Very *many?* How many do you *need?*" Gun said. Cyanide. Sweet God.

The fire snapped weakly and an unkind wind pushed under the canvas and whipped at their ankles. It brought along voices from outside the barrier, the words indistinguishable but the tone saying it clearly: *Come on, let's move it, we're on deadline here.* Pim rose at last. "Do you see why we can't move from here? Why we can't let them in?"

"What's Schell's place in this?" Gun asked.

Pim's eyes closed. "Schell's place, we thought, was one we could trust. If he found gold, he was to inform us of it first. Before he told his company people. We had this worked out: He would tell us about the vein, where it was, and we would try to plan accordingly. Line up some legal representation, get some protection. Do it right. Only Crosley Schell *did* find gold, and for some reason, he didn't keep the bargain. Crosley's *place* turned out to be betrayal."

"Pim." Carol looked at him closely, making his eyes open again. They were dry, determined. "How do you know he found gold? Who told you?"

"May Marks," he said. "She spent time with him. A lot of time. He was going through those old samples, looking for traces the last prospectors didn't have the equipment to see. He found it, all right, but he didn't tell us. He told DDH. Now they've brought the needle, and this line of shit about *exploratory* drilling. You telling me they don't know exactly where to explore?"

Running steps approached the tepee and the sentry poked his head through the flap. He sucked in hard and spoke on the exhale: "People gonna start leavin', Pim"—big breath—"you gotta get out there."

"I'm coming."

"Pim," Gun said. "Maybe Schell wasn't straight with you. It can't matter now. If you've got him, give him back."

Pim stepped outside the tepee and held the flap for Gun and Carol. The wind blew the hood of his sweatshirt up against the back of his head and the cold of the gust seemed to calm him. "Crosley," he said, "is not mine to give."

20

Someone at Spirit Waters had begged or borrowed an old flatbed Chevrolet from the Lakeland Sawmill on the edge of the reservation. The sawmill wasn't sawing a lot these days, and it wasn't changing the oil in its trucks much either, but the old critter had gotten this far and had been parked, like a pregnant tortoise, in front of the pine barricade. It faced the jockeying reporters, the mikes and minicams, with a solidity Gun admired: a good, level flatbed about head-high off the ground. A good place to make a speech.

"Happy you could all make it," Pim was saying now. Without amplification he had to yell, and the rising wind sculpted his voice into swells and dropoffs. The sun was scissoring out from a horsetail cloud and getting him in the eyes and he put up a hand, squinting under the palm.

"We wanted to make a statement," Pim said, "about Mr. Crosley Schell. Some of you seem to think we went out to his place last night and got him. Sorry. We're not responsible."

Gun understood Pim's lie but it got to him anyhow. People who believed in visions weren't supposed to lie. Well, damn this show; he and Carol were poised at

the Miata, ready for takeoff. They'd hear this announcement, for what it was worth, then go out to
May Marks's place, see where she might be.

"What about Gun Pedersen's statement?" a reporter yelled at Pim. Gun craned for a look. Bill Boise.
"He gave eyewitness testimony."

Pim said, "Then talk to *him* about it. I don't speak
for Gun Pedersen." Plenty of cool there and Gun
thought, *Well, thanks for that, hey.*

Carol whispered, "You want to sit down? Or you'll
be next, up there on the stand."

Good idea. Sit down.

"Far from abducting Crosley Schell," Pim went on,
"we have every interest in seeing him back. He has
been a friend to the Ojibwa, and to Spirit Waters. We
have told local law enforcement, and the state police,
that we'll cooperate with them as they mount a search
for Mr. Schell."

Gun noticed for the first time a maroon state-police
sedan, its driver wearing the regulation aviator shades
and Yellowstone hat, parked on the east perimeter of
cars. Next to it, Sheriff Jason Durkins leaned his butt
against the county car, shoulders slumping. In shades
also, Gun saw, hiding those bread bags under his eyes.

"This cooperation you're talking about," a reporter
was shouting. "Is Spirit Waters ready to pack up this
blockade and go home?"

That brought a flurry of follow-ups crowding the air
before Pim could even answer. Foam-padded micro-
phones punched up at him and he backed off, startled.
Like peasants and pitchforks, Gun thought, and then
Pim had got himself back and was shouting, "We will
stay until the mining company takes its business away
from our land and away from our waters. We will
stay!" And it was then that the tan-jacketed woman
from Channel Eight got bumped from the rear by Bill
Boise, the old hard charger, and in turning to give him
some rudeness in return, looked through a face-size
hole in the crowd and saw Gun sitting there in the

open door of the white Mazda Miata. He saw her right back, *nail him first* tooled on her face like flowers on a Mexican saddle, and said, "Carol, drive away."

"What? Pim's not done—"

But the woman was motioning to her cameraman, telling him to get the rest of the main event while she buttonholed a sidebar, and Gun snaked his arm through the car to where Carol's handbag lay on the dash and dug out her keys. He jammed them in the ignition: "Drive away."

Then Carol saw her, too: Channel Eight, smiling and wending toward them, *Trust me* in her eyes. Carol folded her legs into the car and cranked the motor. In her hurry, she blew the horn and set the Arabians screaming in the horse trailer next door. She had her side locked, too, but Gun hadn't thought to do that and Channel Eight, reaching them, didn't even knock on his window, just grabbed the handle and had his door open a foot before he realized it. She was short and very pretty, light brown hair chopped at the shoulder; too-crisp maroon lipstick, though, and a voice too clear with all that practice.

"Mr. Pedersen, a word, please. My cameraman—if you'd just have a comment about your allegations of last night, about the abduction. I won't keep you long."

"No, you won't." Gun gave the door handle a little jerk, pulling the woman off-balance. He said, "I'm sorry, but your fingernails, you'll want to watch them," and she yanked her hands from the door. He shut it, got it locked this time and Carol backed out. Slow enough to be safe, quick enough to water down any other journalistic ambitions that might be creeping up from behind.

Nobody wanted Gun bad enough to follow them out. The last he saw, turning in his seat as they picked up speed, was Pim on the flatbed pointing one finger at the sky as reporters danced like black ants around the queen.

She said, "Well, I guess you're all mine. Exclusive interview."

"What makes you think I'll talk?"

She half-twisted and gave him a smile that was worth a long ride in a short car. Hell, a lot of long rides. She said, "You saw what I did to Ted. Outside of Jack Be Nimble's."

He could only grin. This woman Carol, today she was all surprise.

Gun remembered how you got to May's; the unmarked turnoff from blacktop to sand, the track just about petering out there in the swamp, and finally coming out again and forking off into young growth and then the clearing. He told Carol as she parked not to fret, the dogs were friendly, she could keep her field-goal form a secret here.

"You really think May's going to be home?" she said.

"Nope." They were rounding the first trailer, the white one with long Vs of rust down the sides. The two uneven rows of trailers made a sort of street in between, with May's trailer blocking off the end. "She either had reason to go, or that guy had reason to take her. Nothing's resolved yet—no knifeman, Crosley's still missing, Babe's still missing. Would *you* come back?"

"Gun. What did you make of Pim, back there? Why won't he tell the truth, about Crosley?"

There wasn't much noise around the little Marks community; the same cluckings and hound gladnosings, but no people outside. A face looked out at them from behind a twisted screen door. Man? Woman? Gun nodded, and the face nodded back.

"I don't know. Pim shuts his eyes and sees the future. I suppose if you have visions, they become your absolutes. You protect them, no matter what." Hearing himself say it that way Gun felt some regret.

"You think Crosley's in danger?"

He thought so. Didn't say it. Instead he said, "Trailer's dark," as they approached it, the wind snarling into dusty corkscrews that ran past them on the ground. An empty Marlboro pack got caught in one and deviled into the air, twisting up waist-high before getting hold of gravity again.

May's place was dark all right, and darker for the clouds that had moved up over reservation country like a mourning quilt, soft and smothering. Gun's stomach went watery with remembering the last time he'd been here; the guy had come down those same wooden steps with such deliberation, such sudden speed. It was like visiting a place you've seen before during sleep. Not good sleep. He stood looking, and while he looked Carol climbed the steps and knocked on the screen.

No answer. She opened the screen and banged on the door. Again nothing. Carol looked at Gun, who wanting badly to leave had made no move to join her up there. She saw the wish in his face, he knew it, and it was most likely this that prompted her to play the determined reporter and try the door, and it was unlocked. She put her head in, calling "May?" then disappeared, leaving the door open, and in two seconds came sailing back out with her face the color of autumn clouds and her lips pulled tight against her teeth.

"Gun! Gun . . ." Her voice had the dry shakes and he was on his way, she nearly tumbling down the steps getting to him.

"What's inside?" he muttered, although he knew, because the open door was letting it out, a little at a time.

Carol sobbed, her face in his shoulder, hard, her words muffled. "A smell. An awful smell."

21

He sat with Carol in her big brick-floor kitchen, night trying to come in the windows and one dim yellow lamp almost keeping it out. She'd produced a large bottle of Christian Brothers brandy from a cupboard above the stove. They weren't talking, not yet. Just sitting there at the kitchen table together, letting the brandy work some feeling back into nerves gone numb with overuse.

Gun hadn't wanted to go into that trailer again. He'd done it knowing that every detail, even the ones not messy, would come plowing back at him later, while sleeping maybe, or trying to. The sag of the trailer as he entered it. The strange violet carpeting, fuzzed up in places as if it'd been currycombed. The stiff-legged walk down that same tunnel, the one that led to the bathroom where he'd found Dick, and of course the smell. As a boy, Gun had made pocket change trapping muskrats in the swamp near his Upper Michigan home; the swamp in places had a crust of earth you sometimes dared to walk on, to get out to the larger rat houses. Big for his age and weighted with a burlap sack of traps and stakes and hatchet, he'd stepped through that crust often, and the black stuff that came up on his boots smelled rotten and sulphurous, dangerous. He'd decided then that Hell would probably smell that way—like things that had been dead so long and pressed so hard they'd be coal soon, and then oil. And today he'd smelled it again, in May Marks's trailer house. And she was there in the bathroom, had evidently returned for the contents of her medicine cabinet when the guy got her, using a firearm this time instead of a knife.

"You don't think they're going to catch him, do you?" Carol said.

Gun shook his head. Durkins had arrived with a deputy named Willis something who kept finding excuses to go into the bathroom and look at the body.

"Leave it alone," Durkins had glared. "It's federal. They'll be along soon."

"But I got to take a leak, Sheriff," Willis pleaded.

"Take it in the trees. You touch that toilet before the federals take prints, they'll squeeze your butt till it pops." Willis had moseyed into the trees then and Durkins had gotten out his notebook and asked them the questions. Same ones the federal guys asked twenty minutes later, and it all seemed maddeningly useless to Gun, but what could you do? He listened to Durkins telling the federal guys about the man who'd cut up Dick and who'd probably murdered May.

"What about Babe?" Carol was asking now.

Gun had a small tug of the brandy and felt it whisper comfort to his brain. Babe was the puzzler in all this, more so since Durkins had said why he'd been present at Warrior Pim's press conference earlier that day.

"You missed the main event," he'd told them. "This Pim fellow's quite a dealer. Made a pretty smart play today. Know what it was?"

"Nope."

"First he promised to help look for Crosley, pled innocent to grabbing him. You"—Durkins summoned Gun a smile—"did *not* come off like a good honest boy scout."

"Oh-oh."

"And second, Pim showed his good faith by handing over"—Durkins jogging his eyebrows now but not seeming at all jolly—"Dick Chandler's kid, Babe. You know how it looked, after he disappeared—"

"Babe was *there*? At Spirit Waters? How long had he been there?" Gun was recalling his visit with Pim, Pim saying, "I haven't seen the boy."

Durkins shrugged. "Sounded to me like he'd run straight up there after you found Julius in the ice. Don't know for sure, though, I've not had a chance to ask him. What I heard, Pim called the state boys just this morning and made the offer: 'You let me off the hook, I'll give you the kid everybody's looking for. Give you an eyewitness, too; somebody who saw Babe do in Julius Marks.'"

Grimmer by the second. "Did he say who the eyewitness was, Sheriff?"

"Well, no. I didn't hear about it if he did."

"It was May Marks."

Hearing that, Durkins had opened his mouth and found no words in it at all.

Outside the wind had departed, chased by nightfall, but the clouds had thickened and begun to drop wide, heavy snowflakes. Carol capped the bottle. There was coffee and after the medicinal fire of the brandy, it tasted smooth and sensible. Carol had her steno pad and a black ball-point on the table but she wasn't picking them up.

"What happens now?" she asked. "Does Dick know?"

"Durkins was going to call him."

"And I'll bet he was really anxious to do it. 'Listen, we found your son and he's okay, except we think he killed his best friend, so we're going to hang on to him for a while.'"

"Can they do that? Keep a sixteen-year-old kid locked up?"

Carol picked up the pen. "They can if they have a good enough reason, like suspicion of murder. Besides, they don't want to take him home; his dad's still in the hospital."

"That's right. Home all alone, you think he could handle that?"

She ignored the joke and turned to watch the flakes slanting gently onto the windowpane, big sopping flakes that turned to rain as they hit the glass. She watched them without speaking, tapping the rim of her cup with the pen, giving him a perfect picture of her jawline, straight and tan and resolute. He saw she was deciding something. She said, finally, "Do you think Crosley really found gold? Double-crossed Pim?"

"I doubt if DDH would call it a double cross. Crosley worked for them, after all." He thought about it. "I don't know. Pim seemed sure of it, but his only source was May."

"If Crosley found gold, he'd have documented it," Carol said. "He was going through those old core samples. He had one of those old-fashioned ledger books; he made notes in there about the samples, which ones showed trace amounts of iron sulfide, zinc, copper, lead. He called them indicator minerals —find them, and you may find gold, too."

Gun had a suspicion, the way she was tapping her pen on that cup. He wanted to go home before the suspicion played out, he was so tired. Crawl into bed, turn some of that brandy into dark sleep.

She said, "I think he kept the ledger in the shed. With the samples."

"Then it burned. The rocks survived, but nothing else."

She considered. "Crosley was upset? He was freaking out?"

She knew this part already, he'd told her: how

Crosley'd charged out of the house with the Colt, dropped it in the grass and attacked the fire, made the big effort, then calmed down into his old feel-good self. Practically started an encounter group, just a bunch of guys sitting around a campfire being honest with each other.

"Do you think," she asked, "maybe Crosley knew he could afford to be so calm?"

"What do you mean?" Knowing, though. Eyeing his coat on its hook across the kitchen and thinking how damp it was going to feel, just a minute or so from now.

"He might have kept another copy," she said.

"Might have."

"It might be in his house."

"The cops would have found it."

"The cops wouldn't have known what they were looking at," Carol said.

Probably not. "What about DDH? Wouldn't they have sent someone to get it?"

He saw it, then, same as she did, the same strange tickle coming into both of them at once. "Not if he didn't tell them," said Carol. "Not if he was keeping it all to himself."

The clock on the kitchen counter said 9:15. Gun got up and reached for his coat. It wasn't so damp after all. "Think anyone's home at Crosley's?"

She began to smile and it died in mid-bloom. "After today, I hope not."

When they got there it was close to ten and the warm snow had gone to the sort of slick drizzle that turns a throat into a mucus farm. Schell's place was of course unlit, unseeable in such weather until Gun swung the pickup in close and parked. He'd lost a headlight and the remaining one on high beam settled like a vaudeville spot on the totem pole next to Crosley's front door.

"Gun . . ."

"Second thoughts?"

Carol took her time answering. "I don't know. Maybe it's . . . not the best thing. Going in this way."

She was breathing nervously. It was in her voice. Gun found he wasn't sure about this, either. *It's just the going in,* he told himself. *Do it, look around, get out. There can't be bodies every place you go.* He said, "It's not going to happen again."

"I know that. Maybe I'm just afraid we're right, about Crosley lying, I mean. You understand? I don't *want* to be right. It's like somebody tells you they're working on a cure for cancer, they're *this close,* and it feels so nice to believe them."

The drizzle was starting to shift toward snow again, ten thousand BBs tapping the roof of the Ford. Engine still running and heat starting to pile up in the cab, breath turning the windshield to Amazon fog. Gun waited until she said, "Damn it, are we going in?" then reached across her and opened her door.

Schell's octagon had windows on six sides, doors on two, a dream of cross ventilation unless you had every opening shut—like now. The place was locked up tight except for one window. It was the fourth Gun tried as they worked their way around the house, staying fairly dry beneath the generous overhang. Gun pressed his fingers against the sash, set himself for resistance, and the window went up so fast there was a blistering crack when it met the frame.

"Something's wrong," he said. With the window open his fingers had expected to feel open space but instead there was a wall. He took off his gloves. "Wood. It's blocked. No wonder it wasn't locked."

"Tell me where we are," Carol said. It was so dark her voice came to him like a spirit's. "Round house, I'm confused."

"I think we're on the east side."

His bedroom's on this side. There's a big old

wardrobe, one of those free-standing ones like they used to make. It must be covering the window."

"You've seen the man's bedroom?"

"First time I came out to interview him." She was only a little defensive. "He'd just built the place. He was proud of it. He'd bought a bunch of furniture, and there was a wardrobe." She reached out for him and followed his arm up to the window. She felt the wood, knocked on it.

He felt mildly sheepish, but it's not a feeling that lasts long when you're breaking into another man's home. He put the heels of his hands against the wood and pushed. There was give. He braced his feet, finding little purchase in the muddy ground, and shoved harder, and the wardrobe began a slow, tree-top fall that seemed to last the distance they'd already come tonight, and then it thumped down with not as much crash as seemed necessary.

Gun went in first. He crouched on the back of the overturned behemoth and took off his boots, then felt about and found a bed, a dresser, a lamp. He switched it on and went back for Carol.

There wasn't much in the bedroom. A quick toss of Schell's dresser and bedside table and they decided to close the window, right the overturned wardrobe and take the front door when they left. Their shoes were mucked to cartoon dimensions and they carried them through the house—Crosley's plain pine floor creaking under their socks—to the front door. There was a heavy hemp mat with pine trees stenciled on it. CANOE COUNTRY—GREEN IS CLEAN.

"Never track mud in the home of your host," Gun said. They were inside and undetected and this had him suddenly giddy.

"Always leave your campsite cleaner than you found it," Carol said, and she was laughing strangely. It made Gun nervous and he circled the room until he'd found several light switches, turning them on as he went. Carol's laughter subsided with the brightness. "What are you doing? Someone'll see."

"I wanted to make sure you were all right." That sounded bad somehow. He didn't try to fix it.

"I'm all right!" she snapped. He watched her color rise. "Now let's get it dark again."

They worked the place finally with only the light from Crosley's open refrigerator and the low yellow glow coming from the bedroom. It shone into a corner the man had set up as a free-form office: a small maple desk, two-drawer steel file cabinet, bookcase running one side of the octagon. The Siamese cat, Crystal, eyed them from behind a potted plant. The cat fled when Carol bent to stroke it, thrummed away across the wood floor.

"And Crosley said the two of you would hit it off," said Gun. "Too bad."

There was no ledger in the bookcase; its contents ran mostly to journals on geologic formation and mineral histories—a copy of *Black Elk Speaks* and more self-help books than you'd find in a psych-ward library. He quickly scanned a shelf of cassettes. No surprises, just lots of piano players smiling like they'd really gotten in touch with themselves and couldn't wait to tell you about it. One of a guy called Yanni that Gun remembered having heard once in a restaurant. He'd ordered a sandwich there, and had barely found any meat at all under all those sprouts.

Carol was into the desk and frowning, holding up sheets of loose paper one at a time, catching the soft light from the fridge. "Nothing," she said. "Memos from DDH. This one says, 'Good to see you at the western conference but next time leave your tomahawk at home.'"

"Did you check the file cabinet?"

"Locked."

"Try underneath for the key."

Even with the low light he saw the look she gave him. *You know all about this?*

"It's automatic," he explained. "Like putting your house key on top of the door frame. Or under the mat."

She bent and felt beneath the file cabinet with her fingers. "No key. But there's something else." She worked for a while, tearing at something, tape it sounded like, then slid out a pair of long paper cylinders. She unrolled them on the desk. Gun was at her side.

"Maps," she said. There was a lamp on Crosley's desk and she snapped it on, squinting in the sudden glare. There were half a dozen of them, topographicals of the counties in and around the reservation. "I've seen these before," Carol said, "when he was showing me the old drill cores. The way they were catalogued, you could tell exactly which core came from where."

The map Gun was holding was dotted at random with small circles of color: red, green, yellow. It looked like a blueprint someone had used as a dropcloth, painting a child's room.

"What's the color code?"

Carol rummaged in the file folder. "Traces of whatever minerals were found in the cores. Red is iron sulphide. Green, copper. Blue, zinc—"

"Gold?" Gun said, but she was shaking her head.

"No. Just all these others, the ones that pop up most often *around* gold. He was narrowing it down."

"So these"—Gun nodded at the maps—"are nothing important."

"Probably not. I mean, he showed them to me once."

"So why'd he tape them under the cabinet? Why not stick them in with everything else?"

Carol shrugged.

They looked around for a while longer, then Gun said, "This place have a basement?"

They opened three doors that seemed to have potential and found only closets. Walking through the kitchen, though, Gun sounded a hollow note in the floor and bent to investigate. Beneath a woven rug of Aztec design he found a trapdoor with an iron pull ring, hinged and countersunk. When he yanked on it, a light automatically kicked in below, revealing a narrow stair painted green and configured in an L pattern. The cat followed them down. Gun carried the rolled-up maps they'd found.

The stairway gave into a large room that seemed to comprise about half the basement. The room was nearly empty. A large freezer stood against the outside wall on the north, and next to it, serving apparently as a storage rack for Crosley's summer clothes, was an exercise bike. It was decorated with Hawaiian shirts, silk running shorts, and cotton sweaters.

"Such a house," said Carol. "And no closet space." She lifted a flowered shirt from the seat of the bike and rehung it on the handlebars.

"Shame," Gun said. He nodded toward a door on the inside wall which was paneled in a dark wood. "After you."

Carol tried the knob but it was locked. "You're the snoop," she said.

"You're the journalist." He meant it as a challenge, and Carol took it that way, setting her lips in a line and lifting her eyebrows.

"All right"—going to her purse—"three minutes." Her hand swept noisily through the big leather bag, the one she carried only because her son—grown now—had made it for her in seventh-grade shop class. Keys jangled and paper rattled. A bright gold lipstick cylinder jumped a leather side and hit the floor. She didn't bother to pick it up. She let the whole bag drop beside it and pointed a gold credit card at Gun's chest. Her smile was all shrewd fun and then she went to work on the door, at first with delicate fingers, pinky extended, then with force, her elbow pumping.

"Darn," she said, and held up her gold card. One of its corners had been amputated.

"No more fine restaurants for you," Gun said, but Carol was after the lock again, kneeling down in front of it, holding the doorknob in one hand and playing her card in the jamb with little thrusts of her wrist.

"Okay," she said. "There, there, please? Damn it." She took her hand from the knob and slammed it hard against the door. It fell open and Carol fell into the next room. She was up in a hurry though, and Gun watched her from behind as she registered something that made her take a quick defensive step backward. Then her shoulders relaxed. "Oh—they're not alive," she said.

Gun stepped over her purse and walked through the door, placing his hands on Carol's shoulders. The room was full of Indians. Not real ones, but real enough to make you glad they weren't. Some stood, others crouched or sat. All were life-size and dressed with anthropological impeccability. Their wax bodies were tinted in lovely shades of reddish and olive brown. Calling on his memory of a childhood book of great Indian chiefs, Gun was able to recognize Geronimo, who was pointing at something far in the distance; Sitting Bull, proud and straight, his wrinkle-mapped face lifted to the floor joists above him; Crazy Horse, bare chested; an old man sitting cross-legged with a pipe; a woman, very pregnant, one hand supporting her lower back.

Gun and Carol walked among them, quiet, not daring to touch. Gun thought of the times he'd gone to viewings at funeral parlors. Grandparents, a couple of aunts and uncles. A friend or two.

There were a dozen figures in all—Gun counted quickly—and they seemed to be arranged in no particular pattern. In one corner was a naked one with a blank face. Under construction.

Gun heard a door open upstairs. Then footsteps across the floor above them. He looked at Carol, who made a face like, *We're in for it now.* The footsteps stopped in the kitchen and came down the stairs. Gun and Carol waited, nothing to be done.

Soon a face peeked around the doorframe, cautiously—some hair, a nose, an eye. Then a hand which held a small, black pistol.

"Hi, Izzy," Gun said.

The man ducked back, reappeared. Only this time he brought his body along. He wore a Norwegian sweater with reindeer on it and, over that, a down vest. Gun hadn't noticed the other night, but Izzy's face had a pink spot on each cheek like those of a kid who's been running hard, and freckles across the nose. "You're lucky I didn't call the authorities," Izzy said.

"Why didn't you?" Gun asked.

"Thought I recognized the vehicle." Izzy stood outside the room, arms crossed on his chest, pistol sticking up out of the crook of one elbow. He seemed unwilling to come in. "You shouldn't be here," he said.

"Should you?" Carol asked.

"Crosley's a friend. I'm staying out here."

"We thought it was best if we had a look around," said Gun.

"You could have waited till I was home, then."

"We might've, if we'd known you were staying here."

"I can't imagine what you'll find, anyway," said Izzy. "Let's go upstairs and talk." He scooped Crystal into his arms and nodded toward the stairway.

"Nice museum," Gun said. "What you said about Schell and Margaret Mead, it's not so far off maybe." Gun was standing partly behind Geronimo, and with the hand hidden from Izzy's view he eased the roll of maps into the waistband of the wax Indian's buckskin pants. Slowly, he pushed them down along one leg until they were out of sight.

"Twenty-five years of hard work," said Izzy. "Crosley was a double major in undergrad. Geology and art. Started his work on these guys back then. As you can see, he's still at it. His interest in Native Americans is not recently acquired—as some people have it." Izzy was tapping his fingers on the wood casing of the doorframe.

"That's not the way you sounded last night," Gun said.

"I was upset last night. Tell me, how'd you get in?"

"Window," said Gun.

"And I suppose that's okay, means to an end." The pink spots on Izzy's face got pinker. He looked angry.

"We knocked first," said Carol.

"Right. Now, come on. Crosley doesn't bring people down here. It's personal space, this room. We'll go upstairs to talk." Izzy still held the gun in one hand and now he looked at it, frowned, and shoved it, cowboy style, into his belt.

"Always carry the heater?" Gun asked, as he followed Izzy and Carol up the stairs.

Izzy stepped up into the kitchen and waited until Gun cleared the hatch. He slammed shut the trapdoor and arranged the rug with a foot. "It's Crosley's. Tell you, though, I've been tempted to get my own sometimes. In my business you can get paranoid."

"Teaching *geology?*" Carol scowled hard at Izzy, then even harder at the pistol, which prompted Izzy to pluck it from his belt and lay it on the kitchen table.

He shook his head. "I do consulting in the summertime—for mining companies, investment firms, private parties. People who need to know what's in the ground and what it might be worth. I've been in South Africa, Brazil . . . China. And, I'll tell you, rocks and metals can make people very happy. *Very* happy. Angry too. And nervous. Hey, they can make people want to kill you, if what you happen to know means enough to them."

"Since you bring it up," said Gun, "is this a consulting trip you're on right now?"

Izzy smiled and picked up Crystal again. He walked away into a part of the house furnished with low sectionals and silver-tubed lamps, coffee tables and shelves. He dropped himself into a curveless chair. "This is great," he said. "You wait till I'm gone, you come in through a goddamn window, and then when I get here—by way of the *door*—you treat me like *I'm* the one with something to be ashamed of. No, I'm not here on business. I'm here to visit. It's quarter break, if you must know, and I like to clear out for a few days when the school shuts down." Stroking Crystal's ears with his thumbs, Izzy took a deep breath and rocked his shoulders a couple of times, self-righteous.

"You sure seem comfortable," Carol said.

"And you're going, 'Why isn't this guy worried about his buddy?' " Izzy rocked his shoulders again. His spine cracked.

"Well, yeah," said Carol. "You were here last night, and now the Indians are saying they don't have him, haven't even seen the guy. Doesn't that bother you a little bit?"

"No." Izzy released Crystal onto the floor and looked up at Carol and Gun, who were still on their feet in front of him, then leaned his head against the square top of the chair back and smiled generously. "You were there, Gun. Crosley went along with them willingly. These people, they're his friends, remember."

"You're talking a different story than you were last night, Izzy. What'd you do, have a visit with Schell? He call you up today?"

"No, I just did a little thinking. How Crosley works, how he gets on with these people. And I'll bet this: Everything that's happened in the last twenty-four hours? It'll all make sense before long, a day or two. Crosley'll just show up again, and then everything'll be back to normal. What he's doing right now is what he's got to do if he's going to maintain a relationship with the Indians. Can't you see? Pim and the others, they're in a jam. DDH coming in here and starting to drill—that was bound to make them think Crosley found gold. When in fact he advised the company *against* drilling. Told me so himself. He doesn't want the digging any more than Spirit Waters does. And once he sets the record straight—which you can bet he will—the place'll calm right down."

Izzy laughed, shook his curly head. "This gold-strike nonsense," he said. "Of course, I understand why Pim's upset. He's got every right to be. But he's a reasonable man. An educated man. He'll listen to Crosley, and when they've come to a meeting of the minds, Crosley'll just . . . rematerialize. And nobody will have to know where he's been, either. No law against leaving town for a couple days."

"But there's a law against killing people," Gun said.

"What's that supposed to mean? The Marks kid? What's Crosley have to do with that?"

"I'm not talking Julius. I'm talking May."

"May?" said Izzy. He spoke to a point in space well behind Gun and Carol, and Gun turned, half-expecting to see the dead girl. She wasn't there.

"Found her too late for the evening news," said Carol.

"Somebody killed her," said Gun. "Thoroughly."

"God, no." The man's eyes came back and he blinked. He seemed to be struggling to understand something. "You're not thinking Crosley killed her."

"No," said Gun. He sat down on the end of the sectional closest to Izzy and leaned toward him. "I'd guess, though, that Crosley and May Marks had a few secrets between them, wouldn't you think?"

"I . . . yeah, I suppose," Izzy agreed. He was thinking hard now, his eyes burning calories.

"I mean, if Crosley *does* know something—something people might want to hurt him for—then May might know it, too." Gun glanced over at Carol, who'd taken a seat on the other side of Izzy.

Carol spoke quietly. "Izzy, May's dead—and we've

got to think about what that means. Especially to Crosley right now. You've got to tell us whatever you can that could help."

"No, no," said Izzy, shaking his head. "Like I told you, Crosley didn't have a thing. Anybody thinking different's making a hell of a mistake. And May—I don't know. May was . . . May. She could have done anything. Slept with the wrong guy, most likely. God, how should I know?" He stood up. "Don't look at me like that," he said to Gun. "Shit, like I'm involved somehow. May's a . . . look, things happen to women like her." Izzy started toward the kitchen but Gun grabbed his shoulder.

"Let go of me." He tried to pull free but Gun turned him around and replaced him in the chair.

"Too easy," Gun said. "First it's Julius, who happened to work for your friend. And now May's dead. And you're saying it's coincidence."

Izzy's cheeks were in full bloom. His lips shook as he spoke. "That's all I can say because there's nothing else I know that sheds any light on things. What are you gonna do, shove me around till I make something up?"

Gun stood up and said to Carol, "Let's get out of here."

"You gonna leave by the window you came in through?" said Izzy, livid. "You gonna clean up the mud you tracked in? You gonna—"

A white bomb went off in the back of Gun's brain. He turned and leveled a finger at Izzy's red face. "You gonna keep asking questions till I pull your tongue out of your mouth and strangle you with it?"

Izzy backed up and shut up. His eyes were as big and bright as a wild rabbit's in a trap. He was shaking his head.

"Thank you," Gun said. He felt Carol's hand on the back of his neck, her fingers squeezing hard. He let himself be turned around by her and led out the front door.

22

They drove to Carol's place, Carol going cold beside him in the cab. She didn't ask him to come in.

Fine, she was upset—at him for losing control, at herself for who knew why, or at Death for doing what it did, Gun wasn't sure. They'd just been through a hell of a day together.

Gun drove home and parked his truck in the garage. The weather was still wet and miserable and Gun's clothes were damp all the way through. He took a long hot shower, drank some hot chocolate, put on some clean wool underwear, and still he felt lousy. Decided he didn't want to stay home tonight. Decided that Jack Be Nimble's was the place to lose the blues.

He walked to the garage and climbed back into his truck. It didn't start. Just cranked and cranked without firing. He climbed out of the cab and went around front and lifted the hood. Weather like this, the old V-8 was prone to electrical pneumonia. Gun removed the plug wires and rubbed them dry with a cotton rag, the coil wire too, and while he did this he asked himself if it wasn't about time to break down and buy a new pickup truck. This one he'd had since '71. And weren't twenty years of good service more than somebody could ask for? He slammed shut the hood and got back inside the scratched and battered cab.

Problem was, he could still smell Amanda in here. The vinyl seats had long ago cracked and peeled. The speedometer had Alzheimer's, forgetting what to do half the time, and the springs rocked more than Izzy's poor shoulders. But Amanda's scent had never faded. Why? he wondered. Years ago her smell had disappeared from the house, even from the closet where her clothes had hung for half a decade beyond her death. There was no natural explanation, but plenty of good reasons. Like the fact that she'd been the one Gun had bought the truck for in the first place. She had spent summers here while Gun was playing ball, and he'd insisted she drive something besides a car, something with clearance and power for the bad driveway, and cargo room for the work she did, like building the rock garden south of the house, collecting wood for the fireplace, and hauling home the trophies she bagged at country auctions.

It was funny, but every time Amanda had slammed herself shut inside the Ford's cab, she'd changed—from city woman and oh-so-elegant to country girl and the world be damned. She'd turn up the radio, drive too fast, brake too hard, shift too much. Leave the windows down and let her hair loose to blow around. The Ford was Amanda the summer wife, the wife who surprised Gun one night during late October, Indian summer. Called out for him from the lake, her husky voice reaching in through the open window of their bedroom. She'd refused to leave the water until he joined her for a long swim and a deep, deep dive.

No, the Ford he'd drive for a while longer, and then he'd park it out in the trees, close enough by so he could still go out and sit inside it when he needed to. You had to go out of your way sometimes to preserve continuity, to keep yourself safe from the kind of forgetting that puts you at the mercy of your own blind spots, your intermittent falls from grace.

He turned the key and heard the starter whirr, the engine thunk over, spin, and catch hold. He nudged the gearshift forward into first and set his mind toward Jack Be Nimble's. Jack would be cleaning up now—it was midnight—rubbing down his tables and his bar, polishing glasses, mopping spilled beer from the floor. His clientele tended toward older guys past their fear of the quiet dark, and younger ones with sense enough to stay inside the boundaries of Jack's code of bar behavior.

One time a guy about six and a half feet tall and thick in all the right places, a stranger, had gotten pushy with a fellow he claimed had usurped his stool. Gave the smaller man a shove that sent him to the floor ungently. Gun was there that night, a few stools to the west, and was ready to intervene when Jack burst over the mahogany bar like a mother bear and broke the man's nose with a single right hand. The man went down, got up bleeding and bawling, then tried to muscle Jack around a little to get his self-respect back. What he got instead was a badly wrecked rib cage and a kick out the door. Around Stony, rumor had it that Jack LaSalle had seen time with the French Foreign Legion, and whether that was true or not—Gun suspected not, but had never asked—somebody somewhere had taught him how to fight.

The place was quiet, a few men still hanging on though not too hard. And there was Jack, mopping the hardwood floor. He'd done half of it already, leaving the wooden chairs upside-down on top of the tables. The men at the bar sat with their shoulders humped, resigned to going home. Gun took his usual stool.

"Somehow you don't remind me of a happy man," said Jack. "Or maybe your chest picked tonight to give up and fall down. You're old enough." Jack had on his small grin and a spotless white apron that came down almost to his ankles.

"So give me a strong one, then, with the chaser. We'll celebrate."

Jack went behind the bar and leaned the mop against the back wall. He knocked his knuckles on the dark wood and said to his patrons, "You guys okay for a while?" They moved their heads enough to show they hadn't died. "Gun, pull up a booth in back and I'll join you for a spell. My legs told me an hour ago to sit down." He disappeared into the kitchen.

The booths had high backs and were the same dark wood as the tables. Only the walls, which were knotty pine and gold with age, held any light. Gun tried to decide if he was hungry. Decided he was, but remembered that Jack had turned off the grill for the night.

"This should be just about ripe enough. Had it in the back of the fridge since last summer." Jack winked and set down a pair of glasses in front of Gun. He scratched the top of his skull through the short-cropped black hair. He smiled. "The iced tea is fresh, though."

Gun lifted the glass of yellowish buttermilk and allowed himself a long swallow. The stuff crawled down his throat, promising to coat his insides and keep them warm and safe. He followed it up with the tea. The tips of his fingers started to itch—*ah, nutrients*—and the feeling of satisfaction settled into his chest.

Ten minutes later the buttermilk and the tea were both gone, the men were gone from the bar, and Gun had unloaded himself of his last two days.

"Tell you the truth," Jack said, "I'd be real surprised if any gold's been found, secret maps or no. DDH smells that stuff and they're gonna be playing this thing a whole lot harder. And Crosley—I'm with Izzy on that. He'll turn up. He loves this role of his. Man between cultures. Long about tomorrow or the next day, they'll call a press conference, him and Pim, and read a joint statement, something like that."

"What about May?" Gun asked.

Jack shrugged. "Gold or no gold, she's in a tight place. Teeny-weeny. Or *was* in a tight place. Look at it. Her people are gonna believe anything she says; she gets the pillow talk, right? So Crosley drops a hint or two and suddenly she knows—or thinks she knows— way too much. She spills it, like Crosley probably wants her to, and somebody pops her."

"Hold it," said Gun. "Two questions. First, why would he want her to think there's gold if there isn't? And two, why would somebody want her dead for telling what she thinks is the truth?"

Jack got up and walked to the bar to refill his glass with Coke. "Anything for you?" Gun shook his head and Jack moved slowly back across the floor, the fingers of one hand massaging his temple. "Being brilliant always makes a guy thirsty, you know? And I shouldn't be telling you all this anyway. You're the problem solver, you and Carol. I'm just a heavy."

"Problem solvers've got to gather opinions."

"Fair enough." Jack sat down and took a sip. "To your first question, I say this. Could be that Mr. Crosley Schell is a man with an ache that only politics can cure. He's been in the news a bit now, you might've noticed that. And this gold scare'll be keeping him there for a time to come. Second question's even easier, Gun. You don't get killed for telling the truth as you see it. You get killed for telling bad news, which is what May probably did. Don't you stay up on your clichés?"

The clock above the bar said 1:15 and Gun felt his cells settling earthward. Jack drained his glass and met Gun's eye. "What does Carol think?"

"Don't ask," Gun said. He let out the sigh he didn't know he'd been holding. "She wasn't of a mind to tell me tonight."

"I'll change the subject, then. What does Carol think of *you* these days?"

"Don't ask," Gun said.

"Damn it. You two." Jack looked toward heaven and squinted. "You don't seem to get it, neither of you. And it's so bloody simple. There is a man, see, and there is a woman, and the two of them love each other." Jack lifted his hands palms up above the table. "Okay? You hear me? Don't *think* so much. Your brain can't make you happy, haven't you figured that one out yet? Your brain's up there just fightin' to make trouble. You've got to step in and knock it back down. Listen to this instead—" Jack slapped his broad chest, which made the sound of a drum.

"You should've been a priest," Gun said.

"I know. But I ran into a problem. There was a man, see, and there was a woman . . ." Jack smiled and shut his eyes sweetly. "And well . . . oh baby, am I tired."

23

Gun was beyond tired, and as they'd often done after twi-night doubleheaders in August, the muscles in his legs refused to relax, even in bed. They twitched and tightened and wouldn't let him sleep. His mind went back and forth between Carol Long's temperature drop and Crosley Schell's maps—Geronimo's now. In both cases it was time to act.

Three A.M.

Three-thirty and still awake.

Gun got out of bed, went to his dresser and turned on the multiband radio he'd gotten ten years earlier for nights like this when his mind wouldn't leave him alone. He liked to flip the dial back and forth and try to guess where the voices were coming from. Tonight he found, way over on the right side, a woman talking in a Brooklyn accent about the emotional struggles faced by widowers. Gun fine-tuned the dial and lay back down. *Maybe I can learn something.* He promptly fell asleep.

When he woke the clock said 4:39 and a different signal was coming in. The woman was gone and a man was talking a hundred miles an hour in what— Chinese? Japanese? Oriental, anyway. Then he heard the pure, familiar sound of honest contact, bat on ball, the crescendo of a crowd, and he knew—Japanese. *Did their season last this long?* He didn't know a word of the language but the announcer's partisan voice, together with the other sounds, gave him a series of pictures that required no translation. He listened to half an inning—two hits, one run, a runner wiped out in a double play, then went to sleep until the sun and the radio's static brought him awake at 7:45. He reminded himself to ask someone about the Japanese baseball season, when it started and came to an end. Then he did his push-ups—barely—took a two-minute shower, drank day-old coffee, and rolled a cigarette while waiting for Carol to find her telephone and make it stop ringing.

"Hello, Gun."

"Shower?"

"No. I was in bed. Awake. Relaxing. Testing your patience."

"I passed, then."

"Yes. But I'm not relaxing anymore."

"Aren't you going to ask why I'm calling so early?"

"I guess you want to talk to me. That's good enough."

Gun smiled. "So how are you?"

"Why'd you call, Gun?"

Gun smiled again. "I want you to pull Izzy out of that house. I need to get back in there—"

"For the maps," Carol finished.

"If Geronimo'll stand for it."

"Indian giver."

"Can you do it?" Gun asked.

Carol was quiet for a moment. "I could ask Izzy to come in for an interview and lunch, though I'm not sure he'd accept the offer. After last night."

"Or breakfast," Gun suggested. "You might even apologize for my behavior."

"Think I ought to?"

"No," said Gun. "But it could make breakfast sound better."

"I'll see what I can do." Carol sounded congenial, but a little stingy.

"It'd be a big favor."

"Don't you think I'm as curious as you are?" she asked.

Gun finished his smoke, drank off the last of a buttermilk carton, and popped two halves of English muffin in the toaster. He was applying a liberal coat of rasperry-almond preserves to the liberal coat of cream cheese when the phone rang.

"That was quick," he said.

"I let it ring about thirty times. Izzy's not there."

"Or not answering the phone."

"I doubt if that's it. Crosley might be needing to talk to him." She sucked in air. "Oh, no."

Gun flexed his brain, and what it gave him was Izzy's reaction the night before to news of May's death. Fear. Did the man think *he* was next? "You think he *is* there," Gun said.

"God, I hope not. Look, I'll meet you out there." The pitch of Carol's voice was high, clear, and terminal.

"Twenty minutes," Gun said.

He parked on the shoulder of the road, half a mile short of the driveway that led into Schell's place. Carol's Miata appeared in his rearview mirror and he pulled back onto the grade and led the way in. They parked side by side in the yard and looked at each other. Carol was biting a thumbnail. Her eyes were dark and full of pictures Gun would not allow himself to entertain. He cocked his head toward the spot in the yard where Izzy had parked his vehicle the night before and made his eyebrows say, "A good sign." She smiled enough to let some light into her face. Nodded.

Gun pushed open his door and stepped out of the truck, watching Carol move up and out of her cockpit, gracefully, like an actress liquid before a camera. What she did with her tension he'd not been able to figure out yet.

She wore a leather aviator-style jacket and Levi's that showed off her committment to the stationary bicycle. *But why am I noticing this now?*

They climbed the steps to the door and Gun let Carol be the one to knock. When nothing happened after three more tries, Gun said, "I bet Izzy locked that window." They walked around back and sure enough the window had been made fast.

"Darn," said Carol. Together they were standing at the rear of the house—if an octagonal house could be said to have a rear—the side anyway that didn't face the road. Carol backed up to a window and snapped one elbow backward, shattering a pane. The sound, it occurred to Gun, was just like the sound track in a movie—snap, tinkle. "Always wanted to do that," she said. "You boys grow up doing this stuff. We never get the chance."

Gun cleared away the shards from the window frame, swung a leg over the sill, had a quick look around—nothing—and made himself at home. Carol hurried in after him. "Slow down," she said. "I don't want to find . . . anything by myself."

"We're not going to find anything." Gun wasn't sure he believed this, but it felt good to say it. And at least he couldn't smell anything. Or feel anything. The window shades were open all around—last night they'd been closed—and the house was as bright inside as the day was outside. The wood floors shone like smooth ice, and the flawless white walls were fashionably bare, marked only by reflections of the sun as it played against the restless birch leaves on the morning side of the house.

A search of the main floor turned up a rubber

mouse and half a cold pizza, but no Izzy and no Crystal, either. "Where's the cat?" Gun asked.

"Probably rubbing herself against Sitting Bull." Carol pointed to the Aztec rug on the kitchen floor.

The light went on automatically as Gun lifted the trapdoor. There came a soft rhythm up the steps and Crystal leaped into the kitchen, then made for the living room and disappeared beneath a low-slung couch. Gun listened for a moment, tested with his nose the cool air rising from the basement, and started down the steps. Carol stayed right behind him.

The exercise equipment was still heaped with the summer clothes. Gun walked over to the freezer and had a look inside—a couple of frozen pizzas, some Popsicles, a few packages of processed potatoes. He shut the lid and turned to Carol, "Ready with your credit card?" But she was already kneeling at the door to the next room, starting to wedge the card between the door and the casing.

"You check to see if it's locked?" Gun asked.

Carol put her hand on the knob. The knob turned. She glanced up at Gun, her eyes displeased by this sudden success. She gave the door a push. The room was dim, lit only by the small window high on the opposite wall, and Gun flicked on the overhead light. The Indians were still here, but apparently no one else. Gun heard Carol release her breath.

They moved slowly among the still figures until they came to Geronimo, then Carol, making a silly face, reached into the back of the Indian's buckskins.

"Bold," Gun said.

The look on her face changed then, and she held up her empty hand. "They aren't here."

Gun checked both of Geronimo's pants legs all the way down to the ankle and found no maps. "I'm sure it was this one," Gun said. "Positive."

"He must've seen you hiding them. That guilty face you had. Damn it, he took the maps and ran."

"At least he's alive."

"Thank God," said Carol. "Where did you say he teaches?"

"New York University." Gun switched off the light and followed Carol out the door and up the stairs. "I may have to go talk to the man."

They were standing in the kitchen now and Gun lowered the trapdoor into place. Then he remembered something. "Carol," he asked, "when does the baseball season end in Japan?"

24

She didn't have an answer but humored him and said she'd do some checking. Gun returned home, Carol to the *Journal* office to call around and get the latest on Spirit Waters and Crosley Schell.

Gun went to the phone. It was nine o'clock, ten eastern time. First he tried New York information on Izzy Rolph and learned that his number was unlisted. Next he got the general information number for New York University and dialed that.

"New York University. How may I direct your call?" A male operator, a transplant from the South.

"Rolph," said Gun. "Izzy Rolph. Geology department."

The phone rang six times before the operator came back and remarked on the obvious. "Dr. Rolph seems to be out, sir. Would you care to try again later?"

"No, but could you hook me up with someone in the personnel office?"

At personnel he got a woman who seemed delighted to be able to deny Gun's request for Izzy's home address and telephone number. Gun told her it was nice to run into folks who enjoyed their work. Then he called the university's main number once more and asked for the geology department. The secretary there told Gun that Izzy Rolph was not expected back until the beginning of winter quarter. No, he hadn't left a forwarding number. Gun considered asking for Izzy's home address but knew better than to try. Instead he asked who of the other geology professors were available at the moment.

"Hmmm, it's slow here, quarter break and all. But Dr. Morgan, I believe, is in. And maybe Dr. Biggs."

"Let me have Biggs," said Gun, liking the sound of the name.

He heard a click, followed by a double ring. Then a voice came on that very much fit: deep, confident, and slurring toward careless. Big. "Biggs here. And who's this?"

"Umm, Bill . . . Bill Carlyle," said Gun, a thrill moving through his gut. *Carlyle?* He saw Biggs in his mind—puffy in the face, large nervous hands, clothes with lots of room and wrinkle. A bottle of something standing on a pile of books. Black Tower. "I'm with the personnel department of New Mexico State University, Santa Fe," Gun said.

"You don't say." Biggs snorted, his head turned from the phone, it sounded like.

"I was wondering if you'd feel free to answer a question or two about a colleague of yours."

"That depends on the whos, the what fors, and the whys, Mr. Carlyle. Start with the whos, if you don't mind."

"Dr. Rolph."

"Izzy?" said Biggs, and laughed once. "What the hell for?"

"Dr. Rolph has applied for a position here at NMSU." *Ooh.*

"You're puttin' me on."

"You're surprised?"

"Well, yeah," said Biggs. "But why're you calling me? I'm not his boss. I'm not even department chair."

"I'm calling you in particular for a couple reasons,"

said Gun. "First, because he indicated that he'd rather keep his, umm, intentions to himself at this point. He'd rather that his supervisor and colleagues not be aware that he's looking around."

"I'm his colleague," said Biggs.

"Yes, which brings me to the second reason. You see, when we ask a candidate for supporting materials, we suggest they provide us with the name of the professional colleague whom they most admire." Gun paused. "You're the individual, Dr. Biggs, whose name Dr. Rolph provided us with." Gun delivered the line with as much gravity as he dared, counting on the man's vanity to override his skepticism.

Biggs didn't respond for a few seconds. Then he laughed and said, "Just goes to show, doesn't it? You can never really figure people. Of course, I'm a geologist, not a goddamn shrink, right?" He snorted. "I still don't get it, though, Izzy leaving here."

"I didn't say he was leaving. We haven't offered him a job yet. We may not. Why does it surprise you that he's considering a move?"

"Well, I don't know. Seems to me he's got it made around here. Sabbaticals, research leaves whenever he wants them. Just got himself tenured, too, for that matter. Must be quite the job you got out there. Maybe you want to hire me instead."

Gun couldn't resist and told him they were accepting applications for another two weeks, which earned another snort and laugh from Biggs. They spoke for a few minutes about Izzy, Gun asking the kinds of questions he imagined people asked in situations like this. How did Izzy get along with his students? Was he respected by his peers? What was his commitment to the discipline?

It was apparent from the answers that Biggs didn't know Izzy Rolph very well at all, and Gun brought the conversation to a close as soon as he could.

"One more thing," Gun said. "A personal request. And I have to say I'm embarrassed to ask."

"Sure." Biggs had warmed up now. The more general the questions had become, the more he'd seemed to enjoy the conversation. "Anything."

"I'm calling you from LaGuardia," Gun said. "In fact, I'm on my way to visit Dr. Rolph right now. I happened to be coming here for a conference, so we lined up a time to meet. Save him a trip out, after all, and the university some bucks."

"What conference?" asked Biggs.

"National Association of College Personnel."

"Ah, I forgot. I was thinking you're geology."

"Anyway, I get all the way out here and guess what I left behind in Santa Fe? Izzy's address and phone number, like an idiot. So I'm wondering—you wouldn't have it, would you?"

"Ah, let's see. I got a list here somewhere with the whole frickin' department on it. Gimme a second." Gun heard Biggs shuffling papers and slamming drawers. The phone took a hit, then Biggs was back on the line. "Yeah, I got it here, but hey, I thought Rolph was out of town."

"I believe he's just stopping home for a couple days," Gun said. "Then he's off again. Gosh, I'm glad you found it. I tried information, but he's unlisted. You're saving me a lot of trouble."

"Here it is." Biggs read the address and phone number and Gun took them down. "You know, I'm just thinking here, maybe I really should have a look at that job you got open out there. You wanna send me a position description?"

"I'd be more than happy to," Gun said.

Biggs gave him one more address now, his own. Gun thanked him again.

"You tell Izzy good luck," said Biggs. "But don't mention anything about, you know, me—that I'm interested, too."

"You have my word, I won't say a thing," Gun said, realizing how good it felt, telling the truth.

25

He tried Izzy's number, without success. Of course there was no way of knowing yet if the guy had cut and run or if he hadn't. He might be out for breakfast in Stony or having a chat with Crosley Schell, for all Gun knew. If he *had* taken off, chances were good he was still buckled in at thirty thousand feet. And if he'd gotten home already, he wouldn't be real keen on answering the phone.

A soft rumble disturbed the quiet—the sound of a vehicle turning off the blacktop onto Gun's long dirt-and-gravel drive. Gun rubbed out the butt of his cigarette and went to the cupboard for a clean coffee cup. Out the window he saw Sheriff Durkins' Blazer coming slowly through the curving, elegant shadows cast by the old birch trees lining the drive.

The red was mostly gone from the sheriff's eyes this morning. In fact they looked unhappily sober. He'd managed to find his razor, and his pants were clean though not pressed. His glasses were high on his nose. He was moving stiffly, with great deliberateness. Gun sat the man down and, remembering his preference, added milk and sugar to his coffee. Durkins put his hands around the warm cup but left it on the table.

His mouth was drawn tightly across his teeth and when his tongue darted back and forth, moistening his lips, Gun made himself ready for news.

"Nobody told you," said Durkins.

Gun shook his head. "Izzy Rolph?"

"Babe Chandler."

No. Gun prepared himself. Tightening the muscles across his gut, clenching his molars together, taking hold of Durkins with his eyes. He exhaled.

"You can breathe, Pedersen. He's very much alive. On the loose, in fact."

Gun refilled his lungs, felt oxygen—and hope—spreading through him. "Thanks," he said.

"Kid's like a pig in mud. There's no hanging on to him."

"What, he snuck out of the county jail? That's never happened."

"No, no. Not like that. Hey, I'd be out my job. Reading the classifieds." Durkins smiled, apparently pleased the situation could be worse than it was. He took an appreciative swallow of coffee and nodded his thanks. "You know how it's been since Pim gave him to us, right? Not a word. The kid can't find his tongue."

"Babe's never said much, and I've lived next to him most of his life. He's not a typical kid, sheriff."

"Okay, but he seems to know a lot about what's going on. Or at least he won't deny that he does. Anyway, if Dick was home, we'd probably have to let Babe go. As it is, we gotta hang on to him. We thought it best to send him over to Red Willow—that juvey center in Bear Island."

"I know where it is."

"They're set up for kids the way we aren't. Counselors and shit. So this morning, early, we packed him into the wagon. I sent two guys, Whipper and Lapp. Know 'em?" Gun nodded and Durkins drank more coffee, closing his eyes as it went down. "Mmmm, first cup all day."

154

"So," Gun said.

"We didn't cuff him or anything. Just stuck him in the backseat, behind the, uh, dog screen." Durkins laughed. "They get about halfway there, to that stretch of road with peat bogs on the south and pine barrens on the north, and Babe starts in complaining. Says he's sick, and he's holding his stomach and bending over. Like he's gonna puke, see. And my boys stop the car and let him out. Both of them, mind you, Whipper and Lapp. Four hundred pounds between 'em. More. And they're being careful, knowing how shrewd this kid is. That's what they're saying now, at least." Durkins was shaking his head and rubbing his eyes beneath the glasses. "Whipper had the nightstick out, to be safe, right? Shit. Now he's got a cracked skull." The sheriff tried to wipe the smile off his face with his fingers but it didn't work. He had laugh tears in his eyes.

"The kid's bent down in the weeds like to blow his breakfast and my boys are standing there feeling bad when Babe comes to life. Rams his head up into Whipper's crotch and grabs the stick away and clubs him with it like they do those seals up on the North Pole. Cowboy Lapp goes for his gun, but gets himself brained before he can draw. Lapp's okay. Just a doorknob on his forehead. Concussion for Whipper, though. They tell me he's asking for his dad, who died years ago."

"And Babe?"

"Gone. Lapp and Whipper can't even say which way."

"He take the car?"

"Thank the Lord, no. Boy's on foot. Must be the way he likes it." Durkins took off his glasses and cleaned the lenses on a swatch of his flannel shirt. He squinted across the table at Gun. "All happened about an hour ago. I suppose you've figured out by now what I'm doing here."

"Have you got men out looking for Babe?"

"Of course." Frowning now, his glasses back on, nodding. Durkins was offended. "Yeah, of course. As many as I could pull in. Bunn's deputy from town, a couple of jail guards, and I called up the state boys, who're bringing a dog."

"They won't find him," Gun said. "That country's impossible. No trails, to speak of. Rocks and moss, all up and down—bad for the feet. And you know Babe and the woods."

Durkins didn't argue. Gun stood and went for the coffeepot.

"Like I said before, Gun, I guess you know the reason I'm sitting in your lovely kitchen here when I should be out beating the woods with the rest of 'em."

"It *is* lovely, isn't it?" Glancing around. *Make him ask.* He turned to the windows facing the lake, then back to Jason Durkins, who looked so sheepish Gun softened and gave him what he wanted. "You want me to go and visit with Dick Chandler, ask him where he thinks his kid's heading. And you don't want to go ask Dick yourself because you know the man would have his nurses toss you out of the room."

"Couldn't have said it better myself," said Durkins. He drained his second cup in a hurry and got to his feet. His fingers played the back of the chair he'd been sitting on. His eyes stayed down. "Gun, I look bad right now. Awful. No breakthroughs on Julius Marks. Then it's May. And now Crosley and the frickin' kid. Help me out, huh? I don't wanna bust my balls for nothing."

"All right." Gun stood. "I'll go see Dick, and then you and I'll talk. But you've got to do me a favor, too." He walked past Durkins on his way to the coatrack by the door, where he took down his red parka.

"Anything you want, Pedersen."

"Call up the airport Hertz—Twin Cities International. Ask them if they've gotten this vehicle back yet." He thumbed through his wallet and removed an Amoco charge receipt he'd used to scrawl a note on. It

read, TOYOTA FOUR RUNNER. BLUE. EFX 491. He handed
the note to Durkins, whose eyes narrowed with questions.

Gun said, "Don't ask me now. You're in a hurry,
remember," and he opened the door for Durkins to
leave.

He followed the Blazer until it turned off in the
direction of the county jail, then he continued on to
the one-story brick hospital, serene beneath a high
canopy of well-trimmed white pines at the edge of
town. Yesterday—Gun had learned from Carol—
Dick had been shipped back here from the Cities at
his own insistence, and now Gun found his neighbor
awake and agitated and leaning out of bed toward a
radio which was going at high volume. It was tuned to
the local station, Gun could tell by the DJ's adolescent
yapping.

Dick's right arm was bound in a sling and his chest
was bandaged white. His face had been neatly reas-
sembled, long purple-black seams running everywhere: from above his right eye straight down one
cheek to the jawbone, from his left ear to his nose,
from his nose to his chin by way of the lips.

"They were wrong about Humpty Dumpty," Gun
said.

"Humpty Dumpty's a pantywaist." Dick's face
started to smile, then caught itself. He swore. "Ooo,
all the stretch's gone out of it." He blinked hard a few
times. "You hear about Babe?"

Gun nodded. "Sound like the proud father." He
reached down and lowered the volume on the radio.

"You didn't need to come see me, Gun. Already
told you where he's gonna go."

"I thought you might have a message for him." As
Gun moved to the window ledge beside the bed, his
peripheral vision caught the blue Chevy Blazer turning into the hospital parking lot. He straightened
himself and crossed his arms over his chest, trying to

block Dick's view through the window. "Or some light to shed on what's happening," he added.

"Hell, you probably know more than me."

"They brought your boy up here to talk to you, didn't they?"

"Yeah, they brought him. We had a few minutes. Didn't learn much, though." Dick's finger came up and touched the stitches that cut through the center of both lips. He shook his head. "I asked if he's got a clear conscience, is what I asked him. He said yes. Other than that, he wasn't talking. I'm telling you, though, the way he was? I've never seen him like that before. He's sitting there on the ledge, like you are now, and he's crying. Not for himself. I can tell what he's thinking. He's crying because of the way I look. My face all hacked to pieces and these bandages. He hasn't cried since I had to explain to him about his mom.

"Gun, my Babe isn't the normal sort of boy. He doesn't put his thoughts to words like others do. But I'm telling you now, he's good inside. If he says he doesn't have anything to be ashamed of, then he doesn't. I took hold of him and pulled him right into me and pressed his face here, where that knife went in."

Dick laid a palm on his chest, beneath the heart. "He let go and cried for a couple minutes—not a sound, mind you, but a lot of water. Then he quit, bang, like that, and pulled away. I said to him, 'Babe, what's going on?' and he just stared at me. That look he gave me—I'm telling you, Gun, the way his eyes were. Blank almost, but scared too, like he's seeing a corpse. I wondered for a second if I was dead."

"We've got to find him."

"Before somebody else does," Dick said, and Gun thought of the man with the knife.

"Babe'd be safer locked up."

Dick smiled, barely wrinkling his eyes this time. "That's not how Babe feels. Not how Babe's ever felt.

If he's got to, he'll stay out there till whoever's making this hell gets caught or killed." He moved his head to one side and took a peek past Gun and out the window. "Don't put my boy in the sheriff's hands, Pedersen."

"We'll do what we have to do. You know that, Dick. All of us."

26

Shorty Heller's lodge was an hour and a half north and Gun was there by one in the afternoon. He'd driven past the sign several times before—a battered sign now, almost hidden even at this time of year by untrimmed growth, the paint so faded you could barely make out the familiar silhouette of the hitter wound up tight after his swing: SHORTY HELLER'S, THE BABE'S NORTH-COUNTRY RETREAT. Gun had never driven in until today.

The narrow, rocky, two-rut path climbed through two zags, crowded on both sides with aspens and Norway pines. Then a clearing. What caught his eye immediately wasn't the lodge itself, which was impressive enough—built of barrel-wide logs and standing three stories above Lake Superior. Instead Gun found himself staring at a massive barnlike structure to the south, a building which displaced half again as much sky as the lodge did. It was a good deal higher and longer with sides that bowed out a little like a ship's belly. In fact it looked a ship, except for the conventional barn roof with exaggerated overhangs on both ends and a rounded pitch. The walls of the building were unpainted boards weathered gray.

There were few windows, high on the walls and widely spaced.

Gun parked the Ford in front of the lodge and went through the door marked OFFICE. The room was small, tongue-and-groove pine finished in clear varnish. Gun walked to a counter with a silver bell and tapped it once. All around, he noticed, on every wall, were black-and-white photographs of George Herman Ruth, The Babe: swatting baseballs (in and out of uniform); stroking golf balls; standing with an arm around Lou Gehrig; beaming at a child in diapers; beaming at a little girl in overalls whose hand he was shaking; beaming at the camera; beaming with his big round face at a large fish he was holding at arm's length. Mounted on the wall above this last photograph was a preposterously outsize trout, probably the fish from the picture, its skin and eyes glazed and yellowed with age. Gun went up on his tiptoes to read the metal plaque: 15 POUNDS 10 OUNCES, BABE RUTH, JUNE 1, 1936.

"He caught the damn thing on a little bitty worm," said a tinny voice behind Gun's left shoulder.

Gun turned and said hello to the man who had spoken. "I guess you'd have to be Shorty." He wasn't particularly short though and didn't look as old as Gun had thought he might. He may have looked older if he hadn't been wearing a Yankees cap, Levi's, and a pair of red Converse tennis shoes. And if his posture weren't so good; he stood up straight as an All-Star player for the national anthem. Then the sun broke free from a cloud and entered the room, and Gun saw how the skin hung from the old man's skull like wrinkled parchment, how his smart blue eyes swam in murky fluid, and how his hands, suspended by their thumbs in the waist of his pants, looked hard put to pick up a fork. The large fingers curled and twisted among themselves like dried-out roots.

"You gonna stare at me or tell me what you come for?"

"My name is Gun Pedersen—"

"Yeah, yeah. I *know* your name and why you're here." Shorty's hands were beating the air in front of his face as if Gun had loosed a swarm of bugs on him. He shook his head. "Dick called me up."

"Then I don't need to explain myself."

"You wanna talk to Babe Chandler, and that's gonna be hard considering the fact he might not be here."

"Have you seen the boy?"

"I might've, and I might not've," said Shorty. "What do you *think* of that?" His blue eyes hummed there, under water.

Gun said, "I think you've been out of circulation so long you don't know how to act around people anymore. And I think maybe you don't know what kind of trouble Babe's in."

"Ah. Ha." Shorty had cocked his head, one ear toward Gun's voice, and now he smiled, not just with his mouth but with every line in his worn-out face. His hands went into the air again to beat the invisible swarm of bugs. "Out of circulation, yeah, you got me pegged. But don't try talking to me about Babe Chandler. I know Babe Chandler, and there ain't nothing I wouldn't do for that little boy, so don't try talking to me about him. I gave the boy his name, I did. You know that?"

"Nope," said Gun. He could tell he'd have to wait this one out for a while.

"Well, I did. Ask Dick about it. Oh, it ain't his real name, Babe isn't—not that anybody'd know it. But Dick and Babe's mom, they come up here a month or so after the boy's born. I took one look at the little fart and said, 'That's Babe all over again.' It's all that cheek, see. And that stick-out nose. Just like The Bambino. Skinny little legs, too, underneath of a belly meant for eating. Oh, you shoulda seen how that man could eat when we put it out for him. He caught this trout once off the dock on a grub worm. Weighed about nine, ten pounds, and I fileted it up clean as a whistle, no bones, and that night my wife fried it for him in beer batter. Ate that whole thing, he did. Took him 'bout an hour. That was in the fall, his first night here after the season ended. Cool night. October. Said it was the best food he'd had since spring training. Loved it up here, The Babe did. Loved it."

"I can see why," Gun said.

"You can, can you?" Shorty had moved to a high stool behind the counter. He was sitting there, his body and shoulders hunched so low and small that his head seemed to rest on the counter like a paperweight. "I'd say you're just going along with it. Humoring the old bastard. Waiting for him to die or talk himself out, whichever comes first."

"Some of that too," said Gun.

Quickly the old man came off his stool and around the front of the counter. Standing, his eyes came up to just above Gun's elbow, which he now grabbed hold of with a surprisingly strong set of crooked fingers. "Humor me a little more then, Pedersen, all right? Come on, let's find the barn."

Gun laughed. "Shouldn't be hard."

"That's what The Babe always said to me. 'Let's find the barn.' Thought that was real funny. And it was, the way he said it."

They walked outside together, Shorty with a steel grip on Gun's elbow. The temperature was about ten with frequent gusts that made it seem colder but the old man wore no coat or gloves. The snow cover was deeper up here, a foot or so in most places, and the path they followed looked as if it had been made with feet, not a snow shovel. Just a lot of feet tramping back and forth between the lodge and the big gray ship of a barn.

"Did you build the place?" Gun asked. He signaled with his head that he meant everything, the lodge and barn and the line of cabins down by the lake.

"Bought her already built in '29. Just after the

Crash. I was twenty-five. The guy that put her up lost his shirt, pants, and most of his health in the market. Sold out to stay alive. Sold her for a dream, I can tell you. He started building the place in '19, I believe it was, just after the war. Wasn't nobody up here, then."

"Why the barn?" Gun asked. The closer it grew, the more absurdly large it seemed, blotting out the afternoon light, looming way up there. As high at the peak as some of the Norway pines surrounding it, out of place, yet belonging somehow, too.

"Everybody asks me that, and I guess I can see why. But I get used to it. Sort of like the guy in South Dakota I read about with dinosaurs in his backyard. Everybody thinking, 'Holy cats, dinosaurs,' and to him they're bones."

At the door Shorty picked through a ring of keys with his curled fingers, selected one, and with a dexterity Gun didn't expect, snapped open the padlock. Shorty stepped back and let Gun enter first. All he saw were channels of light from the high windows two or three stories up, galaxies of dust circulating through. Then Shorty hit a switch and the place flashed awake, banks of outdoor lights glaring down from all four corners. Nearly as bright as daylight.

"They say he built her for Ruth to swing in, but it's not true. Fact is, Babe never come up here till I owned the place. Still makes for a damn good story, wouldn't you say? I did put in the lights, though, and we're talking thirty-some years before the indoor parks went up. Babe got a kick out of it." He led Gun toward the north end of the barn. The floor was a hardwood of some kind, wide planking, and their footsteps echoed off the walls and roof.

"I don't rightly know why she was built, though. I asked of course when I bought the place but never got an answer. Some say he wanted a riding stable but never got around to making trails for horses in the woods. Damn big barn for horses, I always thought, but who am I to say? Don't know crap about horses.

Hell, put the racetrack itself in here and then you really got something." Shorty stopped and took off his Yankees cap. He looked straight up. "You can see by the way she's put together there coulda been a hayloft —those joists running along up there?"

"Lots of wasted space," Gun said.

"Others claimed the guy was a fanatic—built her to save himself from the next flood and that's why the walls bow out like they do. The ark. Me, I gave up figurin'. Enjoy what you got, I always say. Don't ask too many questions, there's enough of *them* already. Okay—" Shorty pointed with his baseball cap to a faded white square painted on the floor about ten feet from the wall. They were standing together at the center of the building's north end. "See that? Home plate. That's where he'd stand. Right there. Legs stiff as boards like he did." Shorty smiled and shook his head. His loose old jowls wagged like a dog's. "Now right over there you'll find another mark, if you look. See? Pitching rubber. Sixty feet, six inches from home. I painted 'em in '31. Touched 'em up a few times after that, but not since he died. For all that, there ain't been a whole lot of folks even stepped in this place since he died."

"You pitched to Babe Ruth—in here," Gun said, knowing how impressed he must sound. But how could you be anything else?

Shorty's hands came up and went after the swarm again. "Listen to me now," he said, impatient. "I want you to walk through that door over there in the corner. See it? Storage. I want you to walk over there now. Go inside and reach around behind the door and see what you find."

Gun did as he was told. The sound of his boots against the floor planks roamed through the building, caroming off the distant walls and coming back to him louder than when they'd left. He turned the brass doorknob. The hinges squealed and the door gave into darkness. He stepped inside, carefully. He waited for his eyes to see, but there was no degree of light at all. He felt his heart speed up inside his chest and took a long, controlled breath to slow it back down. He let his hands explore the region behind the door. What he found was smooth and hard and cool against his fingers. It was the handle of a baseball bat.

"Good work," said Shorty. The old man was standing on the mark he'd called the pitching rubber. At his feet was a roasting pan full of baseballs. In his twisted hands, he was rubbing down a ball. "What you've got there is the instrument he used whenever the two of us came out here to hit. The only one he ever used. Never broke it. Always rubbed it down with a Coke bottle after we played. Or else a bone, like a hambone or a big old turkey leg. Claimed it kept the wood hard. The grain good and tight."

Shorty Heller's left hand disappeared beneath his right shoulder and came out wearing a small padded baseball glove that must have been hiding in the excess cloth of his baggy denim shirt. It was the kind of glove Gun hadn't seen since playing ball with his father as a kid. The leather was worn to a dark coffee tone and the webbing was nothing but a crisscrossing of lace, the size of a cigarette pack. "Are you ready?" Shorty asked. He stood on the rubber, his hands together in front of his chest. He'd pulled the visor of his Yankees cap down low above his eyes, throwing his creased face into shadow and cutting decades from his age.

Gun didn't voice the question in his mind. *You sure you can still get the ball up here?* He could do nothing but assume a stance beside the painted home plate, feeling silly but undeniably thrilled. Waiting for an old man to toss an old ball which Gun would hit with an old bat into the stale air of an old barn where the greatest ballplayer in history had done the same thing more than half a century before, against the same old arm. Not so very old then. All on the shores of Lake

Superior. It was inconceivable, but happening just the same. *Here I am, Babe. Hope you can see me.*

Watching Shorty go through his windup was like watching a child's toy low on batteries. Mechanical, creaky, each movement a process of increments. The old man lifting his left foot, rotating his body to the right, and bringing back his arm—everything by the book, but so, so slow. And there were the age-ruined fingers, and there was the ball wedged impossibly inside them, and there was the hand coming down and forward, the fingers opening by some miracle, releasing the ball. And finally, here came the ball itself, free and floating, bigger and slower than any knuckle ball Gun had ever seen. Hypnotized by this new brand of time, he found himself swinging in slow motion, too. It was a waist-high pitch across the middle of the plate and Gun launched a lazy fly toward center. Above where second base would have been, the ball struck a joist and dropped to the floor.

"You're gone," said Shorty. He tipped his cap back and the lines of his face turned upward in a thousand smiles. His eyes blinked. They were wetter than before, the blue irises paler. "Babe usually took about ten swings, that's all. About ten swings a day. Tell you where he aimed for." Shorty came off the rubber and took a few steps toward Gun, waving him forward.

"Kinda hard to see, what with those lights burning away. But see what they're attached to up there?" He pointed toward the bank of lights up in the southeast corner of the barn, then to the lights in the southwest corner, left-center and right-center in a park. The lights were fastened to what looked like overgrown birdhouses, square wooden boxes fixed to the upper corners of the barn.

"That's so when a light burned out I didn't have to kill myself replacing it. Look hard enough, you can see the ladders going up the wall, every corner. I can climb the ladder into the box, reach out through the

windows I cut and replace the bulbs. Nothing to it."
Shorty seemed pleased with himself. "Now, Babe, he
got to figurin', after he'd been hitting in here for a
while, he could tell by the distances and the feel of the
ball on his bat when he hit it. He figured if you
smacked a ball up against one of them boxes, *without*
hitting the roof first—see, if you hit the roof, you
would've undercut the pitch too much and skyed
out—but if you hit one of them boxes, in Yankee
Stadium that'd be a home run. You hit it between the
boxes, to center, then you couldn't be sure, he said. A
dinger to center's gotta travel so far to get out, you just
can't calculate it inside of here. That's what he always
said. Strange conditions. Odd light and dead air.
Makes for distances that don't seem right somehow.
But those light boxes, they're what he aimed for. And
he hit that one in right-center a lot. Almost every day,
I'd say. Like throwing darts for him."

"Give me a couple more swings," Gun said.

"Many as you want," said Shorty. He'd been working his hands together as he spoke, rubbing and
pulling the fingers straight, blowing on them. He
maneuvered his left hand back into the little glove and
walked toward the rubber. Gun took up his stance at
home plate.

Shorty had no trouble with the strike zone, and Gun
adjusted his timing to make use of his wrists. He
banged three pitches against the far wall, line drives
that hit about halfway up. Doubles or outs, depending
on the center fielder's range. The next pitch he got
under a bit and the ball hit the inside of the roof not
more than six feet above the left-field light box.

"Close there, hey, Babe?" Shorty called in his age-
flattened voice. "Warning-track catch." He laughed.
"I'm one of those pitchers that knows how to use the
park. Throw strikes and let the boys go to work.
Defense and pitching, right? The good teams. A Ruth
comes along once every hundred years or so."

One more time Shorty Heller went into his windup.

Slow-motion pump, turn, lean back and let go. *Wait, wait, wait. Now.* Like with all the best swings, Gun barely felt the ball on the bat but knew his wrists had turned at the right instant. The baseball rose in a true line toward the left-field light box, avoiding the joists that ran perpendicular to it, and snuffed out a bulb as neatly as you can pinch out a candle on a birthday cake. Just a pop of glass and the ball arcing backward toward the plank floor and a gentle rain of glass dust falling through a heavy shaft of light.

Shorty planted his hands on his hips and nodded his pleasure at Gun. Then he turned full around and called up toward the box: "Babe, you come on down here now."

27

For the space of a few breaths, during which Gun half-expected Ruth himself, nothing moved except for the baseball rolling on the planks, its seams causing it to hop a little and follow a wandering course as it slowed. It came to a stop and the barn was silent. High up in the corner, beneath the wooden light box, a pair of feet and legs appeared. The feet, sticking down from the inside of the box, caught hold of the ladder attached to the barn wall. Then the whole body was visible, coming down the rungs as quickly as most people descend a stairway. By the nimble quality of his movements, by his compactness of size, by the golden tone of his buckskin jacket, Gun recognized Babe Chandler.

Ten feet off the floor the boy turned himself around on the ladder and jumped. He hit the planking and sprang up gracefully into a walk. He kept his eyes on the old man and the calmness in his face made him seem no more than his age for the first time Gun could remember. A boy like other boys.

"Haven't had a ball hit up there in fifty years," said Shorty, reaching for Babe's shoulder. He pulled the boy close. "Never thought it'd happen again. You coulda caught that one, couldn't you, Babe?"

Babe grinned. His shoulders said maybe.

"Then why didn't ya?"

"Don't know."

Shorty stepped back from the boy but kept a grip on one of his shoulders. He held Babe at arm's length and looked at him with runny eyes. "I want to tell you something now, son, and you'll listen to me, won't you?" Babe nodded and didn't look away. Shorty went on, his voice quiet. "This guy here's not just your neighbor and your friend. He's also the one that can help you right now." Shorty's eyes and head moved toward Gun, then away. "I want you to understand that. I want you to forget how scared you are and I want you to listen to what he's got to say to you. Then I want you to answer his questions. You're a smart boy. You know that it's wisdom to keep your mouth shut most of the time. And knowing that makes you smarter than about ninety-nine percent of the world out there. I admire that, Babe. But this time I want you to talk. I want you to tell Mr. Pedersen what you know about Julius and all the rest. I want you to do it for your sake, son. And for the sake of everybody else that might get hurt if you don't. Do you understand me, Babe? Can you do that?"

The boy looked over at Gun and nodded. His black hair and dark eyes were brilliant beneath the playing lights. His turned-up nose and the roundness of his face were convincing; Babe had been rightly named.

"I'm gonna leave you two alone, then," said Shorty. "When you're done, come on in. I still got some of that moose left from last year. Saved a few tenderloins." He looked at Gun and rubbed water from his eyes with a big twisted finger. "Damn thing wandered into my yard and wouldn't leave. Had to shoot him."

Shorty wandered about the barn for a few minutes gathering baseballs from the floor, then he carried the long bat back to the storage room where Gun had found it. When he left the barn he shut off the playing lights.

The sun had dropped to an angle so that its rays entered the barn's high windows and laid clean bright rectangles on the plank floor. In one of these, next to the wall, sat half a dozen kitchen chairs all in a line. Gun nodded toward them. "First-base dugout," he said to Babe, and the two of them walked over and sat down.

"I guess if we start from the beginning," Gun said, "that'd work best. A lot's happened, and I don't know what you know and what you don't. Your dad thinks you're innocent. That you're running because you're scared. Is he right?"

Babe was sitting on his hands, staring at his lap and shaking his head back and forth—not in answer to Gun's question, it seemed, but in response to the condition of his world. "Both," he said. "Dad's right, and he's not right."

"Did you kill Julius?" Gun asked, trying to speak gently, matter-of-factly.

"No. But it feels like I did." The boy shut his eyes and now his body was moving too, just slightly, in time with his shaking head. "I didn't kill him."

"You were there?" Gun asked.

Babe nodded, then his head returned to its back-and-forth motion.

"Who else?"

"May. Julius. Me."

"May killed him?"

"May," said Babe, and clamped his eyelids even tighter. "Not that she meant to. But it happened. I didn't stop her. Didn't know how."

"They were fighting about what?" Gun asked. He touched the boy's elbow. "Babe. Just talk. Open your eyes and talk. It's all right."

Nodding again, his dark brow pulling upward, as if to lift his eyelids. But his eyes stayed closed.

"Open your eyes, Babe, and you won't have to look at it anymore. Be easier that way. Then you can talk."

Finally they came open, snapped into circles. Clear and scared. Determined. The boy sucked a lungful of air and blew it out in a long sigh. He said, "First it's Crosley's fault, and then May's, and then Julius's and mine. Something like that. I don't really know what order it goes in."

"Forget about whose fault it was and tell me what happened that night. Why were you out on the lake, the three of you? Where'd you been?"

"Crosley's place. Coming back from there. May'd been out there for a few days and Julius wanted to go get her. He wanted me to go with him, so I did. We were bringing her back to my cabin for the night, just to get her away from him."

"From Crosley, you mean."

"Yeah," said Babe, his frown saying, *Of course.*

"Why?"

"Julius got May talking one night when she was drunk. She told him everything. This was a couple days before it happened."

"'Told him everything?'"

"About Crosley. And the gold." Babe smiled, his round face getting rounder. His lips stretched thin, showing a set of very straight white teeth. "There *is* gold. Crosley doesn't want anybody to know it, but there's gold. He told May. He told her lots of things. He told her he's known for a couple years now and hasn't told anybody. He's gonna wait for the right time. Until he can make it pay off good. He doesn't care about the Ojibwa. He doesn't care about the digging. He doesn't give a shit about Spirit Waters or Pim or anything but how rich he's gonna be. White folks call him Red-Ass kisser. And Ojibwa too, some of them call him that. But he's a big lie. Kisses our ass 'cause he's smart and gold-happy. May said so. She told Julius—nobody else. Julius and May, they grew up together and she couldn't hide it from him. Not forever. He found out."

"Why did Julius decide to go get her that night?" Gun asked. "If she told him about the gold earlier, why did he wait?"

"Julius said it was May's truth to tell. Not his. He couldn't do it for her. But then, in town that day, he saw her at the drugstore and she had on sunglasses and a busted lip. She was buying makeup for the bruises on her face. He told her she was a fool, covering for a liar and a bastard besides and he told her she needed to get away before she got hurt. She needed to tell people what she knew; it was time to give up the truth. But May wouldn't talk to him. She walked away like he wasn't even there. That night Julius had some beers and said he'd waited long enough, he was going after her."

"I take it Crosley wasn't home when you got out there."

Babe shook his head and got up from his chair. He said, "Down by the lake's nice this time of day," and started toward the door. Gun followed him out of the barn and through the beaten path in the snow that led first to the lodge then cut down the steep bank to the shoreline. To the south, the lake stretched away beyond sight. To the west, the red sun rode the tops of the trees and started to eat its way down, thinning and burning as it went. Babe watched.

"You love it here," Gun said.

The boy nodded. He turned away and walked a few steps to a large rock and sat on it.

"You and Julius went out to Schell's," Gun said. "What time?"

"Midnight, maybe. Crosley wasn't home, and May didn't want to come with us, but Julius took hold of her and brought her anyway. She kicked him hard a couple times, got him good, and he slapped her face. He said, 'I bet you like that when it comes from the white man,' and that shut her up good. She rode in the backseat with Julius, and I was driving. Julius gave her a couple of beers and everything seemed okay. We got about to your place and I thought we better park down by the access instead of driving into my driveway and maybe waking up Dad. So we parked. And May started acting up again. She started yelling, she was gonna handle it her way, and slugging Julius, and he hit her again and she went down onto the floor of the backseat. She got up with a tire wrench in her hand and swung it but Julius jumped free and laughed at her. He said 'Come on after me, bitch. Come and get me, knock my head in,' and he started running backward down to the lake. She went after him with that wrench, running and slipping on the rocks and I sort of followed after. You know, not knowing what's going on or what to do, and then they're out on the ice and I see her swinging that thing at him and I see Julius breaking through the crust and splashing around, and all of a sudden he's not moving. It's just the top of him sticking out of the lake. And May's standing there looking down at him. I ran out there and he's got a hole in his head, right here. And May's not crying or anything. She's sober as hell. Her eyes like those marbles with colored spirit waves inside, moving a little, and spooky, and she told me it was an accident, but we'd both get the blame if anyone found out. That it was my fault as much as hers because I helped Julius kidnap her."

"And you figured she was right," Gun said.

Babe's face was lit up to a bright red, thanks to the sun, and his breathing was fast from the telling. He wiped his eyes with the heels of his hands. He nodded. "She told me I better stay quiet, then she left in Julius's car. That's the last I saw her."

"What she told you wasn't true," Gun said. "It wasn't your fault. You need to come out and tell people what happened. I think they'll believe you."

"Doesn't matter anymore if they do or don't." Babe looked into Gun's eyes, sure of himself.

"What do you mean?"

"I told Pim everything. About Julius and May, and about Schell. At first he didn't believe me, or I don't think he did. He kept asking the same questions, and had Sparrow ask me too. He had Charles Two Crow put up the Shaking Tent for a conjuring, but Charles couldn't get an answer from the turtle. Then Dad almost got killed, and Crosley started to make more sense. I heard Pim and Sparrow talking. They figured whoever it was that got Dad was waiting for May. And they said how wasn't it strange, Dick getting it in May's trailer. Who'd want her dead? What did she ever have on anybody? Unless my story was true. They said what if Crosley had her marked? They decided they better talk to Crosley and they went to get him."

"And they let you go," said Gun.

Babe nodded, smiling with half his face, shrewd. "Pim said, 'Let the sheriff have him. If somebody wanted May, they might want Babe too, and we don't need that. We don't want Babe dead. And we sure as shit don't want Babe dead on *our* hands.' That's Pim. Joking. But serious too. So they let me go. And May gets it."

"They have any idea who it was?" Gun asked. He brought to mind the man with the knife.

"Don't know. I guess that's what they're asking Crosley."

"Listen, Babe," Gun said, "I've seen him, a couple of times. I don't know who he is, but Pim's right. Whoever he is, he wants you." Gun told about getting cut down from the snare and about the scuffle outside May's trailer.

Babe didn't seem surprised, more like resigned. He tipped his shoulders like a kid shrugging off a Little League loss and shook his head. "That's what I meant when I said it doesn't matter whether they believe me or not. I know somebody out there's looking. For me. I can feel it. I can feel it the same as I can when I'm close to a bear. Or a deer. Like a tingling. There's something telling me, *Be careful and take your time. Listen and watch.* And when I feel that, I don't want nobody else around and I don't want to be in a *boy's* camp. Too much gets in the way. I want to be out where I can hear things, keep track of what's going on. You don't understand. Out here I'm safer. I am." He looked around at the darkening sky and trees and lifted his nose, sniffed the light wind. "And I'm gonna stay." His eyes were blazing, and Gun tried to decide if it was smart, trusting the boy's instincts the way he couldn't help doing. Or whether he should just pack him off back to Durkins, who could put him in a cell for a few days.

"Tell me one more thing," he said to Babe. "Do you know where Pim's got Crosley?"

The boy was quiet for a few moments. Behind his dark eyes there seemed to be calculating going on. "Yes," he said. "And I'll tell you—if *you* tell *me* something."

"What's that?"

"That you won't try to make me leave here."

It wasn't the rational thing, but sometimes in trying to do what seemed right, you had to go up against reason. Praying he wouldn't have regrets, Gun looked at Babe and said, "I won't try to make you leave."

28

It was six o'clock, full darkness and just a sliver of moon, when Gun left the lodge. Shorty's moose tenderloin had been tender indeed. Tenderloins. Gun had eaten three. Plus onions and carrots and boiled tomatoes. Northern vegetables.

Spirit Waters was a hundred and twenty miles west, and Gun drove as fast as the old F-150 could safely carry him over the hilly, winding highway. Babe's directions were precise and easy to follow. North past the Spirit Waters camp, turn right on the gravel road, and go on for a hundred yards to the burned-out tavern. Park behind it. Climb the little hill and there it'll be. A natural cliff going straight up a hundred feet.

He hadn't been aware that such formations could be found in this part of the state. The solid wall of vertical earth made Gun think of fault lines and earthquakes, continental drift, and the way geologic plates pressed against each other until one had to surrender, go up or down.

Along the top of the cliff was a sentry line of oak trees that didn't seem to belong up there. At the base of the cliff ran a snarl of leafless winter lilacs. Gun walked along in front of the bushes until he saw a place where the hedge came apart and showed rock behind. He had to crouch low to get through, and at first he couldn't find it. Then the smell came and pulled him to the right and he squeezed between stiff lilac branches and rock until the rock disappeared. The entrance was around behind the cold, smooth slab, and once inside Gun moved toward the source of light. There was the smell of wood burning, the smell of tobacco. And a low even push of heat coming from within.

The tunnel was high enough to stand up in, though barely, and wide enough so Gun could touch both sides with his fingertips if he stretched hard. Thirty yards in, a room opened to the right.

It was large, at least twenty feet high and probably three times that wide, the floor an approximate square. Off to one side was a fire, the smoke from which rose in a stream and escaped, though Gun couldn't tell how. Three men stood around the fire, their faces toward Gun and lit up by the flames: Pim, Sparrow, and another, older man with gray hair in two braids that hung down in front of both shoulders. Gun hadn't seen him before. The men were sharing a cigar—not long pipes—and laughing among themselves. On the other side of the room was a very small tent, a miniature tepee with wooden poles sticking up at the center.

Gun stepped into the room and walked toward the men. Pim looked over first, his face registering surprise then going flat. The round lenses of his glasses flashed in the firelight. The other men looked up, stopped laughing. They watched Gun come on.

Pim said, "You got Babe to talk." He smiled. His head tipped toward one of his shoulders, comfortable. "Sparrow, you know Gun Pedersen."

The tall man was still, his expressive mouth powerfully uninterested. Gun nodded at him, wondering what he'd done with his rifle.

"And this," said Pim, looking at the old one with

braids, "is Charles Two Crow. Charles—Gun Pedersen."

Gun said, "Babe Chandler mentioned you."

Charles Two Crow took a pull on the cigar and the end of it lit up orange. "A pleasure to meet you, Gun Pedersen," said the old man, smoke trailing from his mouth. "Heard of you plenty."

"Picked an interesting time to come, didn't he?" said Pim to the other two. "What do you say we do?" He looked at Two Crow, then at Sparrow.

"Ask him what he wants." This from Sparrow. His lips hardly moved as he spoke.

"Oh, I think we can guess what he wants," Pim said. "He wants to see the famous Crosley Schell, bring him back out to the world, learn what Crosley can teach him about these dismal killings going on, make this land a safer place to live."

Gun said, "Pim, I'm too tired for bullshit."

"What makes you think he'll talk to you if he hasn't to us? What's the pressure you can bring that we can't?"

"Let's get him out of here," said Sparrow. He looked disgusted, almost ready to be sick. Pim ignored him. The old man handed Sparrow the cigar, which Sparrow scrutinized for a few moments before putting it to his lips and taking a few puffs. Then he withdrew into himself, life evaporating from his eyes.

Like a professor about to say something profound, Pim scowled. He rubbed the palms of his hands together beneath his chin. "Our interests in this matter are different, yours and ours," he said carefully. "Very different. You should have left us alone to play our hand. I would've thought you had that much respect." He took the cigar from Sparrow, who sat down next to the fire. Pim stayed on his feet. He drew on the cigar.

"My concern is for Babe Chandler," Gun said, "and whoever else seems likely to follow Julius and May out the window. Your concern, as I see it, is the gold—whether there is any or not, and if there is, who knows about it and what they're going to do. And I'd bet our concerns intersect about as neat as can be. Wouldn't you agree?"

"I'm not sure. But you do touch on the sensitive point," said Pim, pointing the cigar at Gun. "What matters to us isn't so much whether there *is* any gold, but what's done about it if there is. Now Crosley, he could clear things up for us, and wouldn't that be nice? Problem is, we can't trust ourselves to trust what he says anymore. Too much has happened. Way too much." Pim was quiet for a few moments. His head bobbed slightly, as if he were trying to prompt some judgment to reveal itself. "So," he said, "in the absence of human witnesses, we have no choice but to fall back on . . . other methods." Pim turned suddenly to Sparrow and spoke sharply.

"Go get Schell. It's time for the tent."

29

Sparrow got up from the fire and left by way of the tunnel through which Gun had entered the cave. Pim nodded toward Charles Two Crow and said to Gun, "He's had the power since he was sixteen," speaking without inflection, his face bland, eyes clear and confident.

Gun shook his head. "Maybe your friend Crosley would understand. I don't."

Pim laughed. "Charles is a *tcisaki,* a conjurer. He's our messenger from the spirit world. He can do the Shaking Tent. Charles, tell him."

The old man shrugged and his gray filmy eyes squinted toward the small tepee across the room. "Tell him what?" he asked.

"What happened to you that first time, tell him." Pim seemed excited now. He nodded fast and pushed his glasses higher on his nose.

"He won't understand," said Two Crow.

"Give him a chance," Pim said. "He's here, after all—he's going to see what goes on."

Two Crow had gotten the cigar back from Pim, and he puffed on it now, taking his time, his head and shoulders thrown back, eyes closed. When he opened them and looked at Gun, his eyes were serene. He said, "I was out trapping one day and Manitou came to me as a badger on two legs. He told me, 'Take off your clothes and turn around.' I did. Then he blew into me from behind, into my rectum. And the power came in. It was so strong, and there was so much of it, that I couldn't hold it all, and it flowed out from my mouth and my ears. My nose. And the badger told me the hidden truths would no longer be hidden. All he said. He wasn't lying, either. Sixty years, and I can tell you he wasn't lying." Two Crow shrugged again, lifting one of his eyebrows, as if to dare Gun to challenge this story.

"Explain to me about the tent shaking," Gun said. He felt a strong desire to be any place but right here.

"The Shaking Tent rite," said Pim. "It's how an Ojibwa shaman conjures. How he gets answers for his people from the Manitou. Watch, you'll see." His eyes glistened behind the lenses of his glasses, then he looked toward the entrance of the cave.

Sparrow and Schell were back. But now Sparrow held a gun, a long-barreled revolver with the trademark finish that looked like car chrome, the same revolver Gun had found in the snow, chasing Babe. Schell's Colt Python. It rode easy in Sparrow's right hand, seeming to belong there, and it was aimed lazily at Crosley himself, whose face was pale. He had on the ever-present Crosley smile, though, and his blue eyes were sleepy as usual. He walked right up to Gun and stuck out his hand.

"Gun, nice to see you," as if he were standing in the living room of his own round house. No sarcasm, either.

"People in town are wondering if maybe the earth swallowed you up. Guess it did," Gun said.

Crosley's smile wattage doubled. He laughed generously. "They'll see me soon enough," he said, then dimmed the glow and gestured toward Pim and Two

Crow. "We've been having some good sessions down here. Making progress."

Sessions? "I'm not sure what you mean," said Gun.

"There've been misunderstandings. Not so much between us as, well, in spite of us. Talk, you know. Fears. But I think the time we've had has been beneficial. *I've* learned a lot, anyway."

Pim and Two Crow looked at Schell, their heads cocked sideways like dogs hearing music. Pim cleared his throat and spit into the fire.

"Yes, Pim?" Crosley, polite.

"Let's do it now."

"Wonderful. Yes. I've been looking forward to it." He turned quickly toward the small tent, bumping the Colt in Sparrow's hand.

Two Crow, all the time in the world in his eyes, pointed at Crosley and said, "You'll sit here by the fire and wait. You, too," he said to Gun. Then he and Pim walked together over to the tent. Sparrow sat down a little way off from the fire and began to polish the stainless-steel Colt using a corner of his jacket.

With great care and respect, Pim removed Two Crow's western-style flannel shirt and his white thermal underwear top. He folded them and laid them aside. He undid the button on the old man's green work pants, unzipped them, and brought them down. These, too, he put aside. Two Crow stood there in his briefs, looking old, skinny, and unshamanlike.

"Now he'll crawl inside and consult the messenger turtle," Crosley whispered, leaning toward Gun. "But I think he's got to be tied up first."

"Ah," said Gun.

Sure enough, Pim began to secure Two Crow's wrists with a piece of yellow nylon rope. He seemed confused at first about what kind of knot to use, and after several attempts settled on a series of square knots, which apparently did the job. Two Crow endured it all without speaking. He made no response at all. His eyes were focused on a point in the distance and his head and upper body swayed back and forth in slow rhythm. Pim stepped away from him.

Two Crow knelt to the ground, paused, and lowered himself with his bound hands until he lay flat on the earth. Gun imagined the cold he must feel and shivered. He watched as Two Crow—wiggling forward in a fluid motion that appeared to require little effort—entered the tent on his belly through its small opening.

"Now watch," whispered Schell.

Nothing happened. No sound came from the tent. Nothing moved. Pim sat outside the tent's entrance, six feet from it, his arms resting on his legs, which he'd crossed and pulled up beneath himself. Sparrow no longer polished the Colt but sat still and watched, his mouth less scornful now. Next to Gun, Crosley nodded, as though everything now happening followed a script of his own. Then a tremor passed through the tent's hide, top to bottom. Another. From inside came the single long beat of a rattle, a metallic, trilling *shunk-k-k-k-k.*

"They hang up rattles inside," said Crosley into Gun's ear. "Tin cans with pieces of bone or something. For the, uh, spirits to shake and make noise with when they come." He laughed quietly. "Oh, wow. Great stuff."

The tent began to move. Not much at first, just a series of rapid shakes, the rattle sounding louder with each one, and then it was like a storm erupted, a twisting wind, the tepee's buckskin sides swelling out, flapping, sucking in, shivering up and down, the poles trembling where they were lashed together at the top, and from inside, a mad syncopated beating of the rattles.

"Son-of-a-bitch, how's he do that?" said Crosley— but his last words were stranded in silence. The tepee was still and quiet, the wind gone so fast Gun wondered if he'd imagined it.

Now Pim began to talk. He hadn't moved from his

place in front of the tent, and his voice came like a song without melody, the words blending together, all spoken in the same pitch, no pauses in delivery.

"Call on Mikkinnuk now and tell him we need his aid, we respect his work and we ask that he speak for us to a discerning spirit. We are a humble people and request a simple answer to a single question. Ask our turtle friend Mikkinnuk to find out if the man Crosley Schell is speaking the truth to us when he says he knows of no gold in the earth. Ask him to go and speak to Manitou and bring an answer back to us."

After a minute or two of silence, Two Crow's voice started up inside the tent and Gun heard Crosley, to his left, let out a breath and swear. Two Crow began to sing in a high, nasal tone that made Gun recall a powwow he'd seen at the reservation years ago, with drummers who'd demonstrated traditional Ojibwa chants. Two Crow sang for some time, maybe five minutes, then he stopped abruptly and spoke in his normal voice.

"Mikkinnuk says the white man is not telling us the truth. He is lying. There is gold. This is what Mikkinnuk has learned."

"I hate this Indian shit," whispered Crosley Schell.

30

"No, no, no no no. You don't understand. Don't you see? You're proving my point. You don't believe me, right? That's why I didn't tell you in the first place. I knew you wouldn't. I was scared, damnit."

Crosley wasn't so calm now. His eyes were awake for once and the smile was dead on his face. He sat with his butt on the ground and for the last ten minutes had been sliding backward slowly, away from the fire, as he argued for himself. As he moved, Sparrow followed him with the long, shiny revolver, standing above him, looking down on him like a hunter on a wounded animal. Two Crow was dressed again and sitting across the fire next to Pim. Gun sat off from the rest of them, watching and listening, waiting for the right moment to bring his own knowledge to bear upon the situation.

"Look now, please," said Crosley. He slid backward again, but this time his shoulders butted up against the rock wall. His face was so white there could have been a light bulb turned on inside his head. "If I'd told you before, it wouldn't have been any good. Think of it now. Think. It's last year at this time and I come to you and I say, 'Yeah, there's gold all right, but don't worry, I'm not gonna tell a soul, you're safe.' You wouldn't have bought it. No way. Am I right? You couldn't have trusted me with that."

"That was our agreement, though. That you'd tell us first."

"I know. But when it came right down to it, I didn't think it would work. I didn't feel like you trusted me enough. Look, I'll be honest. I was afraid of what might happen if I told you. God, I don't know. I guess I was thinking it's just safer, keeping it to myself. Safer for me, and for you. And simpler. I mean, who's gonna be harmed if nobody knows? Tell me. The gold stays where it is and everything's fine. Isn't that right? And nobody's upset or even has to think about it. That's what I wanted. You gotta believe me. You've got to."

"No, we don't have to." Sparrow hadn't said a word since the Shaking Tent. He turned and looked at Pim. "Do we have to keep listening to this shit? I'm tired of it. Tired of him and his talk. He's the kind, he could be lying here with a bullet in his heart and still be talking."

Pim raised a hand and his fingers gently strummed the air. "There's more we need to ask. Not much, though. Be patient."

Jefferson Sparrow looked away, let his right arm drop to his side, and with his wrist levered the long barrel of the revolver up close to Crosley's face.

Two Crow said, "May Marks. You didn't tell *her?*"

"Oh, shit," said Schell. "May."

"See?" said Pim. "You *did* tell someone." He was energized now, nodding, his eyes large behind the round lenses. "You told May, and she told Julius. True?"

Crosley bit his lip, knotted his face, blinked once and nodded. "Yes, I told May. But *only* May. You know how it is, with a woman. I didn't intend to tell her. It just happened one night."

Pim said, "Babe Chandler would disagree with this story of yours. He'd say that you told May this gold you found was going to make you a rich man some day."

"That's a lie, Pim. The kid's a thief. Stole one of my guns. This one right here, for God's sake—" He jabbed a finger at the Colt in Sparrow's hand. "He's talking fast to save his own skin is what he's doing and I'd think you'd be able to see that. I don't know what happened between him and Julius on the ice, but you can bet your ass Babe Chandler doesn't want anybody to know. Shit, that kid's no better than an animal, the way he lives. The way he stays out in the woods for weeks and his dad not even knowing where he is."

Pim straightened his back and rubbed his hands together. "Let's say for the moment you're telling the truth, then." He looked over at Two Crow, at Gun. "So we give you the benefit of the doubt here. You're telling the truth, let's say, and you meant to keep the gold a secret from the world. To *protect* us." Pim smiled. "Everything's pretty, yes? But I've still got a problem. I can't help wondering, Crosley, about May. Why is she dead? And don't bring Babe Chandler into it. He was safe here with us—as you are now—when May was murdered."

Crosley shook his head and dropped his shoulders in a show of helplessness. "I don't know. Really. An Indian, probably, who hated the idea of May and I together. You know how people from the Rez said things to her about us. It was ugly sometimes." Crosley shrugged. "Or if May *did* tell Julius about the gold, who knows who else *he* talked to. Then May's the traitor. Shit, I don't know."

Pim and Two Crow sat quietly, calmly watching him. Crosley looked up at them and back down at his lap. He shook his head.

Gun said, "So you don't know a man who carries a

knife with a half-moon blade. No one like that works for you."

Crosley frowned and straightened up against the rock wall of the cave. "Never seen him."

"Too bad," Gun said, "because I think he's the one who killed May. I know he's the one who diced Dick Chandler. I saw him. Fact, I had to be mighty careful to keep from getting cut myself."

"Who is he?" asked Crosley.

"I thought *you'd* be the one telling *me*."

"Sorry."

"Okay." Gun sighed. "Izzy Rolph, then."

"What about him?" said Crosley. "What's Izzy got to do with it?"

"I'm wondering if you told Izzy about the gold. You and Izzy are old pals, of course, and he's been staying at your place."

"Doesn't know a thing," said Crosley. "Like you said, he's a friend. He comes to visit. We talk about old times, shoot the shit. Big deal."

"And he happens to be a geologist," said Gun.

"He's a teacher."

"A geology teacher who also gets paid very well to sniff the ground for money." Gun looked at Pim. "Rolph's a mineral consultant. He goes around checking things out for the people who buy. Investors, speculators. He makes sure that where there's supposed to be gold or diamonds or whatever under the ground, there actually is."

"Where is this Rolph?" asked Sparrow.

"Got a little hot out here for him," said Gun. "He flew home last night."

Sparrow said, "What college did you say?"

"New York University," said Gun. "New York City."

"I'll go after the bastard." Sparrow grinned suddenly. "Pim? I don't feel very nice right now. I feel like a son-of-a-bitch." He leaned down and put the barrel of the revolver against Schell's neck.

Crosley slid his head against the rock, away from the barrel. "I haven't said a word to Izzy. Honest to God. Nothing."

"Sparrow," Pim warned.

"And then there's the matter of the maps." Gun stood up and walked toward Crosley and Sparrow. He knelt down about three feet away, close enough to see the muscles of Schell's left eye ticking away in bad rhythm. The man's lips held the only color left in his face, and they were going pale too. "Do you want to tell these men about your maps, Schell? I will, if you don't."

"Maps." Crosley's smile was brave but he couldn't hold it. "Of course I've got maps."

"And they're a record of what?"

"Of the core samples taken, and the minerals found in each core."

"And you've kept a record of the gold on these maps?" Gun asked.

"No," said Crosley.

"Because you didn't want anyone else to know about it."

"Yes," said Crosley. "But I have a pretty good idea where the gold is, in my head."

"But the gold isn't indicated on your maps."

"No."

"And where do you keep the maps?"

"In a map drawer in my cabinet. Locked. It's in my office in the house."

"That's all there is, then," said Gun. He raised an index finger. "You have a single set of maps in the map drawer. No other record of where the core samples are at. No *other* maps—ones that might help somebody go straight to the gold."

"No."

"Ah. Then what about the ones you hid *beneath* the map drawer? Rolled up and taped to the bottom of the cabinet. Not the smartest place to hide something. Funny how my fingers went under there right away, as soon as I started looking for a key to the drawers."

Crosley was shaking his head quickly, swallowing. Moving along the wall in an effort to keep Sparrow's revolver barrel off his throat. "No, no. Those are extra copies, is all. Just extras."

"And now Izzy's got them," said Gun.

"What?"

"I said, 'Izzy's got them.' I won't explain now, except to say he took them and ran. He seemed very upset when he learned about May Marks. In fact, if you hadn't set us straight tonight, I'd say Izzy knows about the gold and has the scary notion that whoever it was sliced up May could very well be coming after him. Though he wasn't so bad off he wanted to go home without those maps."

"What about the maps?" Pim said to Schell. "What's Izzy gonna do with them?" His voice was hard as slate. "Don't shit on us anymore. We're done with you."

"Answer him!" Sparrow pushed the barrel hard into Crosley's throat but Crosley, instead of ducking back, grabbed the barrel and yanked forward, pulling Sparrow to the ground and the revolver free. Before Gun could act, Crosley had jumped away, spinning the weapon's butt into both fists and leveling the long barrel at Sparrow's midsection. He pulled back the hammer, which made what to him must have been a satisfying steel clicking sound.

"Now everybody just hold on," he said. His fingers were shaking on the gun and there was a fast vibrato in his voice.

Sparrow got up and raised his fist. "You don't have the nuts," he said. "That's mine now and I'll have it back." He took a single step forward before Crosley pulled the trigger.

The sound was overwhelming, a flash flood of noise that came from every direction and silenced the eardrums before receding, and Gun didn't realize until Crosley Schell dropped to his knees that there had been two shots.

Calmly, Schell looked down at his own chest, where a red mark, just off-center, marred an otherwise beautiful white ski sweater. Then his eyes, sleepy again, went to Pim. Gun's did, too. Pim held a small black pistol in his right hand.

Pim turned his head and said, "Sparrow, are you all right?"

Sparrow was on his rear end, holding his right shoulder. He was groaning. "Goddamn. The white man shot me." He pushed himself up a little and looked at Schell. "You shot me," he said.

Schell nodded. He dropped forward. His arms didn't reach out to break his fall.

31

Sleep did not come. He wouldn't let it. Sleep was obsolete. Irrelevant. Wrong.

Sleep now seemed to Gun as criminal as what he'd done last night, after the shooting when—with Crosley Schell on his face and soaking up cold from the cavern floor—Pim said, "Well. We better hide him."

The better angel in Gun's nature had caught up with him, there in the cave, and made him ask why. Pim, blast him, had answered, "Why? Pedersen, look. There's at least one killer who is still loose"—Pim somehow looking more like a schoolteacher than a killer himself, even with the gun still in his fingers—"and we don't know who he is. Okay? But May's dead. And Julius. Two Ojibwas. Now you want to throw a white body to the reporters? Sure, come take pictures, get good and righteous on the ten o'clock news. Turn up the dial on the race-hate machine. Pedersen," Pim said, his voice softening, "we just won't let you."

"So you hide him. What do you gain?"

Sparrow made a step toward Gun but Pim shook his head and he stopped. Pim tossed the pistol down. He took off his glasses and rubbed the lenses on his shirt. He said, "I wish it hadn't happened. It was Crosley's own fault. But I'm sorry. If he goes missing for, say, two days, it hurts no one. We gain time."

And time was what Gun needed, too. Time to get what truth there was from Izzy Rolph. To find May's killer. *Time to follow through on what I've started.* The vultures would descend whenever Crosley Schell came to light, be that now or be it later. He said, "Two days."

"No more," Pim said.

So they had bent down, the four of them, and gotten their grips on the dead man. Lifted him up like taking a struck deer off the highway, Crosley sagging in the middle and his coat riding up and his shirt untucked. Gun had hold of one wobbling knee and Sparrow the other, the Indian sweating hard with his wound but denying himself the good shriek he deserved. They followed the cavern inward until the roof ducked down on them suddenly and a fissure opened on their right. The air here was dry and cold. The crack was a dozen feet long and very low, looking in the coppery light like a black alligator against the wall. A skinny alligator. They worked Crosley Schell into it, Sparrow grunting now and letting his anger do the work. Crosley lost a little skin.

"Two days," Gun told Pim.

"And Crosley turns up. Far, far away."

At two A.M. Gun was leaving the cavern and his better angel collared him again—*hiding a body*. He told the angel, *Shut up,* but had a feeling it wouldn't.

And now it was 4:48 and Gun was up again and dressed. He went to the kitchen and turned on the heat beneath the coffee pot. Sleep or no sleep, it was time to work; first, on Izzy Rolph.

He found the number he'd gotten from the NYU professor and dialed. It rang twice before the answering machine kicked in: Izzy's voice saying he wasn't home but please leave a message after the tone.

All right, then, so Izzy had gotten home—or else had called home to program his machine.

Gun hung up without saying a word. *Don't scare the man away. Better to go out there, talk face to face.* He was just about to lift the receiver and dial the airport for flight times when the phone rang, jumping in his palm, the sound and feel of it going to the roots of his molars. "Damn," he said, and picked it up.

"Gun. Pim here." Pim sounded tired, hollow, dead serious.

"What's going on?"

"Sparrow's gone."

"Sparrow's gone where?"

"We got his shoulder patched up, then left him to watch, uh, Crosley for the night. I went back to check up on him . . . couldn't stay away, I guess. He wasn't there. He'd left a note for me."

"And."

"He's on his way to New York."

"To see Izzy Rolph," Gun said. "That's where I'm heading."

"Thought so." Pim's laugh was desert dry, and Gun got a picture of the man's eyes, ironic slits behind the round lenses. Pim said, "Sparrow's not going out to *see* Izzy, I don't think."

Gun couldn't help himself. "Dumb bastard."

"Impulsive," Pim said. "Dangerous. Not dumb."

"I'll do what I can," Gun said. "At least Izzy's not in the phone book. Sparrow could have some trouble finding him."

"Don't count on it."

Gun hung up. Dialed Izzy again. Got the answering machine. This time he left a message: "Leave your apartment or get yourself a weapon and don't go to sleep. Those maps? They caught up with you already." Then he went outside, climbed into the Ford and left for Twin Cities International, not bothering to check on flights by phone.

Driving seventy-five, he got to the airport at five after ten and learned he'd missed a United flight by fifteen minutes. Northwest had a 737 leaving in an hour. He bought a ticket and walked down the blue concourse to gate 31, where he found a nice soft seat and waited as hard as he could.

32

A full sky above LaGuardia kept Gun in the air until four-thirty in the afternoon, New York time, but the limo driver he bought outside the terminal promised to turn back the clock, looked down at the hundred-dollar bill Gun showed him and said, "We don't touch the ground, buddy, you and me."

It was a miracle of tight corners and green lights, and at five o'clock sharp they pulled up, brakes squealing, in front of an old four-story brick apartment building on the west side of Central Park.

The sun was gone beneath the city's steep horizon. A day gone, thought Gun, and not a thing to show for it.

"This here's the *add*ress," said the driver.

Gun handed him an extra twenty.

"You come here often?" asked the driver, fingering the bill.

"Nope," said Gun.

"Shit." The driver tapped the steering wheel and winked. "Be wanting a ride back, though, right?"

"Sorry."

"Double shit."

"Have a nice evening," Gun said, and he walked up the sidewalk toward the building's front entrance.

Twenties' elegance, neglected. Though what the place had been still showed through. Inside, the maple woodwork was scarred and the old brass mailboxes tarnished. Gun looked for Izzy's name but could not find it.

"Do you believe in *asking* for help?" A quiet, civilized voice from behind.

Gun turned to see the elevator operator peering through the accordion slats of his car. "Sometimes," said Gun. "You offering?"

"As long as it's not a woman you want to see, I'm glad to help. The women—now that's another story." He sat straight in his chair, one bony leg crossed over the other at the knee, and regarded Gun from below a pair of sculpted white eyebrows. His veined nose twitched above a trimmed white mustache. He looked eighty and clear headed.

"I'm looking for Izzy Rolph," Gun said, trying to sound natural about it.

"Number 302. Third floor, southeast corner. But I'm afraid you just missed him. He left, oh, half an hour ago, not more. Four-thirty. Stepped out for his evening meal, I'd think. Usually goes out about this time."

"Ah," Gun said.

"Pleasant young man, Doctor Rolph. Stops to chat now and again. You're a friend of his?"

Gun nodded.

"From the university?" The man's eyes, roaming up and down Gun's six and a half feet, were skeptical.

"No. I'm . . . in minerals." *Aaak.*

"Haven't seen you around, have I?"

"You haven't. I'm from Minnesota."

"Oh, yes." The old man relaxed and smiled. "I understand he did a bit of consulting out there? Told me that's where he was going, before he left. He's only recently back in town, but you must know that.

Enterprising young man, Rolph is. Hmmm . . ." He tapped a finger on his lips. "I'm sure he wouldn't mind my telling you where he normally takes his dinner."

Gun agreed.

"Do you know the city at all?"

"I used to get here quite a bit," Gun said. *Every time we played the Yankees on the road. Seventeen seasons.*

"You must know Columbus Circle, then."

"Sure."

"A little place, across the street from there. A diner, nothing about it too special. But the guy who owns it makes his own ice cream in back. Different flavors every day. You wouldn't believe the people he pulls in with that ice cream of his. They go and eat his food, sure, but it's for the sake of dessert. A loyal clientele, Doctor Rolph one of them. My guess is you'll find him there. Can't miss the place. They've got a neon penguin up in the window. The guy who owns it? His name's Nunn, but with two n's. Get it? Penguin?"

"Thanks," Gun told him. "Oh—" he stepped close and spoke confidentially—"if I don't find him, and he gets back here before me, don't tell him I was here. Kind of a surprise."

"No problem. Not a word." The old man's eyebrows shot together in a frown that sealed their agreement.

Gun left the building and walked along the edge of Central Park, past a little lake—the same one, he realized, where he'd taken Amanda for a boat ride one warm August morning twenty-seven years ago. Uncharacteristically, she'd insisted on following Gun east for the Yankees series, and the two of them had stayed apart from the team at a small midtown hotel, the name of which Gun couldn't recall. She'd been acting funny that day, young and old and silly and wise all at the same time, and she held on to her secret until they were out in the middle of the lake, Gun at the oars, Amanda in the bow, the city way up there and above them to the south.

Gun remembered the way she'd said it. The way she looked when she said it: her lovely, heavy, red blond hair, and how she sat there with most of it gathered into her hands in front of one shoulder, and her eyes watching him, coy, ripe with something she knew and he did not. Dumb, he was, even then.

"What is it?" he'd asked.

"A boy or a girl," she said. A girl, as it happened. They'd named her Mazy. Twenty-six years old now.

Gun turned his eyes from a man lying on the sidewalk, head covered with a newspaper. Of course, what kind of father didn't have memories like these: pretty, and full of things good and ordinary. Or full of regret, depending on the choices you'd made. It was lousy, Gun realized, to forget for a time what matters, and then later remember again. He thought of Carol Long and her patience. When was it going to run out? he asked himself. Then his eyes, moving left, caught sight of a dark blue neon penguin.

The place was all window along the outer wall, tables running alongside it. Gun sat down at the old-fashioned counter with a blue Formica top. He swiveled one way then the other on his stool but saw no Izzy. He ordered coffee and watched the door that said RESTROOMS. A waitress parked in front of him and he ordered a cappuccino. The waitress didn't leave.

"You're Gun Pedersen," she said. She looked to be mid-forties, hanging on to her shape still but rough through the eyes. Her mouth had been pretty once, full lips and a pout you had to admire. "You don't recognize me," she said.

He looked harder. "No."

Her finger scolded him. "I'll be right back," she said, and hustled off toward a corner of the diner.

She came back with a man, who wasn't Izzy, in tow. He had shoulders on him like a pair of radials and he wore a ball cap pulled down over his eyes. "My husband," the waitress said. "You better recognize *him.*"

The man tilted back the visor of the cap and leaned toward his wife. A smile was fighting to get past the hurt look that said, *I bet you won't.* Gun studied the face, began to see old lines and angles beneath the puffiness and potato fat. Finally, he was able to say, "Louie, you're as big and ugly as you ever were."

"Thanks. You, too." Louie Scanlon's smile broke through the hurt and he put out his hand. Gun shook it, surprised by the weakness of grip. Louie's belly hung loose over a belt and his knees, which had given out young and ruined the fine outfielder's career at midpoint, were bent inward and resting against each other.

"How've you been?" Gun asked, and wished he hadn't. He looked over quickly at the restroom door. Where was Rolph, anyway?

"You got a couple hours?" asked Louie's wife, her voice sour. Maggie, Gun remembered.

"Small world, ain't it? Who's ever gonna guess you'd end up in here." Louie spoke loudly and shook his head in big sweeps, as if to make up for his wife's tone. "Come and sit down. Buy you coffee."

"He ordered a cappuccino," his wife put in.

"Buy you that, then. What's it been? Ten, twelve years? You quit in eighty, yeah?"

Gun allowed himself to be led by Louie to the corner booth, keeping an eye on the restroom, which no one had come out of. Izzy, apparently, was not here. This would have to be a quick reunion.

Louie ushered him into the booth and sat down next to him, wrapping a huge arm around Gun's shoulders. Across the little table Maggie slid herself in, slowly, as if it hurt. Gun said, "This is wonderful, but you've got to understand, I've got an appointment tonight. Important one, too. Much as I hate to say it, we're going to have to keep this short."

"Pleasure before business, Gun. We've gotta catch

up on each other. Hey, we're talking Fate here. Capital F. Maggie and me in this place every day—life, you know, pick up your feet and set them down—and now you show up."

"Let's talk fast, then," Gun said. He looked at the big round clock on the wall behind the cash register. Five-thirty, it said. Izzy'd been out of his apartment an hour.

"When you quit the Tigers, things weren't, um, so good for you," said Maggie. She was leaning forward, eager, the light in her eyes all too familiar; there were folks in the world who lived for hard-luck stories. Though of course some needed them to keep their own lives bearable and likely Maggie was one of them.

"Things are better now," said Gun. "But it'd take too long to tell. How about you two? You're together."

Louie's arm had come off Gun's shoulders at Maggie's first question, and now he slumped forward, his arms falling to the table, big shoulders sagging as if he'd been holding his breath and finally run out of air. He said, "What happened was, our son got killed. And that's about all you need to know about us."

Gun was stuck for a sensible reply, but Maggie was there.

"That—and it comes after the knees put Louie out of the Show, and the Yanks didn't give him shit. Nine years. And we needed one more—one more, God. For the pension. But do you suppose they lifted a finger? Uh-uh. No, sir. It was, 'Too bad, Louie. We got it outa you, everything we could. Have a good life.'"

"They didn't owe me a thing," said Louie. "I worked, they paid me. Paid me well. We had a good time. Then one day I couldn't work no more. They quit paying me. That's how it went and that's how it goes." He shrugged.

Maggie laughed, and the anger in it made Gun shiver. "They paid you well, sure," she said. "Too bad you didn't know what to do with that money when you had it. Too bad you had yourself such a good time all the time. Too bad you couldn't have looked ahead a little."

"You had some good times, too, the way I remember it."

It was an old fight, Gun could see that, rehearsed to perfection. He tried to think of a polite way to let them play it through again, by themselves. He cut in on Maggie, saying, "I've gotta go, really. My appointment, it's at six, halfway across town. I'll be late as it is."

"Like I was saying, that's when Stu got killed. He was twenty, you know. In college. Stu was a smart boy. And they could never explain what happened, not to my satisfaction. Not to Louie's either. Stu wasn't the kind of boy to get in a fight like that. Not that kind of a boy at all . . ."

So Gun was caught there for another fifteen minutes, his eyes going up to the clock at every chance, over to the restroom door. You didn't walk out on folks who were telling you about their son's death and their own sorry lives. Especially not if they were old friends. But finally that's what he did. He told them he had to leave, sorry, but he didn't have a choice—which he didn't. He got up from the booth, turned his back to their misery and walked from the diner into the cold New York night.

All the way back to Izzy Rolph's building, he resisted the impulse to run.

It wouldn't have mattered if he had.

The street in front of the building was jammed with official vehicles, their red lights spinning. Four squad cars, a police van, an ambulance. The sidewalks and the park across the street were thick with gawkers—not the polite Minnesota brand either—their heads craning toward the door of the apartment building, bodies pushing in against the yellow tape that sectioned off the front of the building. Yet the scene was oddly silent. Those who talked whispered. Gun wanted to believe it was respect that made them so quiet but he knew better. They were scared to death.

Thinking seemed impossible. He was a pair of eyes, a pair of ears, a nose that smelled the sour curiosity of the crowd. Right here, this was the situation he'd flown out here to prevent. Damn. *Nice work, Pedersen. Just beautiful. Everywhere you go, things turn out for the best.*

Like the others, he stood—crouched, actually—and watched. Not too close, either. An old delivery truck across the street made for good cover. He didn't want to be seen and fingered by the elevator operator. *Yeah, that guy, right over there. Better talk to him. He was here an hour ago. Asked to see Dr. Rolph.*

Wouldn't that be sweet.

Five minutes he waited. Ten. Then in twos and threes the onlookers began to leave. Fifteen minutes. What was taking so long? Finally the front door of the building swung open. Four men and a single stretcher on wheels. The men seemed in no hurry, took their time lifting the stretcher down the brick steps and rolling it toward the ambulance. The body was covered up with a white cloth. All the way up. A sibilant wave moved through the crowd.

"Dead as dead," Gun heard an old woman say, and he blinked away the picture that came to mind—Izzy's face, drained of its usual color, no boyish glow in his cheeks.

The body was stuck into the rear of the ambulance and taken away. People started to move off. Gun stayed. He watched two of the squad cars leave. The police van. He watched a third squad car leave. He watched until there was only a small knot of onlookers left on the sidewalk in front of the building. Soon they wandered off. He worried about being seen, but the place where he sat was in deep shadow. He stayed.

Twenty minutes later the front door came open

again. The first man out was a cop carrying a bolt-action rifle. The second man, followed by one more cop, was Izzy Rolph. Though flanked by policemen, he clearly was not in custody. His wrists were free, and he was saying something to the cop beside him. He was smiling, walking with a bounce—a man happy to be on his feet.

First he went to a cafe close by, where he ate a
hamburger and had the cappuccino they'd forgotten
to bring him in the diner. He drank a second
cappuccino—this was New York—and he walked
back to the building, approaching it from the alley. He
picked out the windows of Izzy's apartment: third
floor and southeast corner, like the elevator man had
said. A steel fire escape climbed the brick wall.

He went up the narrow steps and entered Izzy's
place through a window which he shatter-popped with
his elbow. He did it quietly, covering the pane with his
goose-down parka before administering the blow. The
glass fell without much fuss inside.

In the dark kitchen the smell of gunpowder was
unmistakable, pinching sharp, and walking into the
living room he noticed the smell fading. In the two
bedrooms off the hall it was nothing but memory. He
returned to the kitchen and got the first whiff of a
milder, sweeter scent, one overmatched by the burn
smell, and only then did he think of looking for the
blood, which he found in the hallway between the
kitchen and living room. Just a circle of it the size of a
dinner plate in the carpeting. And above, on the wall,

a smear shaped like a man's necktie blowing free in the wind. In the spot where the knot would be there was a bullet hole. A damn unlikely place for a Minnesota Ojibwa to die.

The way it looked, Sparrow had come in while Izzy was out. Hidden himself in a bedroom, probably, then gotten too anxious and made his move at a perfectly wretched time.

Gun sat down at the kitchen table. The chair he sat on was more like a barstool, with a low back and grooves in the seat to accommodate the human butt. On the refrigerator, lit by the streetlight outside the alley window, was an article cut from a magazine. "Five Great Easy-to-Make Vegetarian Entrees." *Okay, you're hip.*

He considered looking for the maps but decided against it. He was tired, and soon enough the police would be done with Izzy, who would then come home and probably be willing to talk. If not willing, Gun would make him willing. He was not in a mood for detail work, finesse. Not at all.

After a while he went to the fridge and found a quart of skim milk and a brick of Swiss cheese. In a cupboard was whole-wheat bread. He made a sandwich. He was eating it when the key turned in the lock and Izzy came in, switching on lights.

"Always wondered how people could drink this stuff," Gun said, holding up the carton of skim. "Don't leave, now."

Izzy was frozen, the door still halfway open behind him. He looked like a man with a low tolerance for surprise. Gun forgave him for looking that way.

"Shut the door behind you," he told him.

Izzy shut the door. He said shit and put his hands to his face. "I got your message."

"Come and sit down," Gun said. "Swiss cheese?"

Izzy frowned at the ceiling for a moment, then he walked over and dropped into the chair across the table from Gun. "Yeah, okay."

"What was your story? For the police?" Gun sliced rectangles of cheese and laid them across a piece of bread.

Izzy reached for the sandwich. "I shot a prowler. It's not uncommon."

"Any identification on him?" Gun asked.

"Not a thing. No license, no credit cards. Wallet had nothing but money in it. They'll never trace him— unless his people back home want him traced."

"No chance," Gun said.

"Didn't think so." Izzy took a bite of the sandwich, chewed tentatively. "He was going to kill me, whoever he was."

"Jefferson Sparrow," Gun said.

Izzy swallowed. He shut his eyes, took a deep breath and sighed for about ten seconds. "Will there be others?"

"Not if you give me the maps."

"I'll pay you to take 'em."

"And," Gun said, "you'll have to have some good answers for the questions I've got. No getting cute and leaving things out. I want to know everything, and you're the only one left to tell. Your friend Crosley's dead."

Izzy smiled the way people do when they get bad news they've been expecting. More like a facial stretch to relieve tension.

He said, "You think I'm surprised? Look, I just want this over with."

"What did you and Schell have in mind? You knew about the gold, but you weren't telling people. What good was it to you?"

Izzy shook his head. "For now it wasn't any good at all. But a few years down the road, hey, it would've been our ticket to write."

"Go on."

"All right, here's how it went." Izzy got up and took a glass down from the cupboard, poured himself some skim milk and took a couple of swallows. Another long sigh and he sat down. "Crosley found gold in those cores a couple years ago, and ever since, he's been feeding bullshit to DDH. Sending them maps that tell the wrong story. He had to keep them interested enough to let him keep on doing what those were paying him to do, testing and recording those old cores. But not so interested they'd actually expect to find much of anything. So that's how he played it. He fixed the maps. Teased them away from the good spots. Eventually, when he had all the information he needed, he would've let DDH down easy. Would've quit giving them anything at all to go on. Say, a year or two from now. They would've given up, pulled out. And Crosley would've held on to his maps. The real ones, I mean. And that's where I come in."

"Because you know the people who'd pay for them."

"I sure do." Izzy looked up and his face opened, as if at the sight of a green cloud raining paper money. "God, do I."

"I suppose," Gun said, "nobody would've had to know what the two of you had done."

"That's the beauty of it. I know a hell of a lot of people in a hell of a lot of companies, and I can go in the front door or I can go in the back door. We show those maps to the right men—in the right context, of course—and then we just smile, walk to the bank. No one's the wiser. See, we're talking very high stakes and really no risk to speak of."

"Well . . ."

"I mean, no risk if we'd gotten that far."

"And you don't think you'll be tempted to go at it from another direction? A few years from now?"

"Mr. Pedersen," said Izzy Rolph. "Do you think there are many greedy men on Death Row?"

"Greedy for life, maybe."

"Yeah, like me." Izzy's eyes wandered over to the blood on the wall, then came back. He chewed on a fingernail, his forehead bunching. He said, "You want to know whether I'm going to reenter the picture some day, and I understand that. I'm not. I'm young, I have a decent life. Do you understand? I'm done with this. I'm not a fool. But I've got the same question for you. How do I know somebody's not gonna show up here some day and bring it all back to me?"

"Look. You should be dead right now and it's because there's lots of people back there on that reservation who want more than anything to be left the hell alone. They don't want their lives changed in ways they can't control. Or their land carved up. Legally you're free and clear. Nobody's going to bring charges, believe me. Last thing they want is for any of this to go public. But you know that. And as far as your own safety, you should know that Sparrow wasn't acting on any kind of orders. He was on his own. My guess is, you don't do anything to make anybody nervous, you'll be just fine."

Izzy nodded, smiled. "I hate it when people get nervous. Hey, I bend over backward to make folks comfortable."

Gun stayed quiet and watched him for a few moments, until he felt satisfied, then he said, "What can you tell me about the guy who killed May Marks?"

The question put some starch in Izzy's posture. Gun heard the man swallow. "Oh man. I can tell you he scared the crap out of me, all right. And I can tell you his name is Quill, first or last, I'm not sure. Crosley just called him Quill. He came over a couple times last week, sort of hung around at the edge of the yard until Crosley spotted him. Then the two of them'd have a little conference. Crosley wouldn't say much about him. Said he did some work with the cores, I can't imagine what. Crosley didn't want to talk. But after Chandler got hurt and then after May, well, I started thinking. Honest, though, I don't know any more than his name, and the fact that he came around. And I think I saw Crosley give him some cash. That would have been a week or so ago."

"Where does he live?"

"Don't have the foggiest. Really. If I knew, I'd tell you. He gives me the creeps. But you've got to understand something about Crosley. He and I were old friends, and uh, partners in this thing, too. But he was always real close to the vest. Kept a lot of stuff to himself. He was paranoid. The maps, for instance, the ones you found and hid in the Indian's pants and I brought back here with me? They're the ones with the gold markings, I'm sure of it. But I can't read them. Crosley must've used a code. He never showed them to me. Always said there'd be a right time for it, but till then there wasn't any point. The right time never came."

"You're telling me you can't help with the maps."

"I can't. Not beyond handing them over, which I'll do right now," he said, getting up. He left the kitchen and came right back. The maps were still rolled, but the cylinders had been flattened from pressure. "Between the mattress and box spring," said Izzy. "Original, huh?"

"Final question," Gun said. "How'd you get Sparrow? I was out there watching with everybody else, across the street, and I was betting on *you* getting rolled out of here."

Izzy shook his head. "I got that call from you last night. No, this morning. And for the next twelve hours I sat right here in this chair, hardly moving except to shake. I'm serious. I sat here and shook, and got up to take a leak about every fifteen minutes, and I wasn't drinking anything. I mean, I didn't know what the hell to do. Call the cops, right? Call them up and say, 'Hey, me and my buddy've got this gold scam going out in Minnesota and I think it just backfired. I need some help.' Sure.

"So finally about four-thirty this afternoon I

couldn't stand it anymore and I got up and left, walked out of here, thinking I might not come back. I was maybe ten blocks away, trying to think what to do, you know, any damn thing. And I'm starting to wonder if somebody's following me. Not that I saw anybody, but wouldn't it make perfect sense? I'm thinking whoever it is probably'd been just waiting for me to leave the building, and now here I was, target practice. That's about the time I walk past this pawn shop where they've got guns in the window, and one of them catches my eye—a rifle, the same kind I used to see in the war movies when I was a kid—and I thought to myself, *I've got to have that gun.* Which is really dumb because what do I know about rifles? Never owned one in my life, only shot one a couple times out at my cousin's farm when I was ten or eleven. But I went in there and bought it. I was scared shitless. Looking over my shoulder and crippled, I mean crippled with the shakes, and I think the guy in there thought I was gonna go out and kill somebody. But he sold it to me anyway. Showed me how it worked, too. Gave me a little lesson. Then I had him break it down and put it in a bag so it wouldn't look so obvious out in the street.

"I came back here and parked myself on this chair. First thing I did, I put the gun back together and loaded it, just to make sure I remembered what the guy in the shop had taught me. And, my God, I wasn't sitting here five minutes and that bastard came sneaking around the corner from my bedroom. I heard the closet door squeak open first, so I was ready. Had the sights on him even before he was there. When I saw that pistol in his hand, I pulled the trigger. Bang. Then I called the cops. Like that. Simple."

"Didn't the cops ask you about the gun?"

"You don't have to register a hunting weapon in New York. Just handguns. I told them I heard somebody in the next room and got scared, went for the rifle. They didn't have any trouble with that."

"Anybody see you come into the building with it?" Gun asked.

"Not that I know of, and like I said, I had it broken down in two parts and stuck in a bag."

"How about that elevator guy?"

"You met him," said Izzy, smiling. "No, I went in the back way and up the stairwell."

"Then I'd say you don't have a lot to worry about, Izzy. That is, if you can manage to hang on to the attitude you've got. And if the gold'll leave you alone, stop whispering all those sweet things in your ears. You'll probably have to find something to take its place."

Izzy was nodding away, sincere as you can get and still be convincing.

Gun said, "You got a girlfriend?"

This brought his nodding to a stop and lifted him up straight in his chair. "Um, no. Not right now. Why?"

"Might help you get over the gold."

34

Somehow it still surprised Gun to get off a plane and not have to go straight to a ball park, get changed, start pressing the muscles down long and loose again to get the travel out. A lot of guys learned to moan about road trips, once they'd been up long enough to forget how lucky they were. Gun let them complain. To him it had seemed a good deal even then: you got a first-class flight, touched down in a city where guys in jeans and sweatshirts brought their little kids to see you play, and with any luck you brought your good wood along, helped the cause, moved another day toward the long off season or, if you were very blessed, a pennant race. Now he stood in a quiet concourse of the Minneapolis–St. Paul International Airport, looking up at a clock that said three A.M. Instead of the gym bag he'd carried to games, he had Izzy's broad cardboard tube with some maps in it that might lead him someplace or might indeed not. It was the middle of the night and he couldn't remember where he'd parked the truck. Traveling had sure been better with the Tigers.

Second-level ramp, that's where the Ford was, fifth or sixth row in. Then a drive to the North Shore, because that's where Babe was and Babe was first priority now, poor wary kid. Gun had meant to go back to the lodge and get him once Crosley was freed and the gold scheme laid bare as an Iron Range mine, and instead he'd had to chase off to New York.

And all the while Babe was back at the lodge, waiting for news. Maybe getting in some batting practice with the old man. Or maybe, damn it, taking off again. Wondering why Gun hadn't come back, if Gun had sold him out, if the next knock at the door would be a state cop.

There was a phone bank next to an all-night newspaper stand.

Shorty Heller picked up after half a minute of rings. "Wrong damn number!" he shouted. "No damn Carlsons in this house!" and Gun had to shout himself to keep the old man from slamming down the receiver.

"Heller! It's Pedersen. I'm sorry to wake you up."

"Ah. Ah. Heh, heh. Mr. Pedersen." Heller sounded alert enough and a little embarrassed. "The phonebook people wrote my number next to somebody else's name this time around. I don't know who he is, but he plays long hours. Ah. Heh, heh."

"I've had a delay. I'm in the Cities, on my way up. Is Babe Chandler still there?"

Heller said, "That's all you want to know?"

"Yup. Sorry about the time."

"Well, jeez . . ." Heller put the phone down rough enough to smack Gun's ear and went grumping off out of hearing range. There was quiet and then some banging around, kitchen pans for goodness' sakes, and Heller returned. "Young man's sleeping like a winter woodchuck. This is right for this time of night. Me now," Heller said, "I'm all done. Get so many calls for Mr. Carlson I'm turning into him. Gonna throw a little party now, just me and the Hills Brothers."

"You saw his face? Not just a pile of blankets?" Gun

was aware of his paranoia but had come to accept it. Appreciate it, even, dealing with Babe.

"Kid smiles in his sleep. Teenagers."

"Thanks. Heller, can you cook breakfast?"

"Wheaties," the old man said, and hung up.

The North Shore of Lake Superior begins in Duluth, but often you can feel the lake coming miles before that, sending shivers down the spine of Highway 35 toward St. Paul even in early winter, when the whole state's starting to freeze. Four in the morning, last of November, Gun was still twenty minutes from water when the air went to icy gray mash. It congealed on the windshield like a Dairy Queen slush with the color sucked out, and he switched on the wipers. He was grateful for the motion, had been hammering steadily northward for an hour with his mind tucking itself in for the night, nothing to do but settle and watch the old Ford's odometer about to turn forty a second time, and here arose this foul mist like a pal who slaps you awake fifty yards from the cliff.

He didn't have coffee. Needed some, and the first road sign he'd noticed in miles told him he'd already driven past Tobie's, though he didn't remember doing it. He rolled down his window one crank and let some cold slush spit at his temple; turned on the AM hoping for Merle Haggard and got instead, ack, Kenny Rogers, exhaling all over everything. Dialing north he ran into a tape delay of Bruce Williams describing to a caller, poor devil, the proper way to discourage homosexual advances when traveling among the natives in the Yucatan. What was funny, Bruce actually *knew*. Gun let him talk all the way to Duluth, then stopped at a Super America and bought gas and a large coffee that was so bad he dropped it whole and heavy into the trash bin by the pump.

North. Gun had by his own foggy count another ninety miles to go, ninety miles of slow curves and narrow lanes where cliff swallows blinked from the left and Lake Superior wallowed and smoked in its deep bed to the right. The wipers kept sweeping the gray rot off the glass but were no help to his brain anymore, no sir. Just the opposite: what a sweet slow rockabye they made, swoop, rub, swoop some more.

Rub, swoop.

Gun cleared his throat, sagged, and began to dream.

He dreamed of a turtle, a big snapper with Jurassic moss growing on its back, its shell the size of home plate. The turtle moved out of the weeds and into the Ford's low beams, a beast from Superior crawling toward the high ground, and just as Gun swerved to miss it the turtle swiveled and snapped at air. It had a clean, hooked, half-moon beak and Gun jerked awake, his breath coming panicked as a newborn's, and discovered himself another thirty miles along, past pretty Two Harbors and shambling at half the speed limit with the white lines smack between his wheels. Bruce Williams sounded far distant, hawking a no-refusal credit card, his voice fading into the light just starting to stretch in the east. Gun gave in, found a wide piece of shoulder to park on and huddled down into his canvas jacket. The crash and frozen shroud of the lake reached the quiet cab in seconds, pounding him down into the company of dead folks, and snappers.

He opened his eyes two hours later on the bright side of dawn, straightened in his cold-crinkle jacket and was Ice Age man—joints all full of winter rust, fingers curled as if frozen around the handle of a club, eyelids birch-bark crisp. The lake boomed up powerful but friendly again now that it was daylight and Gun eased out of the dormant Ford while the sun peeled strips of yellow from itself and buttered them over water and land.

He walked half a mile up the road. Short steps at first and then longer ones, good pulls of lake oxygen coming in and loosening the carbon dioxide from his blood; putting his mind where it belonged at this time of day, too, which was on his stomach. Hibernation lifting away, he could smell the lake and its atomized tease of trout and crayfish. At his neck, the canvas jacket smelled of sleep and he slipped it off there in the stinging wet wind, balled it down into a taut tan cantaloupe. Turning he beheld his white pickup, at this distance just a young thing sitting jaunty on the shelf above the water. Gun stretched until the aches lost out to limber, then began an easy jog toward the truck. Surprise: the legs wanted to run, and more surprising, the lungs did also, and he shut his eyes and leaned ahead into it, going on the fly to a place across left field, the shout and gasp of the waves his audience, roaring to see the old guy run.

Babe was in Shorty's kitchen when Gun arrived. The kid was puttering around, breaking eggs into a clay bowl big enough to knead bread in, slicing redskinned potatoes and a wrinkled jalapeño while the old man sat grousing on a metal chair in the corner. Seeing Gun, Heller chuckled.

"Boy claims to cook. Ah. Heh."

"Makes sense to me," Gun said.

"Sure it does." Heller had a wood yardstick in his paw and bent forward to prod Babe with it. "Don't tell me Captain Hook's cabin boy don't keep busy."

Babe, at the stove tending the sizzle, grinned, then went impassive. Heller said, "We looked for you yesterday, Pedersen."

Gun pulled up a hard tubular chair that looked right to be making apologies from. "There were troubles."

He spared them what he could, needing to keep quiet about Schell for now. Babe didn't ask about him, though. Didn't seem to want to. Through it the boy kept quiet, his eyes on the stove, his body seeming straighter and slenderer all the time.

"I'm going to need your help now," Gun finished, directing the words to Babe.

The boy looked at him with a glossiness in his eyes Gun hadn't expected.

"I brought back some maps. They may show us what Crosley really had. You worked around his place, didn't you? You and Julius."

Babe nodded, still not speaking.

When they broke their fast at last, Babe hoisting up plates full of scrambled and fried and heavily peppered, Shorty Heller broke the quiet of astonished mouthfuls to say roughly, "Well. Can he cook?"

Could he.

35

"A bargain," Gun said to Carol. Home, one P.M., a fresh-rolled Prince Albert at the kitchen table. Babe in the living room with a copy of *The Sporting News*.

"This has nothing to do with dinner," Carol said. "I'm only guessing."

She hadn't answered her home phone but picked up at the office in the middle of the first ring, a bad omen.

"I have the maps," he told her, "which may verify Crosley's gold."

"I've just been on the phone with DDH. They say exactly what Crosley says. They hope for gold, but nothing yet."

Gun laid Prince Albert in a ceramic saucer. He extracted a map from the cardboard tube and rustled it next to the phone. He said, "What would you give?"

"You can't mean it. If you've got the maps, why wouldn't you let me see them?"

"Because you are the press, and because I have a secret which needs keeping."

He didn't need to rustle again. "Bargain," she said.

"All right. Babe Chandler is with me."

"Babe? Gun, the police are out looking—" She

paused, let a smile climb on board her voice. "I hope you've told Dick, anyhow."

"Dick knows."

"Where was he? And the maps—"

"Part of the bargain. I'm not saying."

There was a silence long enough for the smile to get off and make room for something utterly its opposite. He admired her for keeping it quiet when she said, "Damn it good and hard, Gun, I'm not some jerk columnist you can't trust."

"I know. Can you come out?"

"No." A little petulant, the way she got when she was leaning in his direction. "I'm waiting for some calls."

"Let us come in then."

"You're bringing Babe?"

"He worked for Crosley. We might need some help reading these maps."

"Back door, back alley," she said, and hung up with little forgiveness in her wrist.

The maps were five big blue-veined sheets of newsprint peppered here and there with little black felt-tip circles. Each described, in river lines and topographical swirls, a county adjacent to or containing part of the reservation, and each of the tiny circles was marked with a number and a two-letter code: Fe, Cu, Zn, Ag.

"He explained this once," Carol said. They were in a back corner of the square, fluorescent *Stony Journal* office, Carol and Gun and a Babe-gone-thoughtful. It was early afternoon, two days past edition and no paper due for another four, so Carol's part-time ad seller and copywriter, Azalea, was at home, vacuuming her Orientals. Gun had spread the first of the maps flat over what had been Carol's paste-up table, preMacintosh; the surface was lit from below, the map now oozing blue light.

"The numbers," she said, "are where the drill cores

originated. They match the ones marked on the core boxes in the archives."

"The boxes that burned," Gun said.

"Right. The letters are minerals. He used their elemental symbols—Fe is iron, Cu copper, that way." She pointed. "See, some cores showed traces of several minerals."

Gun looked at the first map, DIBBLE COUNTY printed up top in capitals of bleeding-edged navy. Below, Crosley had penciled "Archive Exploration for DDH, Inc. Commenced 7/1/90." The northwestern tip of the county was designated as reservation land; there were no circles there, but they were pebbled across the rest of the map like haphazard buckshot.

"Didn't they ever drill on the reservation?" Gun asked.

"Nothing in it for them," Babe said, surprising them. "The Bureau of Indian Affairs owns the mineral rights."

Gun wondered how much of Schell's work the kid had soaked up, intentionally or not; he wondered how much Crosley had realized this; how much he'd cared.

Carol pushed the sleeves of a blazing pink sweatshirt up over her elbows and leaned mapward until the blue light painted her face anemic. She said, deciphering: "Iron, copper, lead. Zinc." Paused. "Silver. What's the elemental symbol for gold?"

But chemistry for Gun was just a bad memory. "G-O," he guessed.

"A-U," Babe said.

"Thank you," Carol said, bending further into the map.

Gun narrowed his eyes at Babe, who said, "General science."

"No gold in Dibble County," Carol said. She straightened. "Some of the others are here, though. The iron pyrite and silver, the ones Crosley said were like gold's bitter cousins, always hanging close by."

Gun rolled up Dibble and handed Carol a new

county. This one had a heavy pattern of circles in the southeastern corner and nothing even close to the reservation, which covered a long vertical strip on the western edge. Again, no gold. Lots of bitter cousins.

Gun said, "If there's this much stuff in the ground —copper, silver—why isn't DDH mining already?"

"Traces, Gun," Carol said impatiently. "They're just little bits of clues in the rock. It's like, if you went out looking for a house and found one board."

"Guess I'd leave the realtor at home."

"Yes." Her voice distracted, then addressing Babe: "What does C-H mean?"

"What?"

"C-H. Which element is that?"

Babe didn't know and Gun wouldn't have guessed again for money. Carol pushed herself away from the table saying, "Wait," and went bobbing along the back wall of the office. One thing she had plenty of in her job was facts, and she found the ones they needed now in an eight-pound Webster's, under E for elements.

"There *is* no C-H," she said. The page had a periodic table, something Gun hadn't seen or wished to since the tenth grade. He looked now to satisfy her, and it was true.

"None," he agreed.

"Then it means something else," Carol said simply. "She eyed Babe and he shrugged, exaggerating it, *Don't look at me.*

"Maybe it's shorthand for something else, a combination of mineral traces," Gun said. "Copper and whatever."

She waved him off. "Then he'd have used shorthand for these others, too. Look. Here's a drill site with copper, zinc, and silver. Three minerals, three sets of letters."

"Well," Gun started, and let it die. His brain felt plugged, the good part of it still busy chewing him out over losing Crosley and Jefferson Sparrow. He remembered a ball game in Chicago, stuffy night, the night after Robertson got head shot in his car at a downtown stoplight, "Random Shooter Picks Off Shortstop." He remembered baseballs speeding toward him in left field and ending up somehow in his glove; once catching a shallow fly with a man on third and the guy tagging and scoring while he, Gun, stood there holding the ball, still as a Cooperstown bust. And the Chicago fans screeching their delight at his crazy lapse, not understanding that there were times when you shouldn't have to play.

"Next," Carol said, and Babe unfurled another county.

When she'd scoured them all and found no gold, just a houseful of cousins and three lonesome C-Hs, she reached down and snapped off the blue light, *sans* gentleness.

She said, "Look, there's no gold marked on these maps."

Gun waited for Babe to react, to dispute, but the boy only looked at Carol and then down glancingly at the unlit map.

"Maybe," she said, "Crosley isn't lying."

He's lying all right. Guess where.

Babe shrugged and Gun held carefully to Carol's eyes. They'd avoided talking of Crosley so far. He didn't want to mislead by silence but telling her now, "He's dead," would involve him in ways he couldn't afford.

At the front of the office, a telephone bleeped. Not the battering noise Gun was used to, but the voice of a polite cricket who was sorry to interrupt.

Carol picked up, said, "Journal," and Gun watched her face go the color of curbside snow as a low voice harped on the phone. He turned and saw Babe watching her too, his face like a wary animal's, almost twitching. The boy lowered his eyes when she hung up and looked at them.

"Durkins," she said. Her voice sounded piped through a plastic tube. "He got a call this morning. Crosley's dead."

Gun shut his eyes and heard her say, "Trucker was crossing a narrow bridge over the Marble River. Wisconsin. He looked down to see if it was frozen over yet."

The body rode like memory itself on the insides of Gun's eyelids. He felt his silence squeeze his chest. He thought he might forget to breathe.

"There's a press conference in an hour," Carol said. "Durkins and the FBI. I have to get ready." Her piped-in voice had gone soft and distracted, as if the only chore left to her now was choosing which dark dress to wear for the funeral.

36

"You're the press," he'd told her—a little harshly, it appeared in retrospect. "You go. I'm taking myself out of this one." And he'd hustled Babe out the back door, leaving Carol the maps and thinking selfishly that there was no good to come from this night anyhow; he might as well stew things over at home.

Now, heading that way with a few frantic snowflakes snapping around in the headlights, it seemed important that Carol had wanted him along. She'd been to hundreds of press conferences; had never wanted him there before. They'd been together through a lot of this blasted muddle, and would have been for more of it if not for his obdurate methods, his almost instinctive need to give chase when the color changed and not a second later. Like a mutt in a front yard, going flat out after every passing Dodge, trying to nip the hubcaps. It seemed to him he'd accomplished about as much; Sparrow and Schell were probably sitting together in a dark chamber somewhere, making the same comparison.

Still, Gun thought, getting the guard up, what was he supposed to do with Babe? Take him along to the press meeting? Reintroduce him to Durkins? Besides, the maps he'd taken from Izzy Rolph had proved a disappointment; if there *was* gold, Crosley had wanted to keep the knowledge to himself. The only proof, Gun realized, would be the core samples themselves. There were two living people who might have an idea where to find them. One was Babe. The other was Quill.

But Carol needs you. It was true. Or else, he realized, he wanted it to be true. He proposed himself a compromise: he'd take Babe home, make sure there was bedding in the spare room and milk in the fridge, then drive back into Stony and stand there with Carol and listen while she asked the cops questions no one knew he could answer himself if he wanted to.

"Mr. Pedersen," Babe said, just as Gun was realizing his decision hadn't made him feel better.

"I think you can call me Gun."

The kid seemed to be thinking this over, watching the snowflakes as they danced suddenly thicker in the lights. He said, "What about the dogs?"

"The dogs." Gun still feeling like the front-yard mutt.

"They'll have to eat."

"Oh." *Think.* Last stop to fill the Chandler dogs with carp had been . . . just before New York. He said, "Oh boy."

They were hungry enough, their eyes showing an anxious three-day glitter in the flashlight beam as Gun and Babe slipped down the path with buckets of fish. There was no howling this time, only gravity and hoarse, thick-necked growls as the dogs thrashed the frozen carp, swallowing hammerhead clods of flesh. It took them a half hour of gorging and another of unhitched bounding around the Chandler property to find their old joyous canine natures again, by which time Gun knew he'd not get back to Stony in time for the press conference. It chafed him a little, made him irritable, and for this he stubbornly blamed Crosley

Schell, whose death had been inconvenient enough, and who'd now gone and turned up again, earlier than Gun had anticipated.

Babe was still on the police wish list, for one thing; they wanted him for Julius and, if their usual logic applied, they'd want him for Crosley as well. The body jumbled things, like too much loose fishline in the bottom of a tackle box; you could sort things out, but it took a while, and you had to be mindful of hooks.

When Babe and the huskies were all romped out, the kid's tongue practically hanging out like the dogs', the two of them went up to the house through snow that was looking as if it meant to start winter right here and now. At the back door, Babe overturned a galvanized watering can and picked up a key.

"You can come in if you want. I drink coffee."

It struck Gun: *He thinks he's staying here.* "No, thanks. Just get some extra clothes and we'll head for my place."

That stopped the kid with the key in the lock.

"Safer for us both," Gun said.

"I'll be careful. No one knows I'm here." Babe was on defense now, his voice dropping back in his throat.

"I could use your help," Gun said. "Picking through some of this mess." Thinking, *The boy bolts now and I'll never catch him. Not now nor in worlds to come.*

Babe rocked faintly to and fro, a slow intuitive bobbing motion like a captive animal's at a roadside attraction.

"We'll come back tomorrow, feed the dogs," Gun said.

And Babe nodded, unlocked, and went silently in, not even bothering to turn on a light.

On the highway minutes later, Gun wishing for a load of wood or a few sandbags in the back for traction—no, not sand, come to think of it—Babe drummed tentatively at a Vikings gym bag on his lap and said, "Did you know about Crosley already? When Mrs. Long got the phone call?"

Intuition, hell. Who *was* this kid?

"You didn't jump or nothing. You just shut your eyes, like you didn't want her to see them."

Gun turned into his driveway, took a lot of time bumping in through the pines and killed the motor, rolling to a stop beside the snow-peaked woodpile.

"Yup, I knew." He sat looking across the cab. Let the kid ask some questions, for a change.

Babe said, "They kill him up on the Rez?"

"Yes."

"Were you there?"

"Yes."

"Sparrow."

"What about him?"

Babe was still. A fresh wind loaded with snow charged north across the lake and rammed the pickup on the passenger side. The old truck sloped a little toward Gun with an empty, used-up, settling sound. Like the floorboards of a black-eyed house, at the first of the rising whipstart storm that will finally take it down.

"Why'd Schell trust us so much, anyhow? I mean Pim, and Sparrow? Or Julius, or me. Schell, he read too much."

"Too much of what?" Cold was coming into the cab as if it were a canvas tent, but Babe was talking by himself at last and Gun didn't want to kill it.

"Oh, Indian crap. He had it that we were part of the land, you know, the people of the earth. Like we wouldn't hurt anybody who could look us in the eye."

Gun thought of something to say, watching Babe's profile, his boyish chin as smooth as an apple, and decided to keep his mouth shut.

"You know what he told me? That his only heroes were Indians, from the time he was a kid. He had 'em all, down in that basement. Guys made out of wax, Chief Joseph, Geronimo, Osceola."

"I saw them."

Babe exhaled through his nostrils, a hard disgusted snuff. "Yeah. It was to honor their spirits. He loved talking that way. He said a white man could never be so true."

Crosley'd been speaking for himself, Gun guessed.

"As honest as clay."

"What?"

"That's what he called them. He said a real Indian could not lie, any more than clay could call itself gold."

Pretty damn romantic. The Indian as natural element. And maybe, Gun figured, not so romantic after all; natural elements were something a man could exploit, especially the kind as honest as clay. Where, he wondered, would the Indian fit on Crosley's periodic table?

"You ever hear of a thing like that?" Babe said.

The letters came back to bug Gun some more: C-H. The only spots on the map that weren't explained. *People of the earth.* "Did Crosley have a favorite?" he said, just as Babe seemed to notice the cold in his fingers and was starting to open his door. "A favorite Indian?"

Babe's voice was impatient, wanting to be done with this. "Crazy Horse."

Crazy Horse. The initials of a missing element. If you were stumped enough, such guesses became enough to go on. "The right one," Gun said, and started the truck again, the dome light catching the boy's lifted brows and skeptical upper lip.

"Where are we going?" Babe said.

"To Schell's." Gun's mind felt slightly punch-drunk, as if an answer he'd needed had sneaked up and clubbed him, but it seemed to have swung right over the kid. Babe shook his head, the ten trillionth teenager befuddled by adult folly.

"General science," Gun said.

* * *

Now that Crosley was pure blue for-certain dead, the police had come in with their long yellow tape and turned his house into a foreign country, border un-friendly. There'd been plenty of vehicles in his yard as well, official cars leaving prints of their practical all-seasons, but it was late now and how much could they have expected to find anyhow? A man, a confi-dent one, gets grabbed from his home and it's a surprise, he's not going to hide a note for the authori-ties saying, "Should anyone kill me, check for a motive among the wax Indians downstairs. It's quite a collection. . . ."

And it was, a bigger collection than Gun had remembered, once he and the kid had gone in via the window-wardrobe entrance (how many times, he wondered, could you tip even such a sturdy antique before it burst into a thousand great-grandsplinters?) and found their way to the basement. The rows of fluorescents in the ceiling showed them all without mercy: Geronimo with his map-scarred butt, Osceola smiling as if he hadn't heard of St. Augustine yet, each character nearly life-size, labeled and pedestaled. Not bad pieces either, real enough proportions in those faces and bodies to show Crosley's skill with the wax and apparent admiration for his subjects. *Worship them, rob them,* Gun thought. He tried to stem a sudden disgust for the late Crosley Schell but couldn't do it, his cynicism gland running now like a power juicer—Native American of the Month, *Join today and get three more Indians at no additional cost!*—and then Babe, dodging through the waxes like a freed ape through a crowd of stunned movie Indians, yelped out, "Here he is," and there, indeed, he was.

Crazy Horse.

Old C-H.

The elemental Indian, honest as clay, swaddled in a comb-textured robe Gun assumed was meant to be buffalo, though Crosley hadn't got the color quite right. Too many purple crayons in the vat.

"He's heavy," Babe grunted, dragging Crazy Horse away from the others to a workbench on the west wall.

"Bellyful of gold," Gun said.

The young warrior had a wily look, one black eyebrow stretched up at the side. His mouth had the smug tilt of a child's who knows that his little brother's ice cream has just been licked by the dog. Two pheasant feathers, real ones, splayed down over a bare shoulder.

"Well?" Gun said.

"I think it's nuts." Babe hoisted Crazy Horse to the workbench, the stiff to the slab.

"Look. He finds gold in a few old cores, close to the reservation. Of course he's not going to just mark it on the map," Gun believing this as he spoke it, "because look at everyone who's interested. Your cousin Pim, along with Sparrow, along with Izzy, who can offer a better package than Crosley's own bosses at DDH. He wouldn't be the first prospector to doctor a map. Or to hide his find."

Babe tapped his knuckles on the reclining Horse, who didn't sound hollow. "I guess," he said.

Then there was the awkwardness of knowing what had to come next, the waxen warrior lying on his back with eyes locked to a place on the ceiling like a stoic patient resigned to the scalpel, Babe choosing the silence of a natural adolescent now and Gun understanding that they both knew surgery was the only hope.

"Want to cut?" Gun ventured.

"I guess."

Babe even had a knife, as Gun suspected he would, a lock-back Schrade with a five-inch cutting edge. The boy knew it like a sailor knows knots, the blade showing the raspy shine of frequent whettings and slicing through C-H's ankles as if they were cheese.

The ankles were solid. Gun took the severed feet of Crazy Horse and set them, with pedestal, on the floor.

Babe said, "Knees?"

The operation was giving Gun an odd heaviness of stomach. He nodded.

The knees were solid.

"I don't think the cores are here," Babe said.

Gun didn't either, anymore, but let Babe go ahead just in case, worthlessly performing an abdominal search and finally a crass tracheotomy. Silent, Babe finished at last, blowing wax tailings from the edge of the knife and leaving Gun as exhausted as if he'd done the work himself, with his fingernails. Crazy Horse lay on the workbench, quiet as an innocent bologna, dismembered and betrayed. Gun sighed and stacked the sorry brave up again, knees to gut to crafty head. It was tiring, sometimes, being the white man.

37

Gun woke the next morning to eight inches of fresh snow and a few late-coming flakes sweeping in out of a sky that had lost its threat. No sun yet, but the gray had a definite blue tint to it, like dissipating jet smoke, the whitish blue of a sky that's given up autumn at last and gone to winter. The flakes coming down now looked hard edged, as if they'd make ticking noises upon landing, and the air coming through Gun's bedside window—cracked a half inch for good sleep —was clean as a new Deepfreeze.

The clock said 8:30, later than he'd voluntarily slept in a year. It was—he shut his eyes again, stretched under the quilt, he had to think about this—Saturday morning. It had been a lousy move, the Crazy Horse hunt, based on desperation; the gold, real or not, was at the center of all this pain, Dick's included. Late innings, too many people hoping for too much, the adrenaline leaking out your shoes, sometimes you swung at the wrong pitch.

He rose and stretched again, north and south easy, lowered himself to the floor for push-ups, rolled to his back until the lungs quieted again and crunched his abdominals until they wept. He showered, realized from the flatness of his belly he'd forgotten to eat since noon yesterday, and entered the kitchen in jeans and flannel feeling like a crummy host. A kid sixteen never forgot about food.

Babe was so hard asleep on the davenport that he looked like part of it.

Gun stepped quietly around the kitchen, easing open the whiny woodstove doors, bunching newspapers against his chest to mute the crinkle. He struck a match and lit the paper in three places. The fire grew and huffed. A pot of cold water, a basket of grounds, a pair of mugs—have a little gladness before you start wondering what's next.

It was the telephone, as usual, that screwed things up. He was just pouring the first cup of black through steam when it lost its temper across the room, and he danced toward it protectively, wanting Babe to keep sleeping. A little coffee roamed out over the lip of the cup and stung his thumb on the knuckle.

"Pedersen," he growled.

"It's Carol," she said, sounding like Easter morn.

"Carol. Tell me about the press meeting."

"They didn't say much. Of course they suspect Pim, or at least Spirit Waters. They're going to try to negotiate some kind of surrender."

"Do *you* see Pim suddenly coming out with his hands up?"

Carol said, "Things may change," sounding as if she knew why.

"Tell me."

"I think," she said, "that I know where to find the cores."

Gun sipped coffee, saw Babe sit up over on the davenport, look around, rub his hair. Well, the day was starting.

"Crazy Horse," she said.

Oh no. "We tried that," he said. "The old fellow wasn't carrying."

"What're you talking about? Gun, I was looking

over those maps again last night, late. Really *looking* at them this time, not just at the places Crosley marked. You know how he was about Indians, his childhood heroes."

"People of the earth," Gun said, resigned.

"That's right! Our first interview, he told me he'd grown up worshiping Crazy Horse, the Sioux warrior."

Her tone of voice, a kid at a carnival. She'd been bitten good. Well, he knew how she felt.

She said, "On the map, Gun, Harrow County, way up on the reservation. There's a tiny landlocked lake. Crazy Horse Lake."

"What?"

"It's maybe an hour northeast of the Spirit Waters blockade. Crosley told me about it, said he'd built a Sioux sweat lodge there, he'd go for purification. Don't laugh. He called it a holy place, there's a bald eagle nest, everything. Crazy Horse Lake. I can't believe I didn't think of it."

Gun wasn't laughing.

"The spots on the map that are marked C-H," she said. "You think those cores are there?"

Babe, it turned out, had been there before. "He wanted help building the sweat. Me and Julius went."

Carol said, "Did he go there much? Take things with him?"

"I don't know." Babe's voice dipped. "Quill would be there, sometimes."

A chill entered Gun's insides that made him glad he still rented space under the seat to a .38 Smith & Wesson.

"Does he live near there?" Gun said.

"He lives everywhere," said Babe.

The last thirty miles of road were gravel. Carol had proposed caravanning along in her Mazda and now looked glad she hadn't. They pushed ahead over an unmarked, unused road the snow tricked you into thinking was smooth. The illusion didn't last long. The pickup lurched and complained, past two lonesome-looking farms—one abandoned, the other almost so but with a few bushy sheep nosing the snow.

"It's close now," Babe said. He was watching the woods to the right. "There's a gap in the trees, you can see the big nest, and then there's a trail after a quarter mile or so."

Another ten minutes of slow toil and Babe said, "There," giving Gun and Carol a brief look at where a storm years before had leveled a strip of jack pines fifty feet wide, leaving the heavy Norway visible to the road with its high proud bowl-shaped nest.

"My gracious," Carol said, respectfully.

"Wait till you see it up close," Babe said. "It's as big as Crosley's sweat lodge."

The trail was narrow but mercifully in better shape than the road, and they could see it better; most of the snow here was still in the trees, waiting for a rude westerly to come give it a push. They went in several hundred yards with low-hanging pine branches combing the windshield and arrived at the very base of the eagle tree. It was too late in the season for eagles, and so it was a good place to park.

"Man," Carol said. She was eyeballing the nest from maybe eighty feet straight under it. Just another bird's nest, only the usual twigs and grasses were instead whole limbs, forearm thick. She said, "Eagles are that big? Two *people* could raise kids in there."

But Babe was scowling into the trees, where something bubble bright was reflecting the sun.

"That wouldn't be the lodge," Gun said.

"No." Babe pointed to a spot to the left of the gleam in the trees, a matted-down blackness of dirt and branches that looked from here like someone's stamped-out fire. *"That's* the lodge. Or was."

The .38 hadn't touched human hands in more than two years. It stretched now in Gun's fingers, yawned as he checked the rotating chambers, clicked awake, and was his friend.

They walked slowly toward the bubble and that's exactly what it was, a vintage aluminum Airstream trailer, the smallest of the breed. A bicycle bracket had been attached to the side. The bracket held a generous coil of new half-inch hemp rope, a black pry bar, and the fresh stained skin of a sheep, draped out like an awning over sharp stakes in the earth. Gun recalled the farm, the lonely flock.

They approached without speaking, not needing to guess out loud.

An improvised chimney was thrust up through the trailer's roof and a naked white string of smoke rose straight out as though being reeled in by patient angels.

"He's not inside," Babe said, and Gun saw the tracks leading from the Airstream into the woods and knew they would be the tracks of mukluks.

Forty feet from the trailer they stopped. A tiny window in the side of the trailer that faced them had been blocked from the inside by a taped-up magazine page showing an ad for Cutty Sark, a mighty good boat name blown on whiskey. This close there was a smell—made all the sharper for the cold—of mutton and uncured leather.

"Why is he *here?*" Carol whispered. "Who was he to Crosley anyhow?"

Babe said, turning where he stood to scan the trees and open spaces, "Worked for him."

"Did he *know?* About the cores?"

Gun pointed at the remains of Crosley's sweat lodge. Once a sturdy igloo-shape of branches and boards, it had been leveled and tramped into a circle of chaos. The short handle of a spade leaned up out of the ruin, its blade buried in frozen ground, a topknot of snow balanced on the U-shaped grip.

"I'd say he knew," Gun said. "Stay here." He kept the Smith pocketed, thumb on the hammer, and went forward quickly on the balls of his feet. Quill's tracks left the Airstream and entered the woods to the west. Beyond the trailer a Cadillac was parked at a tilt under the trees—an old one, the scaly green of an aging lizard. Next to the car a tall skinny outhouse angled up tombstonelike from the snow. No tracks showed anywhere near either outhouse or car.

He went back to the trailer and paused at the door. Carol stood at a distance with her arms crossed hard and nightmares on her brow. Babe was next to her, his face unreadable as a melon. Gun took the Smith out of his pocket.

He opened the door to a blast of muttony warmth, and dropped in fast letting the pistol lead the way as he'd seen a cop or two do it in the pictures, and was as glad for human absence as he'd rarely been before. A bunk, a down bag, a tinny stove with a large pan containing water and sheep fat (still hot), and on the slim eating counter, a long plastic tray full of bones, most of them still with thick shreds of meat on them but when you had a whole sheep, who cared whether you cleaned your plate?

"Okay," Gun called. His voice in the tin bubble seemed to stick to him.

They made as thorough a search of the Airstream as they comfortably could, Gun keeping an eye on the trees and wondering if a man who took sheep like a wolf had any use for firearms. Probably so.

If Quill had found the cores, he hadn't stashed them in the trailer. "If he's got them, would he still be here at all?" Carol said. "What's a guy like Quill going to *do* with them, anyhow?"

Babe said, "Crosley hated it when Quill came around if there was folks, but he didn't dare tell him what to do."

"If you know where there's gold," Gun said, "someone'll always buy. He knows that."

They checked the Cadillac, too, prying open the trunk with Quill's own crowbar and finding nothing but the rest of the sheep. Piled, in unwrapped but dumbfoundingly neat-cut steaks and roasts, in the Caddy's deep freezing wheel wells.

"Geez," Babe said.

Carol turned her face away, lips locked shut against the air's suddenly predatory taste, and finally set forth in a dignified lurch for the outhouse.

She seemed to be in there for a long time. Finally Gun walked over and said, "Carol?"

No answer, and Gun didn't blame her. The ewe had been a rare sight and truly so.

"You okay?" He was looking at an inconsistency in Crosley's outhouse. The old boards were gray with time as a barn's, and yet on the corners, the saw cuts showed fresh. Well. It was only an outhouse, and for such projects you sometimes used old wood.

"Gun," came Carol's voice, from down low. There was a bumping within and Gun thought, *It's bad, she's still on her knees.*

"Yes." Sticking the Smith back in his pocket, embarrassed to be holding it now.

"Look," she said, shoving the door open hard enough to bounce it against the wall. She was on her knees all right, and her hands, too. Breathing tough, like a marathoner.

"Here!" She was rocking a board at the foot of the seat, down where your feet would normally go while you were occupied and thinking of anything else. "It was loose, I got down and it just about tipped me over." And then she had it, the board coming up in her hands and underneath it a long narrow box of gray wood. It was unmarked and bound with two frosty steel bands, one at each end. She reached down and lifted one end up out of the hole, dropped it again and gasped.

"It's a ton."

"Let's both," Gun said. He had to bend in at a slant because Carol took up most of the room in the wee privy but they lifted it out, three feet of lead that made them stand up with some extra care once they'd staggered it out and dropped it in the snow.

Babe was hovering on high caution, grinning over the exhumed box as Gun took the pry bar to the bands, but he kept his face to the surrounding woods in a way that made Gun think of a barometer on storm days. Gun said, "Come *on,*" and the first band burst away and then the second, and Carol flung the lid off the box.

"These?" Gun said, aware of disappointment in his voice. Short, split pieces of unpolished rock. Patterns of gray going to black going to brown, and not a glimmer of any winking mineral eye that might be gold. Practically identical to the worthless cores he'd seen at Schell's. Maybe a little rust of iron.

Carol was joyous. "You expected gold bars? Pieces of eight? Krugerands?" she exulted. She picked up a broken piece of core. "This piece was probably drilled out at the turn of the century. The gold in it's so fine they couldn't even tell it was there, let alone mine it. But these days—" she shook her head and the shine of her green eyes made Gun wonder at what gold, even such raw stuff as this, could do to a woman—"these days they can pull the dust out of the rock. It's really here!"

"Crosley really found it," Babe said, sobering her again with the name.

"And then you did," Gun told her.

Carol said, "Thank that poor sheep."

38

Alfred Pim was back living in the green trailer house again, the tepee having taken in quite a bit of snow during the night and the whole spirit of the blockade having gone pretty much to hell anyway once Crosley's remains turned up.

"Sparrow must have heard about it," Pim said, his tone resigned. "He went out to New York, to talk to Mr. Rolph, you know. He still isn't back."

"Did Sparrow kill him, Pim? Did *you?*" Carol was asking the questions, Gun avoiding Pim's eyes and Babe getting some solitude out in the car. Babe had had unhappy feelings about stopping here.

"The responsibility is mine," Pim said. He looked neither better nor worse for the fact. "I'd rather not say more. Did you know this is my last day here?"

Carol didn't speak but gave a tiny nod, the reporter's language for *keep talking.*

"I told the police I'd talk to them tomorrow about Crosley Schell. They wanted me to go with them right away—that was last night—but I held out. Security was still out there," Pim said, waving in the direction of the barricade. "Always negotiate while you still have rifles."

243

"We noticed how quiet it was," Carol said. "We just walked in. There wasn't even a police car."

"Most of our people were gone by midnight. I encouraged them to go. Angel stayed, my daughter. Won't live with me anymore though; took Booger and is off with her Aunt Cooper now, next trailer down. She's still angry over my handling of Babe Chandler." He smiled. "A good girl. I should listen to her more."

"You can tell her Babe's okay," Gun said.

"I'll do that." Pim shook his head. "Don't know why the hell I'm delaying things. Still hoping Sparrow might come back, maybe."

"That would make it easier on you," Gun said, enough understanding there so that Carol shot him a glance.

"Yes. Coffee?"

Carol said, "I thought you were all out. Drinking hot milk now."

"The troopers were good enough to run in a can of Butternut."

"No thanks," Gun said. He was looking around the trailer, which had lost its essential neatness in the absence of Pim's Angel; not that it could be called messy, with its lack of furnishings. It all just seemed to have aged, somehow; gotten yellow, like a dream after you wake up.

"DDH," Carol said, watching Pim as if he might go *poof* and be gone, "tells me they plan to renew their mineral leases here. Even though Crosley didn't find them any gold."

"Let them look," Pim said, with a little too much easiness.

"That's quite a turnaround." She hesitated, probably wondering how hard to shove. "For someone who has visions," she added.

Pim took off his round-rimmed glasses, breathed upon the lenses, chamoised them clean on his shirt. "If Crosley had actually produced proof, if he had shown us samples, as he promised to do, more Ojibwa would have believed in those visions," he said. "The trouble was, with Crosley we got confused. He told the truth some and lied some and his face never showed you the difference."

"You mean you didn't know if the gold was real. Or if he made it up in order to sell it," Gun said.

"He found the gold," Carol said. "In the archives. It would've been enough to put DDH in the right place, but he didn't tell them about it."

Pim shifted forward. "But DDH *is* drilling, even though they've not found anything. What's that supposed to mean?"

"Crosley didn't intend for them to come. He sent them discouraging archive reports. But there are enough other signs of mineral deposits—iron, copper, nickel—that the company decided to come in anyway."

"The hell!" Pim said, suddenly angry. "He *did* try to keep DDH out! That much was true."

"Not because of altruism, though," Gun said. "Because of capitalism."

"Izzy Rolph?" Pim said.

"A different sort of prospector," Carol answered. "His job is, 'Learn who has what, and what their price is.' He was lining Crosley up to sell his knowledge to a higher bidder."

Pim held up his hands, stop. "But DDH holds the leases on that property."

"The leases have to be renewed every year. Crosley doctored his reports, thinking DDH would let the land go."

"So Izzy's people could move right in," Pim finished.

Gun said, "If you'll excuse me, there's something in the car we'd like you to have."

They left Pim the cores, the maps, and in the dark about Jefferson Sparrow. "It's enough," Gun opined, steering the Ford south again. "He knows about the gold, and he knows that we know, and that DDH doesn't. He can do what he likes with the cores."

"I'd bet no one ever sees them again," Carol said. Gun nodded.

He was thinking he knew Carol almost well enough now to tell her things. Like the fact that he'd been there when Crosley died, that he was still trying to paint over the memory of the man's final expression of disbelief. Gun could almost tell her this; but said instead, playing it cautious, "Nope, I'm not assuming it. I suspect Pim's responsible, like he says. Though Sparrow"—careful now—"might've had something to do with it." He explained no more than that, for now, and he loved Carol for not pressing him about it. *Loved her,* he realized. That was some word. He ought to use it, maybe, see what happened.

Babe slept, his head against the passenger window as if it were a davenport pillow on Saturday morning.

Gun braked to a stop on the wrong side of the street in front of the *Journal* office, where Carol wanted out. Babe woke and let her out the passenger door, but before Gun could pull away she was knocking at his window. He cranked it down and smiled.

"Forgot to tell you, Gun. It's all over in Japan."

"Come again?"

"The baseball season. The other day you asked me when it ends over there? I called the librarian. She said a month ago—it's about the same time the season winds down here."

Gun nodded. "Okay."

"Do I want to know why you're wondering?"

"Probably not," he said. As he pulled away he pictured a radio wave—a wiggly line, like a skinny water snake—veering off course and wandering lost for weeks in the solar system before finding its way back to earth. A month ago? All right.

* * *

Gun and Babe went straight to the Chandler place. Dick was home when they pulled in, sitting stiffly at the kitchen table playing host to Jason Durkins, who had dropped by—in gracious forgetfulness of getting decked here only weeks before—and brought supper. A bucket of Extra Crispy. Dick was doing the best he could with his permanent utensils but dropping wings and thighs nonetheless.

"I couldn't think of what to bring," Durkins said. He looked to have slept enough for once, the flesh under his eyes not as billowy as usual. "What do you *eat*, Chandler?"

"Sometimes," Dick said, hooking the air, "I roast marshmallows."

His color was the most startling aspect of him, more so even than the new scars. You live in a place where creation is still good, Gun thought, work in red clay until it calls you Daddy, run dogs in the winter sun, and it all shows in your skin. Turns you a hue that seems genetic; the color Adam must've been, freshly framed up by the Lord out of some handy dirt. Dick, though, looked like a man in whom the breath of life hadn't blown recently. If white was the absence of color, then here was white personified, Dick sitting in his kitchen dropping chicken on the floor, a white man washed clean of ruddiness by pain and dismay. What was left to him was pretty much just his wrinkles and the angry rip-work of scar tissue, as deep and distinct as strips of black ice in a field of snow.

"Babe," Dick said softly, seeing his boy enter slowly behind Gun.

"How you doing, Dad?"

Durkins got up to make way for Babe, who came around the table toward his father in short, awkward steps. A week ago, Gun realized, the reasons for awkwardness between the two of them would've been simple ones: the boy's teenage lust for independence, a general disdain for the older generation. Babe wanting the car keys but not wanting to ask.

"Fine, boy," Dick said. He held his hand up and Babe grabbed on and shook it, the boy's touch alone seeming to shoot a little pink back into his old-man's countenance.

By then, Gun was just about out the door and Durkins, showing sensibility bordering on the uncommon, was right at his heels.

"Pedersen," the sheriff said when they were outside, their breaths wisping away on a light west breeze that wasn't as cold as it seemed, "I'll buy you a beer."

Gun peered up in the direction of the sun. There was an extra ring of brightness around it which, if you squinted enough, blazed into a holy palette of surprising colors, greens and cool blues. Away to the west, a sun dog was growing, just a white space in the sky, and it gave the afternoon a sweet epilogue feel.

"Durkins," Gun said, "I'll drink it." And thought: *Later, I'll see Carol. See her for a long while.* Because there truly were some things she ought to know, and as stories went, Gun favored epilogues.

39

Jack LaSalle had ten bucks' worth of quarters which he used every week, same old coins, to monopolize the jukebox when the young folks arrived. He called it his Saturday night roll and it paid, over and over again, for an evening with Cline and Haggard and Cochrane and Nelson, Willie singing from his short-hair days.

"It's my tavern," Jack said. "My jukebox and my roll. The kids can punch up Alabama all week. Saturday nights belong to me."

Also belonging to Jack LaSalle was the hindmost booth in the place—a small, plain-looking spot, better lit than the other booths by twenty-five watts, which Gun liked for its seats. They were straight-backed hardwood benches, not padded at all but so subtly, presciently curved in the seat that upholstery was unnecessary; it would in fact have been an insult to the craftsman. Gun and Jack were in the booth now, sitting across from Durkins.

"Before you get too comfortable," Gun told the sheriff, "I should tell you—"

"Wait." Durkins raised a hand palm out, lifted his mug in the other and swallowed. It sounded like a sigh going down, it was that happy. He set the beer down. "Okay."

"It's Quill," Gun said. "I know where he's staying."

That brought the beer up again, this time leaving foam on Durkins's upper lip like an outgoing tide. "So the knife guy is real. He eats, he craps."

"Lately, he's been eating mutton."

Jack had been looking into his coffee as if it would show him his reflection from twenty years distant and now, still peering into it, lifted an eyebrow.

"Did you see him? Where?" The sheriff was leaning across the little table as if to show Gun and Jack how pearly were the whites of his eyes.

"Do you know of a little bitty reservation lake called Crazy Horse?"

"The hell," Durkins said. "I know where it's *supposed* to be. Rode along with a guy from Natural Resources once, they sent him out to snatch an eagle. Arrangement with the reservation; they got so many of 'em now, we're kidnapping the chicks and sending 'em to grow up in Georgia. Make a little money. But we never found the nest, nor the lake either. The reservation with those half-assed roads, it's like a maze at midnight." Durkins took another lusty-fellow swig. "The DNR guy didn't mind we got lost. Must of saved him a mighty climb."

"I'd say eighty feet," Gun said. Durkins could stall when nervous and Gun didn't blame him. An encounter with Quill would stall Clint Eastwood.

Durkins hiked his beer once more and it was gone. Jack glanced at him and the sheriff said, "No thanks," mistaking the glance for the barkeep's perpetual. "You probably better tell me," he sighed.

Gun told him. The Airstream, the sheep, everything but the box under the outhouse; along with directions so clear Durkins would have to resign from embarrassment if he didn't find the place this time.

"So how'd *you* find Crazy Horse? And find your way back, for that matter?"

Jack said, "He uses a great big ball of string, unwinds it behind him, like Theseus."

"I read that once," Durkins said.

Gun said, "You going to need some help?" Hoping Durkins would just say, "No."

The sheriff stood from the booth, dropped two bills on the table and shook his head, tired as a bear in December. "Don't see why. Were it just my deputies along, Whipper, Lapp, I'd worry. Thank God they're both hurt. Now I can just go to the city and borrow a couple of cops, you know?"

Gun nodded.

Durkins turned, actually squared his shoulders like Mr. High Noon going forth to get his man, and headed out.

"Sic 'em," Jack called. He waited for the door to swing shut behind the sheriff and said, "You think he will?"

"Arrest Quill?" It was something Gun had a peculiar conviction about. An unexpected faith. "Yup," he said. "He will."

"Here," Jack said, "lies a question." They'd been through plenty in the last hour, through forged maps and mercenary geologists and tents that shook by themselves, and had gone on from coffee and beer to the particular brandy Gun had infrequently imbibed at this favored booth, and nowhere else. Mr. Cochrane was on the music box singing "Make the World Go Away," and it was starting to go, all right.

"What's a boy do, I mean a young kid, who's gone and been a responsible party in something like this?"

"Babe." Gun had been wondering, himself. "He didn't hurt anybody, you know. It wasn't him."

"No, sir. But say you're fifteen—"

"He's sixteen."

"Oh, gosh, well then, no problem."

"Come on, Jack."

"Say you're sixteen, you watch what Babe watched

out on the ice, and then before you can hardly think, your dad's gotten chopped up and then the girl too. Nuts. And finally Crosley. You're thinking: if I'da come clean way back when . . ." Jack's face creased into more wrinkles than Gun had seen there before. "There's a mountain of crap on that boy's conscience."

Gun closed his eyes in the booth. There was cigarette in the air and his forefinger absently touched his thumb, making a smoke. Babe appeared to his mind gradually, like he'd done at Shorty's barn, coming down out of the dark, legs first. At once unsure and hopeful, and only later beaming his Bambino smile, later, when the sun hit that wide piece of water and seemed to show the kid how tiny he was. Gun considered the joy such things gave Babe Chandler and wondered what would be the boy's trail to forgiveness. How long it would take. How tough it would be on Dick, who had his own trail to cut.

"If anyone can do it," Gun said.

"Yeah."

They sat awhile, leaving the brandy alone while the supper crowd thinned and the world started coming back again. Then Jack said, "How May brained Julius that way, left him in the lake, that still scares me."

Gun didn't answer. He didn't feel like thinking of it.

"She was that loyal to Crosley," Jack said.

"Well. We all have our allegiances."

"Right enough," Jack said, and stopped. A tall guy in a bomber jacket was showing his girlfriend to a table close by. She had large black hair and the guy was steering her by one elbow, and not with any tenderness. Showing ownership. They sat down, he with his hand in her lap. The table was very near. His hand was moving.

"Say," Jack said. The guy turned and Jack pointed toward the front of the bar. "That's a better table, up there."

Bomber started to reply, stumbled over something

in Jack's face and looked vaguely away. He said, "Yeah, it's a good one," and stood up, got hold of the girl's elbow, yanked on it.

"Say," Jack said again, as Bomber navigated, "she can walk by herself, maybe?" And the guy dropped his hand, not looking back.

"My own place," Jack said. He relaxed in his booth of gladness. He said, "Allegiance is a peculiar critter. I still don't understand Quill's."

"I'm not sure I do, either. He worked with Crosley, apparently they got along. When Crosley thought he couldn't trust May anymore—"

"Quill was the man for the job," Jack said. "And then Dick happened to come along first. Damn."

Gun raised his glass an inch off the table. "To our man Durkins," he said.

Jack lifted and drank. He set the brandy down again and said, "You'll testify for Pim?"

"I expect."

"Uh-huh." Jack coughed into the back of his hand. "You want him to come through it, don't you?" He leaned back in the booth and drummed his fingers on the tabletop, an odd rhythm because of his missing right index.

Gun didn't answer. Jack had this priest-at-confession side to him.

"For all the weirdness, all the misdirected horseshit, you like the guy."

"I expect," Gun said, and then thought, *Carol,* and the name coming to mind that way, nothing attached to it but a pair of green eyes looking straight and easy at him, cheered him and made him ready to be done here and on his way.

Jack wasn't quite done, though. "Crosley was doing well with DDH, yes?" he said. Some frustration in his voice now, not priestly anymore, which was all to the good.

"Yes."

"Made fine wages, had it pretty damn nice."

"Yes," Gun said.

"So why does a man like that take such chances, try to sell his neighbors down the river?"

Gun didn't know many people who were themselves honest enough to need to ask such a question. He said, "Do you ever want more than you've got, Jack?"

Jack fought it but then grinned. He said, "Always." He snuffed out his brandy. "I'm a lousy person, Gun. You know much of Robert Service? Now he wrote about gold better than anybody. 'There are strange things done in the midnight sun . . .'"

Gun knew the poem.

40

Driving north through Stony, Gun's eye was taken by a green Ford pickup angle parked toward the street at the Standard station. It hadn't been there before, was a genuine looker under the streetlamp in that sea green paint, and was no doubt for sale; the Standard man, Harold Amudson, had taken to selling used vehicles on consignment of late, probably figuring the experience would lead him naturally into a political career. On impulse, Gun pulled over, feeling as he did so a sudden warmth for his own coughing truck, wanting and not wanting to give it up. He sat at the curb and appraised: the green Ford was a sleek late model, front grille nearly the same as his own but this one with all its teeth, and back in the bed a hard-rubber liner. Toss in all the wood you want, the paint stays nice and she sweeps out clean.

Monday, he'd talk to Harold.

Man, it felt good, thinking of such plain tasks again. Talk to Harold, strike a deal, buy a truck.

See Carol. Well, that wouldn't wait for Monday. It was early yet, not nine o'clock. Shower and a bite and he was gone, drive the old Ford one more time to her place and make some things clear to her about the past weeks. He owed her this. He suspected he owed her much more. For the first time since Amanda, Gun found himself believing that there could be great happiness, as well as great obligation, under such a debt.

He had a yard light fixed to his porch but hadn't left it on, and since clouds had crawled up out of the southeast and covered everything but the Great Bear, it was a matter of not using the eyes at all, just letting the feet recall the way—skirt the woodpile, bear to the right, hand going out all by itself for the doorknob and getting it dead center. He opened the door and smelled cold furniture, cold wood, cold stove.

He built a fire for fast heat, using up most of the thin-split kindling in the stove-side box. It caught quick as corncobs and he went into his bedroom, took off his shirt. Sat on the bed, unlaced his boots, peeled away the woolen socks—gracious, the glory of hard-wood boards on feet too long encased. Kept his Levi's on, force of habit, a man alone preferring not to walk naked across the floor to his own bathroom. Then he thought: ah, the push-ups. He owed the old man ninety-six more.

After years of repetition, Gun's mind had become as calloused to the strain as his knuckles had to the bare wood floor. The first ones, maybe one through ten, might be slightly stiff, hurt a little in the shoulders and elbows, but then his brain would start to back off and let the muscles go to it; by forty-five his joints and arms and back would be cranking like a block and tackle, his breathing regular and the old brain not worrying a bit. He supposed it was what others felt, or rather didn't feel, during meditation. Down. Up. By session's end the conscious mind had usually gone off somewhere, found a couch and a good book, and was in no hurry to return. *Aw, go ahead, do some more.* At which point his arms would quiver a little and suggest that mind over matter was, after all, a crappy theory, and he'd rise up off the floor to reward himself with a shower and a bowl of Wheaties. A cigarette.

He was at the block-and-tackle stage tonight, free of thought and cranking, when it seeped through to him that his wrists were getting cold. In mid-hoist he glanced up. The back door, the one he'd come in, was open. Just a few inches; he'd close it when he finished. He shut his eyes, trance ruined, thought of a shower and beyond it to Carol Long. Seven push-ups left. Six. Five. He dipped down to bring up number four and felt something hard sink into his back. A flat anvil weight between the shoulder blades. It drove him to the floor so hard he heard his chest slap the wood. He smelled tart leather and reminiscent mutton. He felt a chilly steel edge against the flesh behind his ear. He remembered the quiet of the man, striding toward him over stiff dead grass, the grass itself bending under his feet as if afraid to make a noise.

41

He got his breath back to where it would support whispering and said, "Do you talk?"

Quill didn't answer.

He had to go two hundred and thirty pounds and all of it coming down through one knee that was trying to reach Gun's heart, the back way. Gun's arms were free but he couldn't move them; he wasn't getting enough air for strength and besides, there was the knife, there behind the ear.

"What do you want?"

Nothing from Quill, but Gun could hear him breathing now, even and quiet as a man not wanting to wake his wife. He felt long fingers at his throat, his neck was arched backward, and the room went from having little air to having none at all. There was a pinprick at his scalp, not even pain, and he heard a new noise, tiny and immense—the clocklike dripping of his own blood upon the floor.

He croaked out, "What!"

"You know where it is," Quill said.

The silence had been distressing. The voice was worse—a low scratching gust of muttony speech. But the fingers on Gun's neck loosened a little, to permit an answer.

"Yes," Gun whispered.

"You found it," Quill said in a soft rasp. "Found it in the shithouse and stole it all away!"

"Yes."

Another pressure at the ear and the clock speeded up. Fast forward, wrong answer, *if I could breathe I could think.*

"And you have the maps," Quill said. "My maps. Showing my gold."

"Yours?" Gun said in a constricted whisper, his neck still arched back toward Quill.

"The old man's great-grampa. He knew it was there. And all of us, right down," Quill said. "Could always tell it. Things got passed."

Gun had nothing to say and couldn't have said it if he had. Quill seemed suddenly offended at the silence and pushed with the knife, it hurting this time and the clock dripping ahead as if it couldn't wait to see how this would turn out.

"Crosley Schell got it from *me,*" Quill roared.

"The gold," Gun choked.

"I told him where to look. I took him out to the hills with my witching rod. I witched it for him."

The fingers eased, barely, and Gun said, "You can witch gold . . . why did you need Schell? You could do it . . . all yourself."

The question seemed to suspend Quill on a high wire between outrage and confusion, and the way he trembled there showed Gun what the man's life had been: a life spent more among trees than people, fine if that's what you desire, but hell if the scant few folks you belong to have kept to themselves for too many years, too many generations, and expect you to do the same. Breed in, breed in, and what's lost is the necessary tameness that makes you livable to others. *Things got passed.* The inbred calf most likely dies, or else goes crazy in the barn and kicks its way out.

"Tell you where they are," Gun said. The man's grip had loosened but he kept his voice a thin croak, hardly audible. At last, he'd said the right thing. Quill leaned forward, letting Gun's head come down to rest on the floor.

"Tell you," Gun whispered.

"Louder."

"Tell you—"

"Louder!"

Gun made a gagging sound as if the air wasn't in him to talk louder, and Quill, still with the blade at Gun's ear, leaned down to listen close.

"They're in my—" Gun started, and then with the cooperation of every fiber built for this moment by every push-up, every press of muscle and stroke of bat, rammed his head backward and into Quill's face. He felt the blade slip against his scalp and the dark silver rush begin; he felt the explosion of cartilage that was Quill's nose against his skull; and most important he felt the weight of the man lose its balance and teeter back, and he twisted up and saw Quill getting to his feet, his fingers having remembered to keep hold of the half-moon blade.

But the blade wasn't going to make any difference, not now. There was too much fog across those eyes, and Gun stepped in and buried a fist in Quill's middle that took memory from the knife hand. Quill doubled and was straightened by an uppercut that Gun later realized, without pride, was pure revenge; the man was already cold, on his feet.

When he finally dropped, half-spinning to land facedown with his head in the bathroom and the rest of him in the hall, Gun let him stay for five minutes, waiting for him to wake up. He didn't, just breathed the breath of a gut-shot bear and bled with his nose all over the tile. Gun picked up Quill's feet, the damned brown mukluks, dragged him out the door, and with more effort than he thought he still owned, flopped Quill, like one more pest, onto the woodpile.

* * *

He got the Smith out from under the truck seat before going back in. It was the first time he'd been barefoot in the snow for years and didn't notice it until he was back inside and calling up Durkins. He'd pulled the kitchen table up close to the window, was sitting there with cotton packed behind his ear and the loaded Smith next to the phone. The porch light was on and showed Quill sleeping the patient sleep, his head pillowed on a half-round of oak.

He kept the call short. Durkins was impressed. He'd just returned from Crazy Horse Lake, where he'd been skunked, of course. Would be out directly, along with an ambulance.

Out on the woodpile the weasel poked up his startled face and Gun smiled. He dialed another number.

She answered after four rings and told him she'd hoped to see him tonight, what was going on?

On the woodpile, the weasel disappeared, then came up again from behind a wedge of birch behind Quill's shoulder. Gun said, "You know? I'm thinking about trading cars."

She was interested. The stars were hidden but there was no wind and it was a blessed night.

Gun said, "Carol, I love you. Very much." Easy like that, just straight ahead. He said, "Marry me."

What she replied, after time, made him smile again and rock his chair back, nodding, looking at the weasel as it danced over Quill, the weasel's black eyes gone now from suspicion to pure joy and finally turning to catch Gun's through the window. Like to say, *Look at this mouse now. Look at this.*

She's been featured in *New York* magazine—
the petite redhead who's applied her considerable acting talent to
tracking down real criminals. Master of disguise, quick-change
artist, Gillian B. Farrell's quick wit and sharp tongue have
won her the respect of New York's finest. Now this multifaceted
performer takes us into the world of murder,
mystery and drama she knows best...

GILLIAN B. FARRELL'S

ALIBI FOR AN ACTRESS

Introducing

Annie McGrogan, P.I.

Available in hardcover from Pocket Books in July 1992

POCKET
B O O K S